Praise for #1 *New York Times* bestselling author

NORA ROBERTS

"When Roberts puts her expert fingers on the pulse of romance, legions of fans feel the heartbeat."
—*Publishers Weekly*

"With clear-eyed, concise vision and a sure pen, Roberts nails her characters and settings with awesome precision, drawing readers into a vividly rendered world of family-centered warmth and unquestionable magic."
—*Library Journal*

"You can't bottle wish fulfillment, but Nora Roberts certainly knows how to put it on the page."
—*New York Times*

"Roberts' style has a fresh, contemporary snap."
—*Kirkus Reviews*

"America's favorite writer."
—*The New Yorker*

"Nora Roberts is among the best."
—*Washington Post Book World*

NORA ROBERTS

ONCE AGAIN

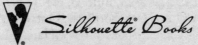

Published by Silhouette Books
America's Publisher of Contemporary Romance

 SILHOUETTE BOOKS

Once Again

ISBN-13: 978-0-373-28248-7

Recycling programs
for this product may
not exist in your area.

Copyright © 2018 by Harlequin Books S.A.

The publisher acknowledges the copyright holder
of the individual works as follows:

Sullivan's Woman
Copyright © 1984 by Nora Roberts

Less of a Stranger
Copyright © 1984 by Nora Roberts

Visit Silhouette Books at www.Harlequin.com

Printed in U.S.A.

CONTENTS

SULLIVAN'S WOMAN

For Don, the most Irish of my brothers.

Chapter 1

Cassidy waited. Mrs. Sommerson tossed a third rejected dress into her arms.

"Simply won't do," the woman muttered and scowled at a midnight-blue linen. After a moment's consideration this, too, was dumped into the pile over Cassidy's arms. Valiantly Cassidy held on to her patience.

After three months as a sales clerk in The Best Boutique, she felt she'd learned patience, but it hadn't been easy. Dutifully she followed the solid bulk of Mrs. Sommerson to another display of dresses. After twenty-seven minutes of standing around like a clothes rack, Cassidy thought, shifting the weight on her arms, her hard-earned patience was sorely strained.

"I'll try these," Mrs. Sommerson finally announced and marched back to the changing room. Mumbling only a little, Cassidy began to replace unsuitable dresses.

She jammed a loose hairpin into her scalp in irritation. Julia Wilson, The Best's owner, was a stickler for neatness. No hair was allowed to tumble over the shoulders of her clerks. Neat, orderly and unimaginative, Cassidy concluded, and wrinkled her nose at the midnight-blue linen. It was unfortunate that Cassidy was disorganized, imaginative, and not altogether neat. Her hair seemed to epitomize her personality. There were shades from delicate blond to rich brown melding into a tone like gold in an old painting. It was long and heavy and protested against the confines of pins by continuously slipping through them. Like Cassie herself, it was unruly and stubborn yet soft and fascinating.

It had been the appeal of Cassidy's slightly unconventional looks that had prompted her hiring. Experience had not been among her qualifications. Julia Wilson had recognized a potential advertisement for her merchandise and knew that Cassidy's long, supple body would set off the bold colors and styles of her more adventurous line. The face was undoubtedly a plus, too. Julia hadn't been certain it was a beautiful face, but she'd known it was striking. Cassidy's features were sharp and angular, undeniably aristocratic. Her brows arched over long, lidded eyes that seemed oversized in her narrow face and were a surprising violet.

Julia had seen Cassidy's face, figure and her well-pitched voice as references but had insisted on having her pin up her hair. With it down around her shoulders, it lent a distressingly wanton quality to the aristocratic features. She was pleased with Cassidy's youth, with her intelligence and with her energy. Soon after hiring her, however, Julia had discovered she was not as pliable as her age had suggested. She had, Julia felt, an unfortunate tendency to forget her place and become overly friendly with the customers. More than once, she'd come upon Cassidy as she asked customers impertinent questions or gave unwarranted advice. From time to time her smile suggested she was enjoying some private joke. And often, far too often, she daydreamed. Julia had begun to have serious doubts about Cassidy St. John's suitability.

After returning Mrs. Sommerson's rejected choices to their proper place, Cassidy took up her post by the changing room. From inside she could hear the faint rustle of materials. Idle, her mind did what it invariably did when given the opportunity. It drifted back to the manuscript that lay spread over her desk in her apartment. Waiting.

As far back as memory took her, writing had been her dream. For four years of college she had studied the craft seriously. At nineteen she'd been left without family and with little money. She had continued to work her way through college in various odd jobs while learning the discipline and art of her chosen profession. Between her education and employment, Cassidy had been left with meager snatches of free time. Even these had been set aside for work on her first novel.

To Cassidy writing was not a career but a vocation. Her entire life had been guided toward it, leaving her room for few other attachments. People fascinated her, but there were few with whom she was deeply involved. She wrote of complex relationships, but her knowledge of them came almost entirely secondhand. What gave her work quality and depth were her sharp talent for observation and her surprising depth of emotion. For the greater part of her life, her emotions had found their release in her work.

Now, a full year after graduation, she continued to take odd jobs to pay the rent. Her first manuscript worked its way from publishing house to publishing house while her second came slowly to life.

As Mrs. Sommerson opened the door of the changing room, Cassidy's mind was deep into the reworking of a dramatic scene. Seeing her standing with proper handmaidenly reserve, Mrs. Sommerson nodded approvingly. She preened ever so slightly.

"This should do nicely. Don't you agree?"

Mrs. Sommerson's choice was a flaming-red silk. The color, Cassidy noted, accented her florid complexion but was an attractively sharp contrast to her fluffy black mane of hair. The dress might have been more appropriate if Mrs. Sommerson had been a few pounds lighter, but Cassidy saw possibilities.

"You'll draw eyes, Mrs. Sommerson," she announced after a moment's deliberation. With the proper accessories, she decided, Mrs. Sommerson might very likely look regal. The silk, however, strained over her ample hips. A sterner girdle, Cassidy diagnosed, or a larger dress. "I think we have this in the next size," she murmured, thinking aloud.

"I beg your pardon?"

Preoccupied, Cassidy failed to note the dangerous arch of Mrs. Sommerson's brows. "The next size," she repeated helpfully. "This one's a bit snug through the hips. The next size up should fit you perfectly."

"This is my size, young woman." Mrs. Sommerson's bosom lifted then fell. It was an awe-inspiring movement.

Deep into solving the accessory problem, Cassidy smiled and nodded. "A splashy gold necklace, I should think." She tapped her fingertip against her bottom lip. "Just let me find your size."

"This," Mrs. Sommerson stated in a tone that arrested Cassidy's full attention, "*is* my size." Indignation seethed in every syllable. Recognizing her mistake, Cassidy felt a sinking sensation in her stomach.

Whoops, she said silently then pulled her scattered wits together. Before she could begin soothing Mrs. Sommerson's ruffled ego, Julia stepped from behind her.

"A stunning choice, Mrs. Sommerson," she stated in her well-modulated contralto. With a noncommittal smile, she glanced from her customer to her clerk then back again. "Is there a problem?"

"This young woman…" Mrs. Sommerson heaved another deep breath. "Insists I've made a mistake in my size."

"Oh, no, ma'am," Cassidy protested, but subsided when Julia arched a penciled brow in her direction.

"I'm certain what Miss St. John meant to say was that this particular style is cut a bit oddly. The sizes simply do not run true."

I should've thought of that, Cassidy admitted to herself.

"Well." Mrs. Sommerson sniffed and eyed Cassidy with disapproval. "She might have said so, rather than suggesting that *I* was a larger size. Really, Julia." She turned back to the changing room. "You should train your staff better."

Cassidy's eyes kindled and grew dark at the tone. She watched the seams of the red silk protest against Mrs. Sommerson's generous posterior. The quick glare from Julia had her swallowing retorts.

"I'll fetch the dress myself, Mrs. Sommerson," Julia soothed, slipping her personable smile back into place. "I'm certain it will be perfect for you. Wait for me in my office, Cassidy," she added in an undertone before gliding off.

With a sinking heart, Cassidy watched Julia's retreat. She recognized the tone all too well. Three months, she mused, then sighed. Oh, well. With one backward glance at Mrs. Sommerson, she moved down the narrow hallway and into Julia's small, smartly decorated office.

She surveyed the square, windowless room, then chose a tiny, straight-backed, bronze cushioned chair. It was here, she remembered, I was hired. And it's here I'll be fired. She jammed another rebellious pin into place and scowled. In a few minutes she'll walk in, lift her left brow and sit behind her perfectly beautiful rosewood desk. She'll look at me a moment, gently clear her throat and begin.

"Cassidy, you're a lovely girl, but your heart isn't in your work."

"Mrs. Wilson," Cassidy imagined herself saying, "Mrs. Sommerson can't wear a size fourteen. I was—"

"Of course not." Cassidy pictured Julia interrupting her with a patient smile. "I wouldn't dream of selling her one, but—" here Cassidy envisioned Julia lifting up one slender, rose-tipped finger for emphasis "—we must allow her illusions *and* her vanity. Tact and diplomacy are essential for a salesperson, Cassidy. I'm afraid you've yet to fully develop these qualities. In a shop such as this—" Julia would fold her hand on the desk's surface "—I must be able to depend, without reservation, on my staff. If this were the first incident, of course, I'd make allowances, but…" Here Cassidy imagined Julia would pause and give a small sigh. "Just last week you told Miss Teasdale the black crepe made her look like a mourner. This is not the way we sell our merchandise."

"No, Mrs. Wilson." Cassidy decided she would agree with an apologetic air. "But with Miss Teasdale's hair and her complexion—"

"Tact and diplomacy," Julia would reiterate with a lifted finger. "You might have suggested that a royal-blue would match her eyes or that a rose would set off her skin. The clientele must be pampered while the merchandise moves. Each woman who walks out the door should feel she has acquired something special."

"I understand that, Mrs. Wilson. I hate to see someone buy something unsuitable; that's why—"

"You have a good heart, Cassidy." Julia would smile maternally then drop the ax. "You simply have no talent for selling…at least, not the degree of talent I require. I shall, of course, pay you for the rest of the week and give you a good reference. You've been prompt and dependable. Perhaps you might try clerking in a department store."

Cassidy wrinkled her nose at this point in her scenario, then quickly smoothed her features as the door behind her opened. Julia closed it quietly then lifted her left brow and moved to sit behind her rosewood desk. She studied Cassidy a moment then gently cleared her throat.

"Cassidy, you're a lovely girl, but…"

Cassidy's shoulders lifted and fell with her sigh.

An hour later, unemployed, she wandered Fisherman's Wharf, enjoying its cheerful shabbiness, its traveling carnival atmosphere. She loved the cornucopia of scents and sound and color. Here there was always a crowd. Here there was life in ever-changing flavors. San Francisco was Cassidy's concept of a perfect city, but Fisherman's Wharf was the end of the rainbow. Make-believe and reality walked hand in hand.

She passed through the emporiums, poking idly through barrels of trinkets, fingering newly imported silk scarfs and soaking up the noise. But the bay drew her. She moved toward it at an easy, meandering pace as the afternoon gave way to evening. The scent of fish dominated the air. Beneath it were the aromas of onions and spice and humanity.

She listened to the vendors hawk their wares and watched as a crab was selected and boiled in a sidewalk cauldron. The wharf was rimmed with restaurants and crammed with stores. Without apology, its ambience was vaguely dilapidated and faintly tawdry. Cassidy adored it. It was old and friendly and content to be itself.

Nibbling on a hot pretzel, she moved through stalls of hanging Chinese turnips, fresh abalone and live crabs. Wisps of fog began to curl at her feet, and the sun sank lower. She was grateful for her plum-colored quilted jacket as the breeze swept in from the bay.

If nothing else, she thought ruefully, I acquired some nice clothes at a tidy discount. Cassidy frowned and took a generous bite of her pretzel. If it hadn't been for Mrs. Sommerson's hips, I'd still have a job. After all, I did have her best interests at heart. Annoyed, she pulled the pins from her hair then tossed them into a trash can as she passed. Her hair tumbled to her shoulders in long, loose curls. She breathed a sigh of relief.

Rats. She chewed her pretzel aggressively and headed for the watery front yard of Fisherman's Wharf. *I needed that job. I really needed that stupid job.* Depression threatened as she walked the dock between lines of moored boats. She began a mental accounting of her finances. The rent was due the following week, and she needed another ream of typing paper. According to her shaky calculations, both of these necessities could be met if she didn't put too much emphasis on food for the next few days.

I won't be the first writer to have to tighten her belt in San Francisco, she decided. *The four basic food groups are probably overrated anyway.* With a shrug she finished off the pretzel. *That could be my last full meal for some time.* Grinning, she stuck her hands in her pockets and strolled to the rail at the edge of the dock.

Like a gray ghost, the fog rolled in over the bay. It crept closer to land, swallowing up the water along the way. It was thin tonight, full of patches, not the thick mass that often coated the bay and blinded the city. To the west the sun dipped into the sea and shot spears of flame over the rim of the water. Cassidy waited for the last flash of gold. Already her mood was lifting. She was a creature of hope and optimism, of faith and luck. She believed in destiny. It was, she felt, her destiny to write. The sale of articles and occasional short stories to magazines kept the dream alive. For four years of college her life had revolved around perfecting her craft. Jobs kept a roof over her head and meant nothing more. Dating had been permitted only when her schedule allowed and was kept casual. As yet, Cassidy had met no man who interested her seriously enough to make her veer from the straight path she had chosen. There were no curves in her scheme of things. No detours.

The loss of her current job distressed her only temporarily. Even as the evening sky darkened and the lights of the wharf fluttered on, her mood shifted. She was young and resilient.

Something would turn up, she decided as she leaned over the rail. Wavelets slapped gently against the hull of a fishing boat beside her. She had no need for a great deal of money; any job would do. Clerking in a department store might be just right. Perhaps something in home appliances. It would be difficult to step on anyone's vanity while selling a toaster. Pleased with the thought, Cassidy pushed worries out of her head and watched the fog tumble closer. Its fingers reached toward her.

There was a chill in the air now as the breeze picked up. She let it wash over her, tossing her hair and waking up her skin. The sounds and calls from the stands became remote, muffled by the mist. It was nearly dark. She heard a bird call out as it flew overhead and lifted her face to watch it. The first thin light of the moon fell over her. She smiled, dreaming a little. Abruptly she drew in her breath as a hand gripped her shoulder. Before she could make a sound, she'd been turned around and was staring up into a stranger's face.

He was tall, several inches taller than Cassidy, with a shock of black curls around a lean, raw-boned face. Her mind worked quickly to categorize the face, rejecting handsome in favor of dangerous. Perhaps it was her surprise and the creeping fog and darkening sky that caused the adjective to leap into her mind. But she thought, as she looked up at him, that his features were more in tune with the Barbary Coast than Fisherman's Wharf. His eyes were a deep, intense blue under black, winged brows, and his forehead was high under the falling black curls. His nose was long and straight, his mouth full, and his chin faintly cleft. It was a compelling, hard-hitting face with no softening features. He had a rangy build accentuated by snug jeans and a black pullover. After her initial shock passed, Cassidy gripped her purse tight and squared her shoulders.

"I've only got ten dollars," she told him, keeping her chin fearlessly lifted. "And I need it at least as badly as you."

"Be quiet," he ordered shortly and narrowed his eyes. They were oddly intent on her face, searching, probing in a manner that made her shiver. When he cupped her chin in his hand, Cassidy's courage slipped away again. Without speaking, he turned her head from one side to the other, all the while studying her with absolute concentration. His eyes were hypnotic. She watched him, speechless, as his brows lowered in a frown. There was speculation in the look. She tried to jerk away.

"Be still, will you?" he demanded. His deep voice sounded annoyed, and his fingers were very firm.

Cassidy swallowed. "Now listen," she said with apparent calm. "I've a black belt in karate and will certainly break both your arms if you try to molest me." As she spoke she glanced past his shoulder and was dismayed to see the lights of the restaurants behind them had dimmed in the fog. They were alone. "I can break a two-by-four in half with my bare hand," she added when his expression failed to register terror and respect. She noted that the fingers on her chin were strong, and that despite his rangy build his shoulders were broad. "And I can scream very loudly," she continued. "You'd better go away."

"Perfect," he murmured and ran his thumb along her jawline. Cassidy's heart thudded with alarm. "Absolutely perfect. Yes, you'll do." All at once the intensity cleared from his eyes, and he smiled. The transformation was so rapid, so startling, Cassidy simply stared. "Why would you want to do that?"

"Do what?" Cassidy asked, astonished by his metamorphosis.

"Break a two-by-four in half with your bare hand."

"Do *what*?" Her own bogus claim was forgotten. Confused, she frowned at him. "Oh, well, it's—it's for practice, I suppose. You have to think right through the board, I believe, so that—" She stopped, realizing she was standing on a deserted dock in the fog holding an absurd conversation with a maniac who still had her chin in his hand. "You'd really better let me go and be on your way before I have to do something drastic."

"You're exactly what I've been looking for," he told her but made no attempt to act on her suggestion. She noted there was a slight cadence to his speech that suggested an ethnic background, but she did not pause to narrow the choices.

"Well, I'm sorry. I'm not interested. I have a husband who's a linebacker for the 49ers. He's six feet five, two hundred and sixty-three pounds and *very* jealous. He'll be along any minute. Now let me go and you can have the blasted ten dollars."

"What the devil are you babbling about?" His brows lowered again. With the fog swirling thinly at his back, he looked fierce. Abruptly, one black brow flew up to disappear beneath the careless curls. "Do you think I'm going to mug you?" A flash of irritation crossed his face. "My dear child, I've no designs on your ten dollars or on your honor. I'm going to paint you, not ravish you."

"Paint me?" Cassidy was intrigued. "Are you an artist? You don't look like one." She considered his dashing, buccaneer's features. "What sort of an artist are you?"

"An excellent one," he replied easily and tilted her face a tad higher. A splash of moonlight found it. "I'm famous, talented and temperamental." The charming smile was back in his face, and the cadence was Irish. Cassidy responded to both.

"I'm desperately impressed," she said. He was obviously a lunatic but an appealing one. She forgot to be afraid.

"Of course you are," he agreed and turned her head to left profile. "It's only to be expected." He freed her chin at last, but the tingle of his fingers remained on her skin. "I've a houseboat just outside the city. We'll go there and I can start sketching you tonight."

Cassidy's eyes lit with wary amusement. "Aren't you supposed to offer to show me sketches, or is this a variation on an old theme?" She no longer considered him dangerous, merely persistent.

He sighed, and she watched the quick annoyance flash over his face. "The woman has a one-track mind. Listen…what is your name?"

"Cassidy," she answered automatically. "Cassidy St. John."

"Oh, no, half Irish, half English. We'll have trouble there." He stuck his hands into his pockets. His eyes seemed determined to know every inch of her face. "Cassidy, I have no need for your ten dollars, and no plans to tamper with your virtue. What I want is your face. I've a sketch pad and so forth on my houseboat."

"I wouldn't go on Michelangelo's boat if he handed me that line." Cassidy relaxed the grip on her purse and pushed her hair from her shoulders. Though he made a swift sound of exasperation, she grinned.

"All right." She sensed the impatience in his stance as he glanced behind him. "We'll get a cup of coffee in a well-lit, crowded restaurant. Will that suit you? If I try anything improper, you can break the table in half with your famous bare hand and draw attention."

Cassidy's lips trembled into a fresh grin. "I think I could agree to that." Before she could say anything else, he had her hand in his and was pulling her toward the cluster of restaurants. She felt an odd intimacy in the gesture along with a sense of his absolute control and determination. He was a man, she decided, who wouldn't take no for an answer. He walked quickly. She wondered if he were perpetually in a hurry. His stride was smooth, loose-limbed.

He pulled her into a small, rather dingy café and found a booth. The moment they were seated he again fixed her with his intent stare. His eyes, she noted, were even more blue than they had seemed in the dim light. Their color was intensified by his thick black lashes and bronze-toned skin. Cassidy met him stare for stare as she wondered what sort of man lived behind that incredible shade of blue. It was the waitress who broke her attention.

"What'll ya have?"

"Oh…coffee," she said when her companion made

no move to speak or cease his staring. "Two coffees." When the waitress clomped away, Cassidy turned back to him. "Why do you stare at me like that?" she demanded. It annoyed her that her nerves responded to the look. "It's very rude," she pointed out. "And very distracting."

"The light's dreadful in here, but it's some improvement over the fog. Don't frown," he ordered. "It gives you a line right here." Before she could move he had lifted a finger and traced it down between her brows. "You have a remarkable face. I can't decide whether the eyes are an advantage or a drawback. One tends to disbelieve violet."

As Cassidy attempted to digest this, the waitress returned with their coffee. Glancing up, he plucked the pencil from her pocket and gave her one of his lightning smiles. "I need this for a few minutes. Drink your coffee. Relax," he directed with a careless gesture of his hand. "This won't hurt a bit."

Cassidy obeyed as he began to sketch on the paper placemat in front of him. "Do you have a job we'll need to work around or does your fictitious husband support you with his football prowess?"

"How do you know he's fictitious?" Cassidy countered and forced her eyes away from the planes of his face.

"The same way I know you'd have a great deal of trouble with a two-by-four." He continued to sketch. "Do you have a job?"

"I was fired this afternoon," she muttered into her coffee.

"That simplifies matters. Don't frown, I'm not a patient man. I'll pay you the standard sitting fee." He glanced up as Cassidy's brows lifted. "What I have in mind should take no more than two months, if all goes well. Don't look so shocked, Cassidy, my intentions were pure and honorable from the beginning. It was only your lurid imagination—"

"My imagination is not that lurid," she tossed back indignantly. She shifted in her seat as she felt her cheeks warm. "When people come looming up out of the fog and seizing other people—"

"Looming?" he interrupted and stopped sketching long enough to give her a dry look. "I don't believe I did any looming or seizing tonight."

"It seemed a great deal like looming and seizing from my perspective," she grumbled before she sipped her coffee. Her eyes dropped to the sketch he made. She set down the cup, her eyes widening with surprised admiration. "That's wonderful!"

In a few bold strokes he had captured her. She saw not just the shape of her own hair, but an expression she recognized as essentially her own. "It's really wonderful," she repeated as he began another sketch. "You really *are* talented. I thought you were bragging."

"I'm unflinchingly honest," he murmured as his borrowed pencil moved across the placemat.

Recognizing the quality of his work, Cassidy became more enthusiastic. Her mind raced ahead. Steady employment for two months would be a godsend. By the end of that time she should have heard from the publishing house that had her manuscript under consideration. Two months without having to sell toasters! She would have her evenings free to work on her new plot. The benefits began to mount and multiply. Destiny must have sent Mrs. Sommerson in search of a dress that afternoon.

"Do you really want me to sit for you?"

"You're precisely what I need." His manner suggested that the matter was already settled. The second sketch was nearly completed. His coffee cooled, untouched. "I want you to start in the morning. Nine should be early enough."

"Yes, but—"

"Keep your hair down, and don't pile on layers of makeup, you'll just have to wash it off. You might smudge up your eyes a bit, but little else."

"I haven't said I'd—"

"You'll need the address, I suppose," he continued, ignoring her protests. "Do you know the city well?"

"I was born here," she told him with a superior sniff. "But I—"

"Well then, you shouldn't have any trouble finding my studio." He scrawled an address on the bottom of the placemat. Abruptly he lifted his eyes and captured hers again.

They stared at each other amid the clatter of cutlery and chatter of voices. What Cassidy felt in that brief moment she could not define, but she knew she had never experienced it before. Then, as quickly as it had occurred, it passed. He rose, and she was left feeling as if she had run a very long race in a very short time.

"Nine o'clock," he said simply; then as an afterthought he dropped a bill on the table for the coffee. He left without another word.

Reaching over, Cassidy picked up the placemat with the sketches and the address. For a moment she studied her face as he had seen it. Was her chin really shaped that way? she wondered and lifted her thumb and finger to trace it. She remembered his hand holding it in precisely the same fashion. With a shrug she dropped her hand then carefully folded the placemat. It wouldn't do any harm to go to his studio in the morning, she decided as she slipped the paper into her purse. She could get a look at things and then make up her mind if she wanted to sit for him or not. If she had any doubts, all she had to do was say no and walk out. Cassidy remembered his careless dominance and frowned. All I have to do, she repeated to herself sternly, is to say no and walk out. With this thought she rose and strolled out of the café.

Chapter 2

The morning was brilliantly clear, with a warmth promising more before afternoon. Cassidy dressed casually, not certain what was *de rigueur* for a prospective artist's model. Jeans and a full-sleeved white blouse seemed appropriate. As instructed she had left her hair loose, and her makeup was light enough to appear nonexistent. She had yet to decide if she would sit for the strange, intriguing man she had met in the fog, but she was curious enough to keep the appointment.

With the address safely copied onto her own notepad and tucked in her purse, Cassidy grabbed a cable car that would take her downtown. The scribbled address had surprised her, as she had recognized the exclusiveness of the area. Somehow she'd expected her artist to have his studio near her own apartment in North Beach. There the atmosphere was informal and enduringly bohemian. Traditionally, clutches of writers and artists and musicians inhabited that section of the city and maintained its flavor. She wondered if perhaps he had a patron who had set him up in an expensive studio. He hadn't fit her conception of an artist. At least, she corrected herself, until she had seen his hands. They were, Cassidy recalled, perhaps the most beautiful hands she had ever seen, long and narrow with lean, tapering fingers. The bones had been close to the surface. Sensitive hands. And strong, she added, remembering the feel of his fingers on her skin.

His face remained clear in her mind, and she brooded over its image for several moments. Something about it tugged at a vague memory, but she couldn't bring her recollection into focus. It was a distinctive face, unique in its raw appeal. She thought if she were an artist, it would be a face she would be compelled to paint. There were good bones there and shadows and secrets, dominated by the terrifying blue of his eyes.

The trolley's bells clanged and snapped Cassidy out of her reverie. Stupid, she thought and lifted her face to the breeze. I didn't even get his name, and I'm obsessed with his face. He's supposed to be obsessed with mine, not the other way around. She jumped from the trolley and stepped onto the sidewalk. She scanned the street numbers looking for the address. I was right, she mused, about the quality of the neighborhood.

Still, like all of the city, it was a fascinating mixture of the exotic and the cosmopolitan, the romantic and the practical. San Francisco's dual personality was as prevalent here as it was in Chinatown or on Telegraph Hill. There remained a blending of the antique and the revolutionary. Cassidy could hear the clang of the old-fashioned trolley as she looked up at a radically new steel-and-glass skyscraper.

The day was fine and warm, and her body enjoyed it while her mind drifted back to the plot that sat on her desk at home. She brought her attention back to the present when she reached the number corresponding to the address in her purse. She stood frowning.

The Gallery. Cassidy scanned the number on the door for confirmation, and her frown deepened. She'd browsed through The Gallery only a few months before, and she remembered quite well when it had opened five years ago. Since its opening it had gained an enviable reputation as a showcase for the finest art in the country. A showing at The Gallery could make a fledgling artist's career or enhance that of a veteran. Collectors and connoisseurs were known to gather there to buy or to admire, to criticize or simply to be seen. Like much of the city it was a combination of the elegant and the unconventional. The architecture of the building was simple and unpretentious, while inside was a treasure trove of paintings and sculpture. Cassidy was also aware that one of The Gallery's biggest draws was its owner, Colin Sullivan. She searched her memory for what she had read of him, then began to put the bits and pieces into order.

An Irish immigrant, he had lived in America for more than fifteen years; his career had taken off when he had been barely twenty. Oil was his usual medium, and a unique use of shading and light his trademark. He had a reputation for impatience and brilliance. He would be just past thirty now and unmarried, though there had been several women linked romantically with him. There had been a princess once, and a prima ballerina. His paintings sold for exorbitant sums, and he rarely took commissions. He painted to please himself and painted well. As she stood in the warmth of the morning sunlight piecing together her tidbits of gossip and information, Cassidy recalled why the face of her artist had jarred a memory. She'd seen his picture in the newspaper when The Gallery had opened five years before. Colin Sullivan.

She let out a long breath then lifted her hands to either side of her head to push at her hair. Colin Sullivan wanted to paint her. He had once flatly refused to do a portrait of one of Hollywood's reigning queens, but he wanted to paint Cassidy St. John, an unemployed writer whose greatest triumph to date was a short story printed in a woman's magazine. All at once she remembered that she'd thought he'd been a mugger, that she had said absurd things to him, that she had told him with innocent audacity that his sketches were good. In annoyance and humiliation she chewed on her lip.

He might have introduced himself, she thought with a frown, instead of sneaking up behind me and grabbing me. I behaved quite naturally under the circumstances. I've nothing to be embarrassed about. Besides, she reminded herself, he told me to come. He's the one who arranged the entire thing. I'm only here to see if I want to take the job. Cassidy shifted her purse on her shoulder, wished briefly she had worn something more dignified or more exotic and moved to the front door of The Gallery. It was locked.

She pushed against the door again then concluded with a sigh that it was too early for The Gallery to be open. Perhaps there was a back entrance. He had spoken of a studio; surely it would have its own outside door. With this in mind Cassidy strolled around the side of the building and tried a side door, which refused to budge. Undaunted, she continued around the square brick building to its rear. When another door proved uncooperative, she turned her attention to a set of wooden steps leading to a second level.

Craning her neck, she squinted against the sun and scanned the ring of windows. The glass tossed back the light. If I were an artist with a studio, she reflected, it would definitely be up there. She began to climb the L-shaped staircase. The treads were open and steep. Faced with another door at the top, she started to test the knob, hesitated and opted to knock. Loudly. She glanced back over her shoulder and discovered the ground was surprisingly far below. A tiny sound of alarm escaped her when the door swung open.

"You're late," Colin stated with a frown of impatience and took her hand, pulling her inside before she could respond. Her senses were immediately assailed with the scents of turpentine and oils. He looked no less formidable in broad daylight than he had in the murky fog. In precisely the same manner he had employed the night before, he caught her chin in his hand.

"Mr. Sullivan…" Cassidy began, flustered.

"Ssh!" He tilted her head to the left, narrowed his eyes and stared. "Yes, it's even better in decent light. Come over here, I want some proper sketches."

"Mr. Sullivan," Cassidy tried again as he yanked her across a high, airy room lined with canvases and cluttered with equipment. "I'd like to know a little more about all this before I commit myself."

"Sit here," he commanded and pushed her down on a stool. "Don't slouch," he added as he turned away.

"Mr. Sullivan! Would you please listen to me?"

"Presently," he replied as he picked up a wide pad and a pencil. "For now be quiet."

Totally at a loss, Cassidy sighed gustily and folded her hands. It would be simpler, she decided, to let him get his sketches out of his system. She allowed her eyes to wander and search the room.

It was large, barnlike, with wide windows and a sky-light that pleased her enormously. The expanses of glass let in all the available sunlight. The floor was wood and bare, except for splatters of paint, and the walls were a neutral cream. Unframed canvases were stacked helter-skelter, facing the walls. Easels were propped here and there, and a large table was scattered with paints and brushes and rags and bottles. There was a couch at the far end of the room, sitting there as if added in after-thought. Three wooden chairs were placed at odd in-tervals as if pushed aside by an impatient hand and left wherever they landed. There were two other stools, two inside doors and a large goosenecked high-intensity lamp.

"Look out the window," Colin ordered abruptly. "I want a profile."

She obeyed. The vague annoyance she felt slipped away as she spotted a sparrow building a nest in the crook of an oak. The bird moved busily, carrying wisps of this and that in her beak. Patient and tenacious, she swooped and searched and built, then swooped again. Her wings caught the sun. Enchanted, Cassidy watched her. A quiet smile touched her lips and warmed her eyes.

"What do you see?" Colin moved to her, and her absorption was so deep she neither jolted nor turned.

"That bird there." She pointed as the sparrow made

another quick dive. "Look how determined she is to finish that nest. The whole thing built from bits of string and grass and whatever other treasures sparrows find. We need bricks and concrete and prefabricated walls, but that little bird can build a perfectly adequate home out of next to nothing, without hands, without tools, without a union representative. Marvelous, don't you think?" Cassidy turned her head and smiled. He was closer than she had imagined, his face near hers in order for him to follow her line of vision. As she turned, he shifted his eyes from the window and caught hers. She felt a sudden jolt, as if she had stood too quickly and lost her inner balance.

"You might be even more perfect than I had originally thought," Colin said. He brushed her hair behind one shoulder.

She suddenly remembered her resolve to be businesslike. "Mr. Sullivan—"

"Colin," he interrupted. He continued to arrange her hair. "Or just Sullivan, if you like."

"Colin, then," she said patiently. "I had no idea who you were last night. It didn't occur to me until I was standing outside The Gallery." She shifted, faintly disturbed that he remained standing so close. "Of course, I'm flattered that you want to paint me, but I'd like to know what's expected of me, and—"

"You're expected to hold a pose for twenty minutes without fidgeting," he began while he pushed her hair forward again then back over her other shoulder. His fingers brushed Cassidy's neck and caused her to frown. He appeared not to notice. "You're expected to follow instructions and keep quiet unless I tell you otherwise.

You're expected to be on time and not to babble about leaving early so you can meet your boyfriend."

"I was on time," Cassidy retorted and tossed her head so that his arrangement of her hair flew into confusion. "You didn't tell me to come to the back, and I wandered around until I found the right door."

"Bright, too," he said dryly. "Your eyes darken dramatically when your Irish is up. Who named you Cassidy?"

"It's my mother's family name," she said shortly. She opened her mouth to speak again.

"I knew some Cassidys in Ireland," he commented as he lifted her hands to examine them.

"I don't know any of my mother's family," Cassidy murmured, disconcerted by the feel of his hands on hers. "She died when I was born."

"I see." Colin turned her palms up. "Your hands are very narrow-boned. And your father?"

"His family was from Devon. He died four years ago. I don't see what this has to do with anything."

"It has to do with everything." He lifted his eyes from her hands but kept them in his. "You get your eyes and hair from your mother's family, and your skin and bone structure from your father's. It's a face of contradictions you have, Cassidy St. John, and precisely what I need. Your hair must have a dozen varying shades and it looks as though you've just taken your head from a pillow. You're wise not to attempt to discipline it. Your eyes go just past Celtic-blue into violet and add a touch of the exotic with the shape of them. They tend to dream. But your bones are all English aristocracy. Your mouth tips the balance again, promising a passion the cool British complexion denies. Pure skin, just a hint of rose under the ivory. You haven't walked through life without having to scale a few walls, yet there's a definite aura of the ingenue around you. The painting I want to do must have certain elements. I need very specific qualities in my model. You have them." He paused and inclined his head. "Does that satisfy your curiosity?"

She was staring at him, transfixed, trying to see herself as he described. Did her heritage so heavily influence her looks? "I'm not at all certain that it does," Cassidy murmured. She sighed, then her eyes found him again. "But I'm vain enough to want Colin Sullivan to paint me and destitute enough to need the job." She smiled. "Shall I be immortal when you've finished? I've always wanted to be."

Colin laughed, and the sound was warm and free in the big room. He squeezed her hands, then surprisingly brought them to his lips. "You'll do me, Cass."

Cassidy's fumbling reply was interrupted as the studio door swung open.

"Colin, I need to—" The woman who swirled into the room halted abruptly and fixed sharp eyes on Cassidy. "Sorry," she said as her gaze drifted to their joined hands. "I didn't know you were occupied."

"No matter, Gail," Colin returned easily. "You know I lock the door when I'm working seriously. This is Cassidy St. John, who'll be sitting for me. Cassidy, Gail Kingsley, a very talented artist who manages The Gallery."

Gail Kingsley was striking. She was tall and thin as a reed with a long, triangular face set off by a spiky cap of vivid red hair. Everything about her was vital and compelling. Her eyes were piercingly green and darkly accented, her mouth was wide and slashed in uncompromising scarlet. Gold hoops poked through the spikes of vibrant hair at her ears. Her dress was flowing, without a definite line, a chaotic mix of greens washed over silk. The effect was bold and breathtaking. She moved forward, and her entire body seemed charged with nervous energy. Even her movements were quick and sharp, her eyes probing as they rested on Cassidy's face. There was something in the look that made Cassidy instantly uncomfortable. It was a purposeful intrusion while it remained completely impersonal.

"Good bones," Gail commented in a dismissing tone. "But the coloring's rather dull, don't you think?"

Cassidy spoke with annoyed directness. "We can't all be redheads."

"True enough," Colin said and, lifting a brow at Cassidy, turned to Gail. "What was it you needed? I want to get back to work."

There is a certain aura around people who have been intimate, Cassidy thought. It shows in a look, a gesture, a tone of voice. In the moment Gail's eyes left Cassidy to meet Colin's, she knew they were, or had been, lovers. Cassidy felt a vague sense of disappointment. Uncomfortable, she tried vainly to pull her hands from Colin's. She received an absentminded frown.

"It's Higgin's *Portrait of a Girl.* We've been offered five thousand, but Higgin won't accept unless you approve. I'd like to have it firmed up today."

"Who made the offer?"

"Charles Dupres."

"Tell Higgin to take it. Dupres won't haggle and he's fair. Anything else?" There was a simple dismissal in the words. Cassidy watched Gail's eyes flare.

"Nothing that can't wait. I'll go give Higgin a call."

"Fine." Colin turned back to Cassidy before Gail was halfway across the room. He was frowning at her hair as he pushed it back from her face. Over his shoulder, Cassidy watched Gail's glance dart back when she reached the door. Gail shut it firmly behind her. Colin stepped away and scanned Cassidy from head to toe.

"It won't do," he announced and scowled. "It won't do at all."

Confused by his statement, shaken by what she had recognized in Gail's eyes, Cassidy stared at him then ran her fingers through her hair. "What won't?"

"That business you have on." He made a gesture with his hand, a quick flick of the wrist, which encompassed her blouse and jeans and sandals.

Cassidy looked down and ran her palms over her hips. "You didn't specify how I should dress, and in any case I hadn't decided to sit for you." She shrugged her shoulders, annoyed with herself for feeling compelled to justify her attire. "You might have given me some details instead of scrawling down the address and bounding off."

"I want something smooth and flowing—no waist, no interruptions." He ignored Cassidy's comments. "Ivory, not white. Something long and sleek." He took her waist in his hands, which threw her into speechless shock. "You haven't any hips to speak of, and the waist of a child. I want a high neck so we won't worry about the lack of cleavage."

Blushing furiously, Cassidy slipped down from the stool and pushed him away. "It's my body, you know. I don't care for your observations on it or your—your hands on it, either. My cleavage or the lack of it has nothing to do with you."

"Don't be a child," he said briskly and set her back on the stool. "At the moment, your body only interests me artistically. If that changes, you'll know quickly enough."

"Now just a minute, Sullivan." Cassidy slipped off the stool again, tossing back her head as she prepared to put him neatly in his place.

"Spectacular." He grabbed a handful of her hair to keep her face lifted to his. "Temper becomes you, Cass, but it's not the mood I'm looking for. Another time, perhaps." The corners of his mouth lifted as his fingers moved to massage her neck. His smile settled lazily over his face, and though Cassidy suspected the calculation, it was no less effective. She was conscious of his fingers on her skin. The essential physicality of the sensation was novel and intrigued her into silence. This was something new to be explored. His voice lowered into a caress no less potent than the hand on her skin. The faint lilt of Ireland intensified. "It's an illusion I'm looking for, and a reality. A wish. Can you be a wish for me, Cass?"

In that moment, with her face inches from his, their bodies just touching, the warmth of his fingers on her skin, Cassidy felt she could be anything he asked. Nothing was impossible. This was where his power over women lay, she realized: in the quick charm, the piratical features, the light hint of an old country in his speech. Added to this was an undiluted sexuality he turned on at will and an impatience in the set of his shoulders. She knew he was aware of his power and used it shamelessly. Even this was somehow attractive. She felt herself submitting to it, drawn toward it while her emotions overshadowed her intellect. She wondered what his mouth would feel like on hers, and if the kiss would be as exciting as she imagined. Would she lose or find herself? Would she simply experience? As a defense against her own thoughts, she placed her hands on his chest and pushed herself to safety.

"You're not an easy man, are you, Colin?" Cassidy took a deep breath to steady her limbs.

"Not a bit." There was careless agreement in his answer. She defined what flicked over his face as something between annoyance and curiosity. "How old are you, Cassidy?"

"Twenty-three," she answered, meeting his eyes levelly. "Why?"

He shrugged, stuck his hands in his pockets then paced the room. "I'll need to know all there is to know about you before I'm done. What you are will creep into the portrait, and I'll have to work with it. I've got to find the blasted dress quickly—I want to start. The time's right." There was an urgency in his movements that contrasted sharply with the man who had seduced her with his voice only moments before. Who was Colin Sullivan? Cassidy wondered. Though she knew finding out would be dangerous, she felt compelled to learn.

"I think I know one that might do," she hazarded while his mood swirled around the room. "It's more oyster than ivory, actually, but it's simple and straight with a high neck. It's also horribly expensive. It's silk, you see—"

"Where is it?" Colin demanded and stopped his pacing directly in front of her. "Never mind," he continued even as she opened her mouth to tell him. "Let's go have a look."

He had her by the hand and had passed through the

back door before she could say another word. Cassidy took care to go along peacefully down the stairs, not wishing to risk a broken neck. "Which way?" he demanded as he marched her to the front of the building.

"It's just a few blocks that way," she said and pointed to the left. "But, Colin—" Before she could finish her thought, she was being piloted at full speed down the sidewalk. "Colin, I think you should know... Good grief, I should've worn my track shoes. Would you slow down?"

"You've got long legs," he told her and continued without slackening his pace. Making a brief sound of disgust, Cassidy trotted to keep up. "I think you should know the dress is in the shop I was fired from yesterday."

"A dress shop?" This appeared to interest him enough to slow him down while he glanced at her. With a gesture of absent familiarity, he tucked her hair behind her ear. "What were you doing working in a dress shop?"

Cassidy sent him a withering stare. "I was earning a living, Sullivan. Some of us are required to do so in order to eat."

"Don't be nasty, Cass," he advised mildly. "You're not a professional dress clerk."

"Which is precisely why I was fired." Amused by her own ineptitude, she grinned. "I'm also not a professional waitress, which is why I was fired from Jim's Bar and Grill. I objected to having certain parts of my anatomy pinched and dumped a bowl of coleslaw on a paying customer. I won't go into my brief career as a switchboard operator. It's a sad, pitiful story, and it's such a lovely day." She tossed back her head to smile at Colin and found him watching her.

"If you're not a professional clerk or waitress or switchboard operator, what are you, Cass?"

"A struggling writer who seems singularly inept at holding a proper job since college."

"A writer." He nodded as he looked down at her. "What do you write?"

"Unpublished novels," she told him and smiled again. "And an occasional article on the effects of perfume on the modern man. I have to keep my hand in."

"And are you any good?" Colin skirted another pedestrian without taking his eyes from Cassidy.

"I'm positively brimming with fresh, undiscovered talent." She tossed her hair behind her shoulders then pointed. "There we are, The Best Boutique. I wonder what Julia will have to say about this. She'll probably think you're keeping me." She bit her lip to suppress a giggle then slid her glance back to his. "Have you any smoldering looks up your sleeve, Colin?" Mischief danced in her eyes as she paused outside the front door of the shop. "You could send me a few and give Julia something to talk about for weeks." She swung through the door, her lovely face flushed with laughter.

True to form, Julia greeted Colin with scrupulous politeness and only the faintest glimmer of curiosity. There was a speculative glance for her former clerk, then recognition of Colin widened her eyes. She lifted a brow at Cassidy's request for the oyster silk dress then proceeded to wait on them personally.

In the changing room Cassidy stripped off her jeans and marveled at the irony of life. Little more than twenty-four hours before, she had been standing outside that very room with discarded dresses heaped over her arms...without a thought of Colin Sullivan in her head. Now he seemed to dominate both her thoughts and her actions. The thin, cool silk was slipping over her head because he wished it. Her heart beat just a fraction quicker because he waited to see the results. Cassidy fastened the zipper, held her breath and turned. Her reflection stared back at her with undisguised awe.

The dress fell from a severely high neck in a straight line, softened by the fragility of the material. Her arms and shoulders gleamed under the thin transparency of its full sleeves. Her hair glowed with life against the delicacy of color. Cassidy let out her breath slowly. It was a wish of a dress, as romantic as the material, as practical as its line. In it she not only looked both elegant and vulnerable but felt it. With taut nerves she moistened her lips and stepped from the changing room.

Colin was charming Julia into blushes. The incongruity of flirtatious color in the cool, composed face turned Cassidy's nerves into amusement. There was the devil of a smile in Colin's eyes as he lifted Julia's hand and brushed his lips over her knuckles. Cassidy schooled her features to sobriety. A hint of a smile lurked on her lips.

"Colin."

He turned as she called his name. The smile that lit his face and brightened his eyes faded then died. Releasing Julia's hand, he took a few steps closer but kept half the room between them. Cassidy, who had been about to grin and spin a circle for inspection, stood still, hypnotized by his eyes.

Very slowly, his eyes left her face to travel down the length of her then back again. Cassidy's cheeks grew warm with the flurry of her emotions. How could he make her feel so vitalized then so enervated with just a look? She wanted to speak, to break her own trance, but the words were jumbled and uncooperative. She found she could only repeat his name.

"Colin?" There was the faintest hint of invitation in the word, a question even she did not understand.

Something flashed in his eyes and was gone. The intense concentration was inexplicably replaced by irritation. When he spoke it was brisk and dismissive.

"That will do very well. Have it packed up and bring it with you tomorrow. We'll start then."

Cassidy's mind raced with a hundred questions and a hundred demands. His tone stiffened her pride, however, and hers was cool when she spoke. "Is that all?"

"That's all." Temper hovered in his voice. "Nine o'clock tomorrow. Don't be late."

Cassidy took a deep breath and let it out carefully. In that moment she was certain she despised him. They watched each other for another minute while the air crackled with tension and something more volatile. Then she turned her back on him and glided into the changing room.

Chapter 3

Cassidy spent most of the night lecturing herself. By morning she felt she had herself firmly in hand. There had been absolutely no reason for her to be annoyed with Colin. His brisk, impersonal attitude over the dress was only to be expected. As she rode the trolley across town, she shifted the dress box into her other arm and determined to preserve a cool, professional distance from him.

He's simply my employer. He's an artist, obviously a temperamental one. She added the modifier with a sniff. Deftly she jumped from the cable car to finish the trip on foot. He's a man who sees something in my face he wants to paint. He has no personal feelings for me, nor I for him. How could I? I barely know Colin Sullivan. What I felt yesterday was simply the overflow of his personality. It's very strong, very magnetic. I only imagined that there was an immediate affinity between us. Things don't happen that way, not that fast. All there is between us is the bond between artist and subject. I was writing scenes again.

Cassidy paused at the base of the stairs that led to Colin's studio. Still, he might have thanked me for finding the dress he was looking for, she thought. Never mind. She made an involuntary gesture with her hand as she climbed the steps. He's so self-absorbed he probably forgot I suggested the shop in the first place. With a quick toss of her head, Cassidy knocked, prepared to be brisk and professional in her new employ. Her resolve wavered a bit when Gail Kingsley opened the door.

"Hello," she said and smiled despite the cool assessment in Gail's eyes. For an answer Gail made a sweeping arm gesture into the room that would have seemed overdone on anyone else. Flamboyance suited her.

Gail was just as striking today in a shocking-pink jumpsuit no other redhead would have had the courage to wear. Colin was nowhere in sight. Cassidy was torn between admiration for the redhead's style and disappointment that Colin hadn't answered the door. She felt juvenile and ragged in jeans and a pullover.

"Am I too early?"

Gail placed her hands on her narrow hips and walked around Cassidy slowly. "No, Colin's tied up. He'll be along. Is that curl in your hair natural or have you a perm?"

"It's natural," Cassidy replied evenly.

"And the color?"

"Mine, too." Gail's bold perfume dominated the scents of paint. When she came back to stand in front of her, Cassidy met her eyes levelly. "Why?"

"Just curious, dear heart. Just curious." Gail flashed a quick, dazzling smile that snapped on and off like a light. It was momentarily blinding, then all trace of it vanished. "Colin's quite taken with your face. He seems to be drifting into a romantic period. I've always avoided that sort of technique." She narrowed her eyes until she seemed to be examining the pores of Cassidy's skin.

"Want to count my teeth?" Cassidy invited.

"Don't be snide." Gail touched a scarlet-tipped finger to her lips. "Colin and I often share models. I want to see if I can use you for anything."

"I'm not a box lunch, Miss Kingsley," retorted Cassidy with feeling. "I don't care to be shared."

"A good model should be flexible," Gail reproved, stretching her slender arms to the ceiling in one long, luxurious movement. "I hope you don't make a fool of yourself the way the last one did."

"The last one?" Cassidy responded then immediately wanted to bite off her tongue.

"She fell desperately in love with Colin." Gail gave her quick light-switch smile again. Her sharp, rapid gestures skittered down Cassidy's nerves. She was a cat looking for something to stalk. "Worse, she imagined Colin was in love with her. It was really quite pathetic. A lovely little thing—milky skin, dark gypsy eyes. Naturally Colin was beastly to her in the end. He tends to be when someone tries to pin him down. There's nothing worse than having someone mooning and sighing over you, is there?"

"I wouldn't know," Cassidy returned in mild tones. "But you needn't worry that I'll be mooning and sighing over Colin. He needs my face, I need a job." She paused a moment. Perhaps, she thought, it's best to be clear from the start. "You won't have any trouble from me, Gail. I'm too busy to orchestrate a romance with Colin."

Gail stopped her pacing long enough to fix her with a speculative frown. The frown vanished, and she moved swiftly to the door. "That simplifies matters, doesn't it? You can change through there." She flung out an arm to her left and was gone.

Cassidy took time to inhale deeply. She shook her head. Artists, she decided, were all as mad as hatters. Shrugging off Gail's behavior, she moved to the door indicated and found a small dressing room. Closeting herself inside, Cassidy began to change. As before, the gown made her feel different. Perhaps, she thought as she pulled a brush through her hair, it's the sensation of real silk against my skin, or the elegant simplicity of the line and color. Or is it because it's the image of what Colin wants me to be?

Whatever the reason, Cassidy couldn't deny that she felt heightened when she wore the gown—more alive, more aware, more a woman. After giving herself one last quick glance in the mirror, she opened the door and stepped into the studio.

"Oh, you're here," she said foolishly when she saw Colin scowling at a blank canvas. She had only a side view of him, and he didn't turn at her entrance. His hands were stuffed in his pockets, and his weight was distributed evenly on both legs. There was an impression of sharp vitality held in check—waiting, straining a bit for release. He was dressed casually, as she was now accustomed to seeing him, and the clothes seemed to suit his rangy, loose-limbed build. His face was in a black study: brows lowered, eyes narrowed, mouth unsmiling. The thought crossed Cassidy's mind that he was unscrupulously attractive and would be a terrifying man to care for. She remained where she was, certain he had not even heard her speak.

"I'm going to start on canvas straight away," he said. Still he did not turn to acknowledge her. "There're violets on the table." With one shoulder he made a vague gesture. "They match your eyes."

Cassidy looked over and saw the small nosegay tossed amid the artistic rubble. Her face lit with instant pleasure. "Oh, they're lovely!" Moving to the table, she took them then buried her face in their delicate petals. The fragrance was subtle and sweet. Touched and charmed, Cassidy lifted her smile to thank him.

"I want a spot of color against the dress," Colin murmured. His preoccupation was obvious and complete. He did not glance at her or change expression.

Pleasure shattered, Cassidy stared down at the tiny flowers and sighed. It's my fault, she thought ruefully. He bought them for the painting, not for me. It was ridiculous to think otherwise. Why in the world should he buy me flowers? With a shake of her head and a wry smile, she moved over to join him. "Do you see me there already?" she asked. "On the empty canvas?"

He turned then and looked at her, but the frown of his concentration remained. He lifted the hand that held the flowers. "Yes, they'll do. Stand over here, I want the light from this window."

As he propelled her across the room, Cassidy twisted her head to look up at him. "Good morning, Colin," she said in the bright, cheerful voice of a kindergarten instructor.

He lifted a brow as he stopped by the window. "Manners are the least of my concerns when I'm working."

"I'm awfully glad you cleared that up," Cassidy replied, smiling broadly.

"I've also been known to devour young, smart-tongued wenches for breakfast."

"Wenches!" Cassidy's smile became a delighted grin. "How wonderfully anachronistic. It sounds lovely when you say it, too. I do wish you'd said lusty young wenches, though. I've always loved that phrase."

"The description doesn't fit you." Colin lifted her chin with one finger and brushed her hair over her shoulder with his other hand.

"Oh." Cassidy felt vaguely insulted.

"Once I've set the pose, don't fidget. I just might throw an easel at you if you do." While he spoke, he moved her face and body with his hands. His touch was as impersonal as a physician's. *I might as well be a still-life arrangement,* Cassidy thought. By his eyes, she saw that his mind had gone beyond her and into his art. She recognized his expression of absolute concentration from her own work. She, too, had a tendency to block out her surroundings and step into her own mind.

At length he stood back and studied her in silence. It was a natural pose and simple. She stood straight, with the nosegay cupped in both hands and held just below her right hip. Her arms were relaxed, barely bent at the elbows. He had left her hair tumbled free, without design, over both shoulders. "Lift your chin a fraction higher." He held up a hand to stop the movement. "There. Be still and don't talk until I tell you."

Cassidy obeyed, moving only her eyes to watch him as he strode behind the easel again. He lifted a piece of

charcoal. Minutes passed in utter silence as she watched
the movements of his arms and shoulders and felt the
probing power of his eyes. They returned again and
again to her face. She knew he could look into her eyes
and see directly into her soul, learning more perhaps
than she knew herself. The sensation made her not nervous so much as curious. What would he see? How
would he express it?

"All right," Colin said abruptly. "You can talk for the
moment, but don't move the pose. Tell me about those
unpublished novels of yours."

He continued to work with such obsessed concentration that Cassidy assumed he had invited her to talk only
to keep her relaxed. She doubted seriously if her words
made more than a surface impression. If he heard them
at all, he would forget them moments later.

"There's only one actually, or one and a half. I'm
working on a second novel while the first bounces from
rejection slip to rejection slip." She started to shrug but
caught herself in time. "It's about a woman's coming of
age, the choices she makes, the mistakes. It's rather sentimental, I suppose. I like to think she makes the right
choices in the end. Do you know it's very difficult to
talk without your hands? I had no idea mine were so
necessary to my vocabulary."

"It's your Gaelic blood." Colin frowned deeply at the
canvas then lifted his eyes to hers. By the movement
of his shoulders she knew he continued to work. "Will
you let me read your manuscript?"

Surprised, Cassidy stared a moment before gather-
ing her wits. "Well, yes, if you'd like. I—"

"Good," he interrupted and slashed another line on
the canvas. "Bring it with you tomorrow. Be quiet now,"

he commanded before Cassidy could speak again. "I'm going to work the face."

Silence reigned until he put down the charcoal and shook his head. "It's not right." He scowled at Cassidy then paced. Unsure, she held the pose and her tongue. "You're not giving me the right mood. Do you know what I want?" he demanded. There was impatience and a hint of temper in his voice. She opened her mouth then closed it again, seeing the question had been rhetorical. "I want more than an illusion. I want passion. You've passion in you, Cassidy, more, by heaven, than I need for this painting." He turned to face her again, and she felt the room vibrate with his tension. Her heart began to quicken in response. "I want a promise. I want a woman who invites a lover. I want expectation and the freshness that springs from innocence. Untouched but not untouchable. It's that you have to give me. That's the essence of it." In his frustration, the cadence of his native land became more obvious. The fire of his talent flickered in his eyes. Fascinated, Cassidy watched him, not speaking even when he stopped directly in front of her. "There would be a softness in your eyes and just a trace of heat. There would be a giving in the set of your mouth that comes from having just been kissed, from waiting to be kissed again. Like this."

His mouth took hers quickly, stunningly. He framed her face with his hands, thumbs brushing her cheeks while he took the kiss into trembling intimacy with terrifying speed. His lips were warm and soft and experienced. His tongue plundered without warning. Somewhere deep within her came an answer. Passion, long overlooked, smoldered then kindled then licked tentatively into flame. She tasted the flavor of power. As quickly as his mouth had taken, it liberated.

Though she was unaware of it, her expression was exactly what he'd demanded of her—expectant, inviting, innocent. Fleetingly he dropped his gaze to her mouth; then, taking his time, he removed his hands from her face. Impatience flickered in his eyes before he turned and strode to his easel.

Cassidy tried to steady her spinning brain. Reason told her the kiss had meant nothing, a means to an end, but her heart thudded in contradiction. In a few brief seconds he had stirred up a hunger she hadn't been aware of having, had stirred up desires she hadn't been aware she had. It was more a revelation, she thought bemusedly, than a kiss. Forcing her breathing to slow, she tried to keep the quick encounter in perspective.

She was a grown woman. Kisses were more common than handshakes. It was her treacherous imagination that had turned it into something else. *Only my imagination,* she decided as she calmed, and his utter effrontery. He'd taken her totally by surprise. He'd kissed her when he'd had no right to do so, and in a way that had been both proprietary and intimate. No man had ever been permitted either of the privileges, and his seizure of them had left her shaken. Cassidy could justify her reaction to Colin by intellectually dissecting the scene, its cause and results. She turned her emotions over to her mind and plotted the scene. She examined motivations. Still, something lingered inside her that could not quite be rationalized or explained away. Disturbed, she tried to ignore it.

"We'll stop now," Colin stated abruptly and put aside the charcoal. He glanced up as he cleaned his hands on a paint rag. She thought perhaps he saw Cassidy St. John again for the first time since he had set the pose. "Relax."

When Cassidy obeyed, she was surprised to find her muscles stiff. "How long have I been standing there?" she demanded as she arched her back. "A good bit more than twenty minutes."

Colin shrugged, his eyes back on the canvas. "Perhaps. It's moving nicely. Do you want coffee?"

Cassidy scowled at his casual dismissal of the time. "Twenty minutes is quite long enough to stand in one position. I'll bring a kitchen timer with me from now on, and yes, I want coffee."

He ignored the first two-thirds of her statement and headed for the door. "I'll fix some."

"Am I allowed to look?" She gestured toward the canvas as he drew back the bolt.

"No."

She made a sound of disgust. "What about the others?" Her gesture took in the canvases against the wall. "Are they a secret, too?"

"Help yourself. Just stay away from the one I'm working on." Colin disappeared, presumably to fetch the promised coffee.

Making a face at the empty doorway, Cassidy set down the nosegay and wandered toward the neglected canvases. They were stacked here and tilted there, without order or design. Some were small while others were large enough to require some effort on her part to turn them around. Within moments, whatever minor irritation she'd felt was eclipsed by admiration for his talent. She saw why Colin Sullivan was considered a master of color and light. Moreover she saw the sensitivity she had detected in his hands and the strength she had felt there. There was insight and honesty in his portraits, vitality in his city scenes and landscapes. A play of shadows, a splatter of light, and the paintings breathed his mood. She wondered if he painted what he saw or what he felt, then understood it was a marriage of both. She decided that he saw more than the average mortal was entitled to see. His gift was as much in his perception as in his hands. The paintings moved her almost as deeply as the man had.

Carefully she turned another canvas. The subject was beautiful. The woman's undraped body lounged negligently on the couch that now sat empty at the far end of the studio. There was a lazy smile on her face and a careless confidence in the attitude of her naked limbs. From the milky skin and gypsy eyes, Cassidy recognized the model Gail had spoken of that morning.

"A lovely creature, isn't she?" Colin asked from behind. Cassidy started.

"Yes." She turned and accepted the proffered mug. "I've never seen a more beautiful woman."

Colin's brow arched as he moved his shoulders. "Of a type, she's nearly perfect, and her body is exquisite."

Cassidy frowned into her coffee and tried to pretend the stab of irritation didn't exist.

"She has a basic sexuality and is comfortable with it."

"Yes." Sipping her coffee, Cassidy spoke mildly. "You've captured it remarkably well."

Her tone betrayed her. Colin grinned. "Ah, Cass, it's an open book you are and surely the most delightful creature I've met in years." The thickened brogue rolled easily off his tongue. Better women than she, Cassidy was certain, had fallen for the Gaelic charm.

She tossed her head, but the glare she had intended to flash at him turned of its own volition into a smile. "I can't keep up with you, Sullivan." She studied him over the rim of her mug. Sunlight shot through her hair and shadowed the silk of the dress. "Why did you settle in San Francisco?" she asked.

Colin straddled one of the abandoned wooden chairs, keeping his eyes on her. She wondered if he saw her as a person now or still as a subject. "It's a cross section of the world. I like the contrasts and its sordid history."

"And that it trades on that sordid history rather than apologizing for it," Cassidy concluded with an agreeing nod. "But don't you miss Ireland?"

"I go back now and then." He lifted his coffee and drank deeply. "It feeds me, like a mother's breast. Here I find passion, there I find peace. The soul requires both." He glanced up at her again and searched her face. The violet of her eyes had darkened. Her expression revealed her thoughts. They were all on him. Colin turned away from the innocent candor of her eyes. "Finish your coffee. I want to perfect the preliminary outline today. I'll start in oil tomorrow."

The morning passed almost completely in silence while she took advantage of Colin's absorption to study him. She had read of the dark devil looks and fiery blue eyes of the volatile black Irish, and now she found them even more compelling in the flesh. She wondered at the strange quirk in her own personality that caused her to find moodiness appealing.

With only the barest effort she could feel the swift

excitement of his lips on hers. Warmed, she drifted with the sensation. For a moment she imagined what it would be like to be held by him in earnest. Though her experience with men had been limited, her instincts told her Colin Sullivan was dangerous. He interested her too much. His dominance challenged her, his physicality attracted her, his moodiness intrigued her.

Gail Kingsley's scathing comment about Cassidy's predecessor came back to her. She had a quick mental picture of the redhead's demanding beauty and the model's sultry allure. Cassidy St. John, she mused, is at neither end of the spectrum. She isn't strikingly vivid nor steamily sexy. Feminine extremes apparently appeal to Colin both as an artist and as a man. She caught herself, annoyed with the train of her own thoughts. It would not do to get involved or form any personal attachments with a man like Colin Sullivan. Don't get too close, she cautioned herself. Don't open any doors. *Don't get hurt.* The last warning came from nowhere and surprised her.

"Relax."

Cassidy focused on Colin and found him staring down at the canvas. His attention was concentrated on what only he could see. "Go change," he directed without glancing up. Cassidy's thoughts darkened at his tone. Rude, she decided, was a mild sort of word for describing Sullivan the artist. Controlling her temper, Cassidy went back to the dressing room.

My worries are groundless, she told herself and closed the door smartly. No one could possibly get close enough to that man to be hurt.

A few moments later Cassidy emerged from the dressing room in her own clothes. Colin stood, facing the window, his hands jammed into his pockets, his eyes narrowed on some view of his own.

"I've left the dress hanging in the other room," Cassidy said coldly. "I'll just be off, since you seem to be done." She snatched up her purse from the chair. Even as she swung it over her shoulder and turned for the door, Colin took her hand in his.

"You've that line between your brows again, Cass." He lifted a finger to trace it. "Smooth it out and I'll buy you some lunch before you go."

The line deepened. "Don't use that patronizing tone on me, Sullivan. I'm not an empty-headed art groupie to be patted and babied into smiles."

His brow lifted a fraction. "Quite right. Then again, there's no need to go off in a tiff."

"I'm not in a tiff," Cassidy insisted as she tried to jerk out of his hold. "I'm simply having a perfectly normal reaction to rudeness. Let go of my hand."

"When I'm through with it," he replied evenly. "You should mind your temper, Cass my love. It does alluring things to your face, and I'm not one for resisting what appeals to me."

"It's abundantly clear the only appeal I have for you is on that canvas over there." Cassidy wriggled her hand in an attempt to free it. With a quick flick of the wrist, Colin tumbled her into his chest. Mutinous and glowing, her face lifted to his. "Just what do you think you're doing?"

"You challenge me to prove you wrong." There was amusement in his eyes now and something else that made her heart beat erratically.

"I don't challenge you to anything," she corrected with a furious toss of her head. Her hair swung and lifted with the movement then settled into its own appealing disarray.

"Oh, but you do." His free hand tangled in her hair and found the base of her neck. "You threw down the gauntlet the night I found you in the fog. I think it's time I picked it up."

"You're being ridiculous." Cassidy spoke quickly. She realized her temper had carried her into territory she would have been wise to avoid. As she began to speak again, he caught her bottom lip between his teeth. The movement was sudden, the pressure light, the effect devastating.

Though she made a tiny sound of confused protest, her fingers clutched at his shirt instead of pushing him away. The tip of his tongue traced her lip as if experimenting with its flavor. When he released it, she stood still. Her eyes locked with his.

"This time when I kiss you, Cass, it's to pleasure myself," he said as his mouth lowered to take hers. Knowing he would meet no resistance, he circled her waist to mold her against him. Cassidy responded as if she'd been waiting for the moment all of her life. Her body seemed to know his already and fitted its soft, subtle curves to his firm, taut lines. Her hands traveled from his neck to tangle in his hair, while her mouth grew more mobile under his. For one brief instant, he crushed her to him with staggering force, ravishing her conquered mouth. Just as swiftly, her lips were freed. Her breath came out in a quick rush as she gripped him for balance. He held her close, keeping their bodies as one, his eyes boring into hers. Only the sound of their mixed breathing disturbed the silence.

The weakness Cassidy felt was a shock to her. Her

knees trembled beneath her and she shook her head in a quick attempt to deny what he had awakened. Something deep and secret was struggling for release. The strength of it alarmed and fascinated her. Still, her fear outweighed her curiosity. Instinct warned her it was not yet time. Even as she found the will to draw away, Colin pulled her closer.

"No, Colin, I can't." She swallowed as her hands pushed against his chest. She watched his eyes darken as his lips lingered just over hers.

"I can," he murmured, then crushed her mouth. She swirled back into the storm.

Nothing in her experience had ever prepared her for the new demands of her own body. With innocent allure, she moaned against his mouth. She felt his lips move against hers as he murmured something. Then he plundered, pulling her down into a world of heat and darkness. A quickening fear rose with her passion. When he released her mouth, her breath came in short gasps. Her eyes clouded with desire and confusion.

"Please, Colin, let me go. I think I'm frightened."

He was capable of taking her, she knew, and of making her glad that he had. His eyes were blazing blue, and she kept hers locked on them. To let her eyes drift to his mouth would have been her downfall. The fingers at her neck tightened, then relaxed and dropped away. Seizing the moment, Cassidy stepped back. The narrowness of her escape shook her, and she dragged her hand through her hair.

Colin watched her, then folded his arms across his chest. "I wonder if you had more difficulty fighting yourself or me."

"So do I," Cassidy replied with impulsive candor.

He tilted his head at her response and studied her. "You're an honest one, Cassidy. Mind how honest you are with me—I'd have few qualms about taking advantage."

"No, I'm sure you wouldn't." After blowing out a long breath, Cassidy straightened her shoulders. "I don't suppose that could have been avoided forever," she began practically. "But now that it hasn't been, and it's done, it shouldn't happen again." Her brow furrowed as Colin tossed back his head and roared with laughter. "Did I say something funny?"

"Cass, you're unique." Before she could respond, he had moved to her and had taken her shoulders in his hands. He kneaded them quickly in a friendly manner. "That streak of British practicality will always war with the passionate Celt."

"You're romanticizing," she claimed and lifted her chin.

"The door's been opened, Cassidy." She frowned because his words reminded her of her earlier thoughts. "Better for you perhaps if we'd kept it locked." He shook her once, rapidly. "Yes, it's done. The door won't stay closed now. It'll happen again." He released her then stepped back, but their eyes remained joined. "Go on now, while I'm remembering you were frightened."

The strong temptation to step toward him alarmed her. In defense against it, she turned swiftly for the door. "Nine o'clock," he said, and she turned with her hand on the knob.

He stood in the room's center, his thumbs hooked in his front pockets. The sun fell through the skylight, silhouetting his dark attraction. It occurred to Cassidy that if she were wise, she would walk out and never come back.

"Not a coward, are you, Cass?" he taunted softly, as if stealing her thoughts from her brain.

Cassidy tossed her head and snapped her spine straight. "Nine o'clock," she stated coolly then slammed the door behind her.

Chapter 4

As the days passed Cassidy found herself more at ease in the role of artist's model. As for Colin himself, she felt it would be a rare thing for anyone to remain relaxed with him. His temperament was mercurial, with a wide range of degrees. Fury came easily to him, but Cassidy learned humor did as well. As she began to uncover different layers of the man, he became more fascinating.

She justified her concentrated study of Colin Sullivan as a writer's privilege. It was a personality like his—varied, unpredictable, bold—that she needed as grist for her profession. There was nothing between them, she told herself regularly, but an artistic exchange. She reminded herself that he hadn't touched her again, except to set the pose, since the first day he had begun work on the canvas. The stormy kiss was a vivid memory, but only that…a memory.

Sitting at her typewriter in her apartment, Cassidy told herself she was fortunate—fortunate to have a job that kept the wolf from the door, and fortunate that Colin Sullivan was absorbed in his work. Cassidy was honest enough to admit she was more than mildly attracted to him. It was much better, she mused, that he was capable of pouring himself into his work to the extent that he barely noticed she was flesh and blood. *Unless I move the pose.* She frowned at the reflection of her desk lamp in the window.

Being attracted to him is perfectly natural, she decided. I'm not behaving like my predecessor with the milky skin and falling in love with him. I'm much too sensible. *Don't be so smug,* a voice whispered inside her head. Cassidy's frown became a scowl. I *am* sensible. I won't make a fool of myself over Colin Sullivan. He has his art and his Gail Kingsley. I have my work. Cassidy glanced down at the blank sheet of paper in her typewriter and sighed. But he keeps interfering with it. No more, she vowed then shifted in her seat until she was comfortably settled. I'm going to finish this chapter tonight without another thought of Sullivan.

At once the keys on her typewriter began to clatter with the movement of her thoughts. Once begun, she became totally involved, lost in the characters of her own devising. The love scene developed on her pages as she unconsciously called on her own feelings for her words. The scene moved with the same lightning speed as had the embrace with Colin. Now Cassidy was in control, urging her characters toward each other, propelling their destinies. It was as she wanted, as she planned, and she never noticed the influence of the man she had vowed to think no more about. The scene was nearly finished when a knock sounded on her door. She swore in annoyance.

"Who is it?" she called out and stopped typing in midsentence. She found it simpler to pick up her thoughts when returning to them that way.

"Hey, Cassidy." Jeff Mullans stuck his friendly, red-bearded face through her door. "Got a minute?"

Because he was her neighbor and she was fond of him, Cassidy pushed away the urge to sigh and smiled instead. "Sure."

He eased himself, a guitar and a six-pack of beer through the door. "Can I put some stuff in your fridge? Mine's busted again. It's like the Mojave Desert in there."

"Go ahead." Cassidy spun her chair until she faced him, then quirked her brow. "I see you brought all your valuables. I didn't know your six-string needed refrigeration."

"Just the six-pack," he countered with a grin as he marched back into her tiny kitchen. "And you're the only one in the building I'd trust with it. Wow, Cassidy, don't you believe in real food? All that's in here's a quart of juice, two carrots and half a stick of oleo."

"Is nothing sacred?"

"Come next door and I'll fix you up with a decent meal." Jeff came back into the room holding only his guitar. "I got tacos and stale doughnuts. Jelly-filled."

"It sounds marvelous, but I really have to finish this chapter."

Jeff's fingers pawed at his beard. "Don't know what you're missing. Heard anything from New York?" After glancing at the papers scattered over her desk, he settled Indian-fashion on the floor. He cradled his guitar in his lap.

"There seems to be a conspiracy of silence on the East Coast." Cassidy sighed, shrugged and tucked up her feet. "It's early days yet, I know, but patience isn't my strong suit."

"You'll make it, Cassidy, you've got something." He began to strum idly as he spoke. His music was simple and soothing. "Something that makes the people you write about important. If your novel is as good as that magazine story, you're on your way."

Cassidy smiled, touched by the easy sincerity of the compliment. "You wouldn't like to apply for a job as an editor in a New York publishing house, would you?"

"You don't need me, babe." He grinned and shook back his red hair. "Besides, I'm an up-and-coming songwriter and star performer."

"I've heard that." Cassidy leaned back in her chair. It occurred to her suddenly that Colin might like to paint Jeff Mullans. He'd be the perfect subject for him—the blinding red hair and beard, the soft contrast of gray eyes, the loving way the long hands caressed the guitar as he sat on her wicker rug. Yes, Colin would paint him precisely like this, she decided, in faded, frayed jeans with a polished guitar on his lap.

"Cassidy?"

"Sorry, I took a side trip. Have you got any gigs lined up?"

"Two next week. What about your gig with the artist?" Jeff tightened his bass string fractionally, tested it then continued to play. "I've seen his stuff…some of it, anyway. It's incredible." He tilted his head when he smiled at her. "How does it feel to be put on canvas by one of the new masters?"

"It's an odd feeling, Jeff. I've tried to pin it down, but…" She trailed off and brought her knees up, resting her heels on the edge of the chair. "I'm never certain it's me he's seeing when he's working. I'm not certain I'll see myself in the finished portrait." She frowned then shrugged it away. "Maybe he's only using part of me, the way I use parts of people I've met in characterizations."

"What's he like?" Jeff asked, watching her eyes drift with her thought. The glow of her desk lamp threw an aura around her head.

"He's fascinating," she murmured, all but forgetting she was speaking aloud. "He looks like a pirate, all dashing and dangerous with the most incredible blue eyes I've ever seen. And his hands are beautiful. There's no other word for them; they're perfectly beautiful."

Her voice softened, and her eyes began to dream. "He exudes a thoughtless sort of sensuality. It seems more obvious when he's working. I suppose it's because he's being driven by his own power then, and is somehow separate from the rest of us. He tells me to talk, and I talk about whatever comes into my head." She moved her shoulders then rested her chin on her knees. "But I don't know if he hears me. He has a dreadful temper, and when he rages his speech slips back to Ireland. It's almost worth the storm to hear it. He's outrageously selfish and unbearably arrogant and utterly charming. Each time I'm with him I find a bit more, uncover another layer, and yet I doubt I'd really know him if I had years to learn."

There was silence for a moment, with only Jeff's music. "You're really hung up on him," he observed.

Cassidy snapped back with a jolt. Her violet eyes widened in surprise as she straightened in the chair. "Why, no, of course not. I'm simply…simply…" *Simply what, Cassidy?* she demanded of herself. "Simply interested in what makes him the way he is," she answered and hugged her knees. "That's all."

"Okay, babe, you know best." Jeff stood in an easy fluid motion, the guitar merely an extension of his arm. "Just watch out." He smiled, leaned over and cupped her chin. "He might be a great artist, but if the gossip columns are to be believed, he's very much a man, too. You're a fine-looking lady, and you might as well be fresh from the farm."

"I'd hardly call four years at Berkeley fresh from the farm," Cassidy countered.

"Only someone utterly naive could evade every pass I make and still make me like her." Jeff closed the distance and gave her a gentle invitation of a kiss. It was as pleasant and as soothing as his music. Cassidy's heartbeat stayed steady. "No dice, huh?" he asked when he lifted his head. "Think of the rent we could save if we moved in together."

Cassidy tugged on his beard. "You're only lusting after my refrigerator."

"A lot you know," he scoffed and headed for the door. "I'm going home to write something painfully sad and poignant."

"Good grief, I'm always inspiring someone these days."

"Don't get cocky," Jeff advised then closed the door behind him.

Cassidy's smile faded as she stared off into space. Hung up on, she repeated mentally. What a silly phrase. In any case, I'm not hung up on Colin. Can't a woman express an interest in a man without someone reading more into it? Thoughtfully she ran her fingertip over her bottom lip and brought back the feel of Jeff's kiss. Easy, undisturbing, painless. What sort of chemistry made one man's kiss pleasant and another's exhilarating? The smart woman would go for the pleasant, Cassidy decided, knowing Jeff would be basically kind and gentle. Only an idiot would want a man who was bound to bring hurt and heartache.

With a quick shake of her head she swung back to her typewriter and began to work. Her fingers had barely begun to transfer her thoughts when a knock sounded again. Cassidy rolled her eyes to the ceiling.

"You can't possibly be finished writing a painfully sad and poignant song," she called out and continued to type. "And the beer certainly isn't cold yet."

"I can't argue with either of those statements."

Cassidy spun her chair quickly and stared at Colin. He stood in her opened doorway, negligently leaning against the jamb and watching her. There was light amusement on his face and male appreciation in his eyes as they roamed over her skin. It was scantily covered in brief shorts and a T-shirt that had shrunk in the basement laundry. His lazy survey brought out a blush before she found her tongue.

"What are you doing here?"

"Enjoying the view," he answered and stepped inside. He closed the door at his back then lifted a brow. "Don't you know better than to keep your door unlatched?"

"I'm always losing my key and locking myself out,

so I…" Cassidy stopped because she realized how ridiculous she sounded. One day, she promised herself, I'll learn to think before I speak. "There isn't anything in here worth stealing," she said.

Colin shook his head. "How wrong you are. Wear your key around your neck, Cass, but keep your door locked." Her brain formed an indignant retort, but before she could vocalize it he spoke again. "Who did you think I was when I knocked?"

"A songwriter with a faulty refrigerator. How did you know where I lived?"

"Your address is on your manuscript." He gestured with the thick envelope before setting it down.

Cassidy glanced at the familiar bundle with some surprise. She had assumed Colin had forgotten her manuscript as soon as she'd given it to him. Suddenly it occurred to her why she hadn't asked him before if he had read it, or what he'd thought of it. His criticism would be infinitely harder to bear than an impersonal rejection slip from a faceless editor. Abruptly nervous, she looked up at him. Any critique she was expecting wasn't forthcoming.

Colin wandered the room, toying with an arrangement of dried flowers, examining a snapshot in a silver frame, peering out of the window at her view of the city.

"Can I get you something?" she asked automatically then remembered Jeff's inventory of her refrigerator. She bit her lip. "Coffee," she added quickly, knowing she could provide it as long as he took it black.

Colin turned from the window and began to wander again. "You have a proper eye for color, Cass," he told her. "And an enviable way of making a home from an apartment. I've always found them soulless devices, lacking in privacy and character." He lifted a small mirror framed with sea shells. "Fisherman's Wharf," he concluded and glanced at her. "It must be a particular haunt of yours."

"Yes, I suppose. I love the city in general and that part of it in particular." She smiled as she thought of it. "There's so much life there. The boats are all crammed in beside each other, and I like to imagine where they've been or where they're going." As soon as the words were spoken Cassidy felt foolish. They sounded romantic when she had been taking great pains to prove to Colin she was not. He smiled at her, and her embarrassment became something more dangerous. "I'll make coffee," she said quickly and started to rise.

"No, don't bother." Colin laid a hand on her shoulder to keep her seated then glanced at her desk. It was cluttered with papers and notes and reference books. "I'm interrupting your work. Intolerable."

"It seems to be the popular thing to do tonight." Cassidy shook off her discomfort and smiled as he continued to pace the room. "It's all right because I was nearly done, otherwise I suppose I'd behave as rudely as you do when you're interrupted." She enjoyed the look he gave her, the ironical lift of his brow, the light tilt of a smile on his mouth.

"And how rudely is that?"

"Abominably. Please sit, Colin. These floors are thin, you'll wear them through." She gestured to a chair, but he perched on the edge of her desk.

"I finished your book tonight."

"Yes, I thought perhaps that's why you brought the manuscript back." She spoke calmly enough, but when he made no response she moaned in frustration. "Please,

Colin, I'm no good with torture. I'd confess everything I knew before they stuck the first bamboo shoot under my fingernail. I'm a marshmallow. No, wait!" She held up both hands as he started to speak. She rose and then took a quick turn around the room. "If you hated it, I'll only be devastated for a short time. I'm certain I'll learn to function again…well, nearly certain. I want you to be frank. I don't want any platitudes or cushioned let-downs." She pushed her mane of hair back with both hands, letting her fingers linger on her temples a moment. "And for heaven's sake, don't tell me it was interesting. That's the worst. The absolute worst!"

"Are you finished?" he asked mildly.

Cassidy blew out a long breath, tugged her hand through her hair and nodded. "Yes, I think so."

"Come here, Cass." She obeyed instantly because his voice was quiet and gentle. Their eyes were level, and he took her hands in his. "I haven't mentioned the book until now because I wanted to read it when I wouldn't be interrupted. I thought it best not to talk about it until I finished." His thumbs ran absently over the back of her hands. "You have something rare, Cass, something elusive. Talent. It's not something they taught you at Berkeley, it's something you were born with. Your college years polished it, perhaps, disciplined it, but you provided the raw material."

Cassidy released her breath. Astonishing, she thought, that the opinion of a man known barely a week should have such weight. Jeff's opinion had pleased her; Colin's had left her speechless.

"I don't know what to say." She shook her head helplessly. "That sounds trite, I know, but it's true." Her eyes drifted past him to the disorder of papers on her desk.

"Sometimes you just want to chuck it all. It just isn't worth the pain, the struggle."

"And you would choose to be a writer," Colin said.

"No, I never had any choice." She brought her eyes back to his. The violet glowed almost black in the shadowed light. "If anything, it picked me. Did you choose to be an artist, Colin?"

He studied her a moment, then shook his head. "No." He turned her hands, palms up, and looked at them with lowered brows. "There are things that come to us whether we ask for them or not. Do you believe in destiny, Cass?"

She moistened her lips, finding them suddenly dry, then swallowed. "Yes." The single syllable was little more than a breath.

"Of course, I was certain you did." He lifted his eyes and locked them on hers. Cassidy's heartbeat jumped skittishly. "Do you think it's our destiny to be lovers, Cassidy?" Her mouth opened but no words came out. She shook her head in mute denial. "You're a poor liar," he observed; then, cupping her chin in his palm, he moved his lips to hers. In direct contrast to the ease and pleasantness of Jeff's kiss, this brought a pain that seemed to vibrate in every cell of her body. Defensively Cassidy jerked her head back.

"Don't!"

"Why?" he countered, and his voice was soft. "A kiss is a simple thing, a meeting of lips."

"No, it's not simple," Cassidy protested, feeling herself being pulled to him by his eyes only. "You take more."

He kissed one cheek, then the other, barely touching her skin. Cassidy's eyelids fluttered down. "Only as much as you'll give me, Cass. That much and no more." His lips moved over hers, teasing, persuading, until her blood thundered in her brain. His fingers were gentle on her face. "You taste of things I'd forgotten," he murmured. "Fresh, young things. Kiss me, Cass, I've a need for you."

With a moan, half despair, half wonder, she answered his need.

The flames that leapt between them were intense and wild. Her brain sent out quick, desperate protests and was ignored. A hunger for him drove her; her mouth became urgent and searching as his hands began to explore her soft curves. The fear she felt only added to her excitement, the exquisite terror of losing control. She was overwhelmed by a primitive need, an ageless necessity. When their lips parted and met again, hers ached for the joining.

Abruptly he tore his mouth from hers and buried it against her neck. Cassidy shuddered from the onslaught even as she tilted back her head to offer him more. With his teeth he brought her skin alive with delicious pain. His hands found their way under her shirt, running up her rib cage. With his thumbs he stroked the sides of her breast while she strained against him.

Her joints went fluid, leaving her helpless but for his support. For a moment, when their lips met again, there was nothing she had that was not his. The offer was complete and unconditional. Slowly, with his hands on her shoulders, Colin drew her away. Her lashes fluttered up then down, before she found the strength to open her eyes. His expression was dark and forbidding. Briefly his hands tightened.

"It seems you were right," he began in a voice thick

with desire. "A kiss isn't a simple thing. I want you, Cass, and you'd best know nothing in heaven or hell will keep me from taking you when I've a mind to." His hands relaxed, the grip becoming a caress. "When the painting's finished, we'll have no choice but to meet our destinies."

"No." Frightened, disturbed by feelings that were too intense, Cassidy pulled out of his arms. She dragged a trembling hand through her hair, and her breath came quickly. "No, Colin, I won't be the latest in your string of lovers. I won't! I think more of myself than that. That's something you'd best understand." She stepped away from him, her shoulders straightening with inherent pride.

Colin's eyes narrowed. She could see his temper rising. "It should be an interesting contest." He took a step forward and grabbed a handful of her hair. With a quick jerk he brought her face to his, then gave her a hard, brief kiss. Cassidy's breath trembled out, but she kept her eyes steady. "Time will tell, Cass my love. Now it's late, nearly midnight, and I'd best be on my way." Lifting her hand, he brushed her fingers with his lips. "Sinning is much more appealing after midnight." With another careless smile, he turned for the door. Reaching it, he pushed the latch so that it would engage when he shut it. "Find your keys," he ordered and was gone.

Chapter 5

Another week passed without any clash between Colin and Cassidy. She had returned to his studio the day after his visit to her apartment determined to resist him. She'd spoken the truth when she'd told him she wouldn't be one of his lovers.

All her life she had waited for a relationship with depth and permanence. Her own ideals and her dedication to her studies had kept her aloof from men, and her aloofness had prolonged her naiveté. She'd grown up with only a father and had never closely witnessed the commitment of a man and a woman to each other. She had watched her father enjoy several light relationships as she'd grown up, but none of the women in his life had become important to him. Watching him drift through life with only his work, Cassidy had vowed she would find someone one day to share hers.

She didn't consider her vow romantic, but as necessary to her soul as food was to her body. Until she found what she searched for, she would wait. Before Colin there had never been any temptation to do otherwise. Still, when she returned to his studio, she was prepared to stand firm against him. Her preparation proved unnecessary.

Colin spoke to her only briefly, and when he set the pose his touch was impersonal. But there seemed to be some surge of emotion just under the surface of his face, something that just stirred the air. Whether it was temper or passion or excitement, Cassidy had no way of knowing. She knew only she was vitally aware of it…and of him.

They passed the days with only what needed to be said, and long gaps of silence filled the sessions. By the end of the week Cassidy's nerves were stretched taut. She wondered if Colin felt the tension, or if it was simply within her. He seemed intent only on the painting.

The sun fell over Cassidy warmly, but her muscles were growing stiff from holding the pose. Colin stood behind his easel, and she watched his brush move from palette to canvas. He could work for hours without a moment's rest. Cassidy tried to imagine how he had painted her.

Will I hang in The Gallery or face the wall in a corner up here until he decides what to do with me? she thought. Will I be sold for some astronomical price and hang in a manor house in England? What will he title me? *Woman in White. Woman with Violets.* She tried to imagine being discussed and pondered over by an art class in a university. A century from now, will someone see me in some dusty gallery and wonder who I was or what I was thinking when he painted me?

The idea gave Cassidy an odd feeling, one she was not certain wholly pleased her. How much of her soul could Colin see, and how much would be revealed with oil and canvas? Would she, in essence, be as naked as the model who'd lounged on the couch?

Colin swore roundly, snapping her attention back to him. Her eyes widened as he slammed down his palette.

"You've moved the pose." He stalked toward her as her mouth opened to form an apology. "Hold still, blast you," he ordered curtly, adjusting her shoulders with impatient hands. His brows were lowered in annoyance. "I won't tolerate fidgeting."

Cassidy's mouth snapped shut on her apology. Swift and heated, her temper rose. With one quick jerk she pulled out of his hands. "Don't you speak to me that way, Sullivan." She threw her nosegay on the windowsill and glared at him. "I was not fidgeting, and if I were, it would be because I'm human, not a—a robot or a dime-store dummy." She tossed her head, effectively destroying his arrangement of her hair. "I'm sure it's difficult to understand a mere mortal when one is so lofty and godlike, but we can't all be perfect."

"Your opinions are neither requested nor desired." Colin's voice was as cold as his eyes were heated. "The only thing I require from a model is that she hold still." He took her shoulders again, firmly. "Keep your temper to yourself when I'm working."

"Go paint a tree, then," she invited furiously. "It won't give you any back talk." Cassidy turned to stalk to the dressing room, but Colin grabbed her arm and spun her around. His face was alive with temper.

"No one walks away from me."

"Is that so?" Cassidy lifted her chin, infuriated with his arrogance. "Watch this." She turned her back on him only to be whirled around again before she had taken two steps. "Let go of me," she ordered as blood surged angrily under her skin. Nerves that had been stretched for a week strained to the breaking point. "I've nothing more to say, and I'm through holding your blasted pose for the day."

His grip on her arm tightened. "Very well, but there's more between us than painting and talking, isn't there?" He bit off the words as he dragged her against him.

Cassidy's heart jumped to her throat when she felt the violence of his fingers against her skin. She saw that temper ruled him now, a temper sharp enough to cut through any protest she could make. He was a man of passion, and she was aware that his darker side could carry them both past the turning point. In a desperate attempt to hold him off, Cassidy arched away from him. Even as she made the move, his mouth crushed hers. She tasted his fury.

Her sounds of protest were muffled, her arms pinioned by his. In her throat, her heart thudded with the knowledge that she was totally at his mercy. His lips were bruising, unyielding, as his tongue penetrated her mouth. The kiss became as intimate as it was savage. When she tried to turn her face from his, he gripped her hair tightly and held her still. His mouth was hard and hot and ruthless. Behind her closed lids, a dull red mist swirled. For the first time in her life, Cassidy feared she would faint. Her protests became slighter. Colin took more.

He was pulling her too deep too quickly, down dark

corridors, beyond the border of thought and into sensation. There was no gentleness on the journey, only hard, uncompromising demand. Unable to fight him any longer, Cassidy went limp. She made no struggle when his hand moved to unfasten the dress. Her body was consumed by fire, instinctively responding to his touch. The knock on the studio door vibrated like a cannon through the room. Ignoring it, Colin continued to ravish her mouth.

"Colin." Dimly Cassidy heard Gail Kingsley's voice and the sound of another knock. "There's someone here to see you."

With a savage oath, Colin tore his mouth from Cassidy's. He released her abruptly, and freed of support she staggered and fell against him. Cursing again, he took her arms and held her away, but his words halted as he studied her wide, frightened eyes.

Her mouth was trembling, swollen by his demands. Her breath sobbed in and out of her lungs as she clung to him for balance.

"Colin, don't be nasty." Gail's voice sounded with practiced patience through the door. "You must be pretty well finished by now."

"All right, blast it!" he called out brusquely to Gail but kept his eyes on Cassidy. Leading her by the arm, he walked to the dressing room. Inside he turned her again to face him. In silence she looked up, struggling to balance her system and discipline her breathing. The need to weep was tearing at her.

An expression came and went in Colin's eyes. "Change," he said in a quiet voice. He seemed to hesitate, as if to say more, then he turned away. When he shut the door, Cassidy turned to face the wall.

She let the trembling run its course. Several minutes passed before the voices in the studio penetrated.

There was Gail's quick, nervous tone and Colin's, calm now, without any trace of the temper of passion that had dominated it before. An unfamiliar voice mixed with theirs. It was light and male with an Italian accent. Cassidy concentrated on the voices rather than the words. Turning, she stared at her own reflection. What she saw left her stunned.

Color had not yet returned to her cheeks, leaving them nearly as white as the dress she wore. Her eyes were haunted. It was the look of utter vulnerability that disturbed her the most; the look of a woman accepting defeat.

No. No, I won't. She pressed her palm over the face in the glass. He'll win nothing that way, and we both know it. Quickly she stripped out of the dress and began to pull on her clothes. The straight, uncompromising lines of her khakis and button-down shirt made her appear less frail, and she began a careful repair of her face. The conversation in the outer room started to penetrate her thoughts. The first moments of eavesdropping were unconscious.

"An interesting use of color, Colin. You seem to be working toward a rather dreamlike effect." Hearing Gail's comment, Cassidy realized they were discussing the painting. She frowned as she applied blusher to her cheeks. He lets her look at it, she thought resentfully. Why not me? "It seems almost sentimental. That should be a surprise to the art world."

"Sentimental, yes." The Italian voice cut in while Cassidy now eavesdropped shamelessly. "But there is passion in this play of color here, and a rather cool practicality in the line of the dress. I'm intrigued, Colin—I can't figure out your intention."

"I have more than one," Cassidy heard him answer in his dry, ironic tone.

"How well I know." The Italian chuckled then made a sound of curiosity. "You have not begun the face."

"No." Cassidy recognized the dismissal in the word, but the Italian ignored it.

"She interests me…and you, too, it appears. She would be beautiful, of course, and young enough to suit the dress and the violets. Still, she must have something more." Cassidy waited for Colin's reply, but none came. The Italian continued, undaunted. "Will you keep her hidden, my friend?"

"Yes, Colin, where is Cassidy?" Gail's question held an undertone of amusement that made Cassidy's eyes narrow. "You know she'd adore meeting Vince." She gave a light laugh. "She is rather a sweet-looking thing. Don't tell me we ran her off?"

Thoroughly annoyed with the condescending description, Cassidy turned and opened the door. "Not at all," she said and gave the trio by the easel a brilliant smile. "And of course I'd adore meeting Vince." She saw Gail's eyes glitter with a quick fury then shifted her gaze to Colin. His face told her nothing, and again her gaze shifted.

The man beside Colin was nearly a head shorter, but his lean build and proud carriage gave the illusion of height. His hair was as dark as Colin's, but straight, and his eyes were darkly brown against the olive of his skin. He had smooth, handsome features, and when he smiled he was all but irresistible.

"Ah, *bella*." The compliment was a sigh before he

crossed the room to take both of Cassidy's hands in his. *"Bellisima.* But of course, she is perfection. Where did you find her, Colin?" he demanded as his eyes caressed her face. "I will go and set up camp there until I find a prize of my own."

Cassidy laughed, amused by his undisguised flirtation. "In the fog," she told him when Colin remained silent. "I thought he was a mugger."

"Ah, my angel, he is much worse than that." Vince turned to Colin with a grin but retained Cassidy's hand. "He is a black Irish dog whose paintings I buy because I have nothing better to do with my money."

Colin lifted a brow as he moved to join them. "Vince, Cassidy St. John. Cass, Vincente Clemenza, the duke of Maracanti."

At the introduction Cassidy's eyes grew wide. "Ah, now you have impressed her with my title." Vince's teeth flashed into a grin. "How accommodating of you." With perfect charm he lifted both of Cassidy's hands to his lips. "My pleasure, *signorina.* Will you marry me?"

"I've always thought I'd make a spectacular duchess. Do I curtsy?" she asked, smiling at him over their joined hands. "I'm not certain I know how."

"Vince normally requires that one kneel and kiss his ring." At the comment, Cassidy let her eyes drift to Colin. His gaze was dark and brooding on her face. Fractionally, she lifted her chin. Though he said nothing, she sensed his acknowledgment of the gesture.

"You exaggerate, my friend." Vince released Cassidy's hands then laid his own on Colin's shoulder. "As never before, I envy you your gift. You will give me first claim on the portrait."

Colin's eyes remained fixed on Cassidy's face. "There's been a prior claim."

"Indeed." Vince shrugged. The movement was at once elegant and foreign. "I shall have to outbid my competition." There was an inflection in his tone of a man used to having his own way. Hearing it Cassidy wondered how he and Colin dealt together with such apparent amiability.

"Vince wanted to see *Janeen*," Gail cut in and moved across the room to a stack of canvases.

"If you'll excuse me, then," Cassidy began, but Vince scooped up her hand again.

"No, *madonna,* stay. Come peruse the master's work with me." Without waiting for her assent he urged her across the room.

Gail took a canvas then propped it on an easel. It was the portrait of the nude with the milky skin. Cassidy glanced up to see Gail smiling.

"Cassidy's predecessor," she announced then stepped back to stand with Colin. Cassidy recognized the proprietary nature of the gesture. She turned her attention back to the portrait without looking at Colin.

"An exquisite animal," Vince murmured. "One would say a woman without boundaries. There is quite an attractive wickedness about her." He turned his head to smile at Cassidy. "What do you think?"

"It's magnificent," she replied immediately. "She makes me uncomfortable, and yet I envy her confidence in her own sexuality. I think she would intimidate most men…and enjoy it."

"Your model appears to be an astute judge of character." Vince rubbed his thumb absently over Cassidy's knuckles. "Yes, I want it. And the Faylor Gail showed

me downstairs. He shows promise. Now, madonna…"
He turned to face Cassidy again. His eyes were dark and
appreciative. "You will have dinner with me tonight?
The city is a lonely place without a beautiful woman."

Cassidy smiled, but before she could speak Colin
laid a hand on her shoulder. "The paintings are yours,
Vince. My model isn't."

"Ah." Vince's one syllable was ripe with meaning.
Cassidy's eyes narrowed with fury. Smoothly Colin
turned to take the painting from the easel.

"Have someone package this and the Faylor for
Vince," he told Gail as he handed her the canvas. "I'll
be down shortly and we'll discuss terms."

Without a word Gail crossed the studio and swung
through the door. Vince watched her with a thoughtful
eye then turned back to Cassidy.

"*Arrivederci,* Cassidy St. John." He kissed her hand
then sighed with regret. "It seems I must find my own
dream in the fog. I will expect a bargain price to soothe
my crushing disappointment, my friend." He shot a look
at Colin as he moved to the door. "If you are ever in
Italy, madonna…" With a final smile he left them.

Trembling with rage, Cassidy turned on Colin the
moment the door closed. "How *dare* you?" Now she had
no need of blusher to bring color to her cheeks. "How
dare you imply such a thing?"

"I merely told Vince he could have the paintings but
not my current model," Colin countered. Carelessly he
moved across the room and covered Cassidy's portrait.
"Any implication was purely coincidental."

"Oh, no!" Cassidy followed him, propelled by fury.
"That was no coincidence. You knew precisely what
you were doing. I won't tolerate that sort of interfer-

ence from you, Sullivan." She took a finger and poked
him in the chest. "I'm perfectly free to see whomever
I choose, whenever I choose, and I won't have you implying otherwise."

Colin hooked his hands in his pockets. For a moment
he studied her face in silence. When he spoke it was
with perfect calm. "You're very young and remarkably
naive. Vince is an old friend and a good one. He's also
a charming rake, if you'll forgive the archaic term. He
has no scruples with women."

"And you do?" Cassidy retorted in an instant of blind
heat. She saw Colin stiffen, saw his eyes flare and the
muscles in his face tense. For the first time she witnessed his calculated control of his temper.

"Your point, Cass," he said softly. "Well taken." His
hands stayed in his pockets as he watched her. "Don't
come back until Thursday," he told her and turned to
walk to the door. "I need a day or two."

Cassidy stood alone in the empty studio. I may have
scored a point, she thought wretchedly, but this victory
isn't sweet. She was drained, physically as well as emo-
tionally. She returned to the dressing room for her purse.
Colin wasn't the only one who needed a day or two.

"Oh, what luck, I've caught you." Gail swept into
the studio just as Cassidy emerged from the dressing
room. "I thought we might have a little chat." Gail shot
her a quick, flashing smile and leaned back against the
closed door. "Just us two," she added.

Cassidy sighed with undisguised weariness. "Not
now," she said and shifted her purse to her shoulder.
"I've had enough temperament for one day."

"I'll make it brief, then, and you can be on your way."

Gail spoke pleasantly enough, but Cassidy felt the antagonism just below the surface.

It's best not to argue, Cassidy decided. It's best to hear her out, agree with everything she says and go quietly. That's the sensible thing to do.

She gave her what she hoped was an inoffensive smile. "All right, go ahead, then."

Gail took a quick, sweeping survey. "I'm afraid perhaps I haven't made myself clear...about myself and Colin." Her voice was patient—teacher to student. Cassidy ignored a surge of annoyance and nodded.

"Colin and I have been together for quite some time. We meet a certain need in each other. Over the years he's had his share of flirtations, which I'm quite capable of overlooking. In many cases these relationships were intensified for the press." She shrugged a gauze-covered shoulder. "Colin's romantic image helps maintain the mystique of the artist. I'll sanction anything when it helps his career. I understand him."

As if unable to remain still for more than short spurts, Gail began to roam the room.

"I'm afraid I don't see why you're telling me this," Cassidy began. The last thing she needed to hear at the moment was how experienced Colin Sullivan was with women.

"Let's you and I understand each other, too." Gail stopped pacing and faced Cassidy again. Her eyes were hard and cold. "As long as Colin's doing this painting, I have to tolerate you. I know better than to interfere with his work. But if you get in my way..." She wrapped her fingers around the strap of Cassidy's purse. "I can find ways of removing people who get in my way."

"I'm sure you can," Cassidy returned evenly. "I'm

afraid you'll find I don't remove easily." She pried Gail's fingers from her strap. "Your relationship with Colin is your own affair. I've no intention of interfering with it. Not," she added as a satisfied smile tilted the corner of Gail's mouth, "because you threaten me. You don't intimidate me, Gail. Actually, I feel rather sorry for you."

Cassidy ignored Gail's harsh intake of breath and continued. "Your lack of confidence where Colin is concerned is pathetic. I'm no threat to you. A blind man could see he's only interested in what he puts on that canvas over there." She flung out a hand and pointed to the covered portrait. "I interest him as a *thing,* not as a person." She felt a quick slash of pain as her own statement came home to her. She continued to speak, though the words rushed out in desperation. "I won't interfere with you because I'm not in love with Colin, and I have no intention of ever being in love with him."

Whirling, she darted through the back door of the studio, slamming it at her back. Only after she had gulped in enough air to steady her nerves did Cassidy realize she had lied.

Chapter 6

For the next two days Cassidy buried herself in her work. She was determined to give herself a time of peace, a time of rest for her emotions. She knew she needed to cut herself off from Colin to accomplish it. The disruption of their day-to-day contact wasn't enough. She knew she needed to block him from her mind. In addition, Cassidy forced herself not to consider the knowledge that had come to her after the scene with Gail. She wouldn't think of being in love with Colin or of the circumstances that made her love impossible. For two days she would pretend she'd never met him.

Cassidy wrote frantically. All her fears and pain and passion were expressed in her words. She worked late into the night, until she could be certain there would be no dreams to haunt her. When she slept, she slept deeply, exhausted by her own drive. More than once she forgot to eat.

On the second day it began to rain. There was a solid gray wall outside Cassidy's window of which she remained totally unaware. Below, pedestrians scrambled about under umbrellas.

Cassidy's concentration was so complete that when a hand touched her shoulder, she screamed.

"Wow, Cassidy, I'm sorry." Jeff tried to look apologetic but grinned instead. "I knocked and called you twice. You were totally absorbed."

Cassidy held a hand against her heart as if to keep it in place. She took two deep breaths. "It's all right. We all need to be terrified now and again. It keeps the blood moving. Is it your refrigerator?"

Jeff grimaced as he ran a finger down her nose. "Is that where you think my heart is? In your refrigerator? Cassidy, I'm a sensitive guy, my mother'll tell you." Cassidy smiled, leaning back in her chair.

"I've got that gig in the coffeehouse down the street tonight. Come with me."

"Oh, Jeff, I'd love to, but—" She began to make her excuses with a gesture at the papers on her desk. Jeff cut her off.

"Listen, you've been chained to this machine for two days. When are you coming up for air?"

She shrugged and poked a finger at her dictionary. "I've got to go back to the studio tomorrow, and—"

"All the more reason for a break tonight. You're pushing yourself, babe. Take a rest." Jeff watched her face carefully and pressed his advantage. "I could use a friendly face in the audience, you know. We rising stars are very insecure." He grinned through his beard.

Cassidy sighed then smiled. "All right, but I can't stay late."

"I play from eight to eleven," he told her then ruffled her hair. "You can be home and tucked into bed before midnight."

"Okay, I'll be there at eight." Cassidy glanced down at her watch, frowned then tapped its face with her fingertips. "What time is it? My watch stopped at two-fifteen."

"A.M. or P.M.?" Jeff asked dryly. He shook his head. "It's after seven. Hey." He gave her a shrewd look. "Have you eaten?"

Cassidy cast her mind back and recalled an apple at noon. "No, not really."

With a snort of disgust Jeff hauled her to her feet. "Come on with me now, and I'll spring for a quick hamburger."

Cassidy pushed her hair back out of her face. "Golly, I haven't had such a generous offer for a long time."

"Just get a coat," Jeff retorted, stalking to her door. "In case you haven't noticed, it's pouring outside."

Cassidy glanced out her window. "So it is," she agreed. She pulled a yellow slicker out of the closet and dragged it on. "Can I have a cheeseburger?" she asked Jeff as she breezed past him.

"Women. Never satisfied." He closed the door behind them.

The rain didn't bother Cassidy. It was refreshing after her hibernation. The hurried cheeseburger and soft drink were a banquet after the scant meals of the past two days. The smoky, crowded coffeehouse gave her a taste of humanity that she relished after her solitude.

Seated near the back, she drank thick café au lait and listened to Jeff's soothing, introspective music. The evening had grown late when she realized she had relaxed her guard. Colin had slipped over her barrier without her being aware. He stood clearly in her mind's eye. Once he had breached her defenses, Cassidy knew it was useless to attempt to force him out again. She closed her eyes a moment, then opened them, accepting the inevitable. She could not avoid thinking of him forever.

Colin Sullivan was a brilliant artist. He was a confident man who twisted life to suit himself. He had wit and charm and sensitivity. He was selfish and arrogant and totally dedicated to his work. He was thoughtless and domineering and capable of violence.

And I love him completely.

Cassidy trembled with a sigh, then stared into her coffee. I'm an idiot, a romantic fool who knew the pitfalls then fell into one anyway. I see he has a lover, I understand he sees me as important only as a subject for his painting. I'm aware he would make love to me without his heart ever being touched. I know there've been dozens of women in his life, and none of them have lasted.

No, not even Gail, she mused, for all her claims. She's just another woman who's touched the corners of his life. Colin's never made a commitment to a woman. Knowing all this, and wanting a healthy, one-to-one relationship with a man, I fall in love with him. Brilliant.

It's insane. He'll trample me. So what do I do? Slowly Cassidy lifted her coffee and sipped. She drifted away from her surroundings.

I have to finish the portrait; I gave my word. It would be impossible to be in the studio together day after day and not speak. I'm not capable of feuding in any case. Her elbows were propped on the table, the cup held between her hands, but her eyes were staring over the rim and into the distance.

Fighting with him is too dangerous because it brings the emotions to the surface. I don't know how deeply inside me he's capable of seeing. I won't humiliate myself or embarrass him with the fact that I've been stupid enough to fall in love with him. The only thing to do is to behave naturally. Hold the pose for him, talk when he asks me to talk and be friendly. The painting seems to be moving well; it should be finished in a few more weeks. Surely I can behave properly for that amount of time. And when it's finished…

Her thoughts trailed off into darkness. And when the painting's finished, what? I pick up the pieces, she answered. For a moment her eyes were lost and sad. When the painting's finished and Colin drops out of my life, the universe will still function. What a small thing one person's happiness is, she reflected. What a tiny, finite slice of the whole.

With a sigh Cassidy shook off her thoughts and finished the coffee. Setting down the cup she let herself be stroked by Jeff's quiet music.

Cassidy pulled her jacket closer as she stood outside the studio door and searched her bag for the key Colin had given her.

Blasted key, she grumbled silently as she groped for it. She blew her hair from her eyes then pulled out a notepad, three pencils and a linty sourball.

"How did that get in there?" she mumbled. Her eyes flew up when Colin opened the door. "Oh. Hello."

He inclined his head at the greeting then dropped his eyes to her laden hands. "Looking for something?"

Cassidy followed his gaze. Embarrassed, she dumped everything back into her bag and fumbled for poise. "No, I...nothing. I didn't think you'd be here so early." She shifted her purse back to her shoulder.

"It appears it's fortunate I am. Have you lost your key, Cass?" There was a smile on his face that made her feel foolish and scatter-brained.

"No, I haven't lost it," she muttered. "I just can't find it." She walked past him into the studio. Her shoulder barely brushed his chest and she felt a jolt of heat. It wasn't going to be as easy as she'd thought. "I'll change," she said briefly then went directly to the dressing room.

When she emerged, Colin was setting his palette and gave her not so much as a glance. His ignoring of her brought a wave of relief. There, you see, she told herself, there's nothing to worry about.

"I'm going to do some work on the face today," Colin stated, still mixing paints. His use of the impersonal pronoun was further proof his thoughts were not on Cassidy St. John. She denied the existence of the ache in her chest. Keeping silent, she waited until he was finished then stood obligingly while he set the pose. She would, she determined, give him absolutely no trouble. But when he cupped her chin in his hand, she stiffened and jerked away.

Colin's eyes heated. "I need to see the shape of your face through my hands." He set the pose again with meticulous care, barely making contact. "It's not enough to see it with my eyes. Do you understand?"

She nodded, feeling foolish. Colin waited a moment then took her chin again, but lightly, with just his fingertips. Cassidy forced herself to remain still. "Relax,

Cassidy, I need you relaxed." The patient tone of the order surprised her into obeying. He murmured his approval as his fingers trailed over her skin.

To Cassidy it was an agony of delight. His touch was gentle, though he frowned in concentration. She wondered if he could feel the heat rising to her skin. Colin traced her jawline and ran his fingers over her cheekbones. Cassidy focused on bringing air in and out of her lungs at an even pace. She tried to tell herself that his touch was as impersonal as a doctor's, but when his hand lingered on her cheek she brought her eyes warily to his.

"Hold steady," he commanded briskly, then turned to go to his easel. "Look at me," he ordered as he picked up his palette and brush.

Cassidy obeyed, trying to put her mind on anything but the man who painted her. Even as her eyes met his, she realized it was hopeless. She could not look at him and not see him. She could not be with him and not be aware of him. She could not block him out of her mind with any more success than she could block him out of her heart.

Would it be wrong, she wondered, to let myself dream a little? Would it be wrong to look for some pieces of happiness in the time I have left with him? Unhappiness will come soon enough. Can't I just enjoy being near him and pay the price after he's gone? It seemed a small thing.

Cassidy watched him work, memorizing every part of him. There would come a time, she knew, when she would want the memories. She studied the dark fullness of the hair falling on his forehead and curling over his collar. She studied the black arched brows which were capable of expressing so many moods. The planes of his face fascinated her. His eyes lifted again and again to her face as he painted. There was a fierce concentration in them, an urgency that intensified an already impossible blue.

She couldn't see his hands, but she envisioned them, long and narrow and beautiful. She could feel them learning her face, seeing what perhaps she herself would never see, understanding what she might never understand. If one has to fall foolishly in love, she decided, there couldn't be a more perfect man.

They worked for hours, taking short breaks for Cassidy to stretch her muscles. Colin was always impatient to begin again. She sensed his mood, his excitement, and knew something exceptional was being created. The studio was alive with it. Eagerness, anticipation, tingled in the air.

"The eyes," he muttered and set down his palette. Quickly he stalked over to her. "Come, I need to see you closer." He pulled her to just behind the easel. "The eyes can be the soul of a portrait."

Colin took her by the shoulders, and his face was barely an inch from hers. The smell of paint and turpentine was sharp in her nostrils. Cassidy knew she would never smell them again without thinking of him.

"Look at me, Cass. Straight on."

She obeyed, though the look of his eyes nearly undid her. It was deep, intruding, reaching past what was offered and seeking the whole. Reflected in his eyes, she saw herself.

I'm a prisoner there, she thought. His. Their breaths mingled, and her lips parted, inviting his to close the minute distance. Something flickered and nearly caught flame. Abruptly he stepped back to his canvas.

Cassidy spoke without thinking. "What did you see?"

"Secrets," Colin murmured as he painted. "Dreams. No, don't look away, Cass, it's your dreams I need."

Helplessly Cassidy brought her eyes back. It was far too late for resistance. Setting down his palette and brush, Colin frowned at the canvas for several long moments, then he stepped toward Cassidy and smiled.

"It's perfect. You gave me what I needed."

Cassidy felt a tiny thrill of alarm. "Is it finished?"

"No, but nearly." He lifted her hands and kissed them one at a time. "Soon."

"Soon," she repeated and thought it an ugly word. Quickly she shoved back depression. "Then it must be going well."

"Yes, it's going well."

"But you're not going to let me see it yet."

"I'm superstitious." He gave her hands a gentle squeeze. "Humor me."

"You let Gail see it." Unable to prevent herself, Cassidy let resentment slip into her tone.

"Gail's an artist," Colin pointed out. He released her hands then patted her cheek. "Not the model."

With a sigh of defeat Cassidy turned to wander the room. "You must have painted her…at one time or other," she commented. "She's so striking, so vital."

"She can't hold a pose for five minutes," Colin said. He began to clean his brushes at the worktable.

Smiling, Cassidy leaned on the windowsill. "Do you have a hard time with your seascapes?" she asked him. "Or do you simply command the water and clouds to stop fidgeting? I believe you could do it." She stretched then lifted the weight of her hair from her neck. With an expansive sigh, she let it fall again to tumble as it chose. The sun shimmered through its shades.

When she turned her head to smile at Colin again, she found him watching her, the brush he was cleaning held idly in one hand. Something pulled at her, urging her to go to him. Instead, she walked to the other end of the room.

"The first painting of yours I ever saw was an Irish landscape." Cassidy kept her back to him and tried to speak naturally. "It was a small, exquisite work bathed in evening light. I liked it because it helped me imagine my mother. Isn't that odd?" She turned back to him as the thought eclipsed her nerves. "I have several pictures of her, but that painting made her seem real. She rarely seems real to me." Her voice softened with the words; then, suddenly, she smiled at him. "Are your parents alive, Colin?"

His eyes held hers for a moment. "Yes." He went back to cleaning his brushes. "Back in Ireland."

"They must miss you."

"Perhaps. They've six other children. I don't imagine they find much time to be lonely."

"Six!" Cassidy exclaimed. Her lips curved at the thought. "Your mother must be remarkable."

Colin looked over again, flashing a grin. "She had a razor strap that could catch three of us at one time."

"No doubt you deserved it."

"No doubt." He scrutinized the sable of his brush. "But I recall wishing a time or two her aim hadn't been so keen."

"My father lectured," Cassidy remembered, taking a long breath in and out. "I'd often wish he'd whack me a time or two and be done with it. Lectures are a great deal more painful, I think, than a razor strap."

"Like Professor Easterman's at Berkeley?" Colin asked with a grin. Cassidy blinked at him.

"How did you know about him?"

"You told me yourself, Cass my love. Last week, I think it was. Or perhaps the week before."

"I never thought you were listening," she murmured. Cassidy tried to remember all she had rambled about since the sittings had begun. Her teeth began to worry her bottom lip. "I can't think of half the things I talked about."

"That's all right, I do...well enough." After wiping his hands on a rag, Colin turned back to her. She was frowning, displeased. "You've got those lines between your brows again, Cass," he said lightly and smiled when she smoothed them out. "Well now, I've made you miss lunch, and that's a crime when you're already thin enough to slip under the door. Shall I poison you with whatever's in the kitchen, or will you settle for coffee?"

"I think I'll pass on both those gracious invitations." She swung around and glided toward the dressing room. "I'll take my chances at home. I have a neighbor who hoards stale doughnuts."

Cassidy closed the door behind her and smiled. That wasn't so bad, she told her reflection. The ground was only shaky a couple of times. Now that the worst of it's over, the rest of the sittings should be easy.

Humming lightly, she began to strip out of the gown. Everything's going to be all right. After all, I'm a grown woman. I can handle myself.

After she had slipped out of the dress, Cassidy held it aloft to shake out the folds. When the door opened, her humming turned to a shriek. In a quick jerk she pressed the dress against her naked skin and held on with both hands.

"What about dinner?" Colin asked and leaned against the open door.

"Colin!"

"Yes?" he asked in a pleasant tone.

"Colin, go away. I'm not dressed." She hugged the dress close and hoped she was somewhat covered.

"Yes, so I see, but you haven't answered my question."

Cassidy made an anxious sound and swallowed. "What question?"

"What about dinner?" he repeated. His eyes skimmed over her bare shoulders.

"What about dinner?" she demanded.

"You can't eat stale doughnuts for dinner, Cass. It's not healthy." He smiled at the incredulity on her face. She shifted the dress a bit higher.

"He keeps tacos as well," she said primly. "Now, would you mind shutting the door on your way out?"

"Tacos? Oh, no, that won't do." Colin shook his head and ignored her request. "I'll have to feed you myself."

Cassidy began to demand her privacy again then stopped. For a moment she studied him thoughtfully. "Colin, are you asking me for a date?"

"A date?" he repeated. For a moment he said nothing as he appeared to consider the matter. One brow arched as he studied her. "It certainly seems that way."

"To dinner?" Cassidy asked cautiously.

"To dinner."

"What time?"

"Seven."

"Seven," she repeated with a nod as she shut her ears on her practical side. "Now, close the door so I can get dressed."

"Certainly." A wicked gleam shot into his eyes, making her clutch the dress with both hands. She took one wary step in retreat. "By the way, Cass, you'd never've been a successful general."

"What?"

"You forgot to cover your flank," he told her as he shut the door behind him.

Twisting her head, Cassidy caught the full rear length of herself in the mirror.

Chapter 7

As Cassidy dressed that evening she blessed her short skip into the boutique business. The wisteria crepe de chine was worth all the hours she had practiced patience. It was a thin, dreamlike dress with floating lines. Her shoulders were left bare as the bodice was caught with elastic just above her breasts. The material nipped in at the waist then fell fully to the knees. She slipped on the cap-sleeved matching jacket and tied it loosely at the waist. The color was good for her eyes, she decided, bringing out the uniqueness of their shade. This was a night she didn't want to feel ordinary.

You shouldn't even be going. Cassidy brought the brush through her hair violently in response to the nagging voice. I don't care. I am going. *You'll get hurt.* I'll be hurt in any case. Moving quickly, she fastened small gold lover's knots to her ears. Doesn't everyone deserve one special moment? Aren't I entitled to a glimpse of real happiness? I'll have my one evening with him without that blasted painting between us. I'll have my moment when he's looking at me, seeing me, and not whatever it is he sees when we're in the studio.

She lifted her scent and sprayed a cloud as delicate as the wisteria. I won't think about tomorrow, only tonight. The painting's almost finished and then it'll be over. I have to have something. One evening isn't too much to ask. I'll pay the price later, but I'm going to have it. After tossing her hair behind her shoulders, Cassidy glanced at her watch.

"Oh, good grief, it's already seven!" Frantically she began to search for her key. She was on her hands and knees, peering under the convertible sofa that doubled as her bed, when the knock came. "Yes, yes, yes, just a minute," she called out crossly and stretched out for something shiny in the dark beneath the sofa.

She pulled it out with an "Aha!" of triumph, then sighed when she saw a quarter and not a key in her fingers.

"I said I'd buy," Colin told her, and Cassidy's head shot up. He stood inside her door, looking curiously at the woman on her hands and knees. Cassidy straightened up, blew her hair from her eyes and studied him.

He wore a slimly tailored black suit. Its perfect cut accentuated the width of his shoulders and leanness of his build. His shirt was a splash of white in contrast and opened at the throat. Cassidy concluded Colin Sullivan would never restrict himself with a tie. She leaned back on her heels.

"I've never seen you in a suit before," she commented.

The lamplight fell softly on her upturned face. "But you don't look too conventional. I'm glad."

"You're an amazing creature, Cassidy." He held out a hand to help her up, touching the other to her hair as she rose.

Standing, she tilted her head back and smiled at him. "Do you think so?"

A smile was his answer as he stepped back, keeping her hand in his. "You look lovely." The survey he made was quick and thorough. "Perfectly lovely." Taking her other hand, he turned it palm up and revealed the quarter. "Cab fare?" he asked. "It won't take you far."

Cassidy frowned down at her own hand. "I thought it was my key."

"Of course." Colin took the quarter and examined it critically. "It looks remarkably like one."

"It did in the dark under the sofa," Cassidy retorted then resumed her search. "It has to be here somewhere," she muttered as she shuffled through papers on her desk. "I've looked everywhere, positively everywhere."

"Where's the bedroom?" Colin asked, watching her shake out the pages of a dictionary.

"This *is* the bedroom," Cassidy informed him and poked through the leaves of a fern. "And the living room, and the study and the parlor. I like things all in one place, it saves steps." She found an eraser under a pile of notebooks and scowled at it. "I looked all over for this yesterday." With a long sigh she set it down.

"All right, just a minute," she said to the room in general as she leaned back on the desk. "I'll get it." Her eyes closed as she rubbed the tip of her finger over the bridge of her nose. "Last time I had it, I'd been to the market. I came in," she said, pointing to the door, "and

I took the bag into the kitchen. I put a can of juice into the freezer, and…" Her eyes widened before she scrambled into the next room.

When she came back, she bounced the key from palm to palm. "It's cold," she explained and flushed under Colin's amused glance. "I must have been thinking of something else when I left it in there." Picking up a small gold bag, Cassidy dropped the frozen key inside. "That should do it." She moved to the door and engaged the lock. Gravely, Colin walked to her then cupped her face in his hands.

"Cass."

"Yes?"

"You don't have any shoes on."

"Oh." She lifted her shoulders then let them fall. "I suppose I'll need them."

He kissed her forehead and let her go. "It's best to be prepared for anything." A grin accompanied the gesture of his arm. "They seem to be by your desk."

In silence, Cassidy walked to the desk and slipped into her shoes. Her eyes were smiling as she returned to Colin. "Well, have I forgotten anything else?"

He took her hand, interlocking their fingers. "No."

"Do you like organized people particularly, Colin?" She tilted her head with the question.

"Not particularly."

"Good. Shall we go?"

Cassidy's first surprise of the evening was the Ferrari that sat by the curb. It was red and sleek and flashy. "That must be yours," she murmured, taking her eyes from bumper to bumper then back again. "Or my neighbor has suddenly inherited a fortune."

"One of Vince's bribes." Colin opened the door on the passenger side. "For this I did a portrait of his niece. A remarkably plain creature with an overbite. Shall I put the top up?"

"No, don't." Cassidy settled into the seat as she watched him round the hood. Cinderella never had a pumpkin like this, she thought and smiled. "I thought you didn't paint anyone unless you were particularly interested in the subject."

"Vince is one of the few people I have difficulty refusing." The Ferrari roared into life. Excitement vibrated under Cassidy's feet.

"Did you know you can buy a three-bedroom brick rambler in New Jersey for what this car costs? With a carport and five spreading junipers."

Colin grinned and swung away from the curb. "I'd make a lousy neighbor."

Colin drove expertly through the city. They skirted Golden Gate Park, and avoided the labyrinthine stretches of freeway. They took side roads, narrow roads, and he maneuvered through traffic with smooth skill.

Cassidy could smell the varied scents from the sidewalk flower vendors and hear the brassy clang of the trolley bell. Tilting her head back, she could see the peak of a slender skyscraper. "Where're we going?" she asked but cared little as the breeze fluttered over her cheeks. It was enough to be with him.

"To eat," Colin returned. "I'm starving."

Cassidy turned to face him. "For an Irishman, you're not exactly talkative. Look." She sat up and pointed. "The fog's coming in."

It loomed over the bay, swallowing the bridge with

surprising speed. As Cassidy watched, only the pinnacles of the Golden Gate speared the tumbling cloud.

"There'll be foghorns tonight," she murmured then looked at Colin again. "They make such a lonely sound. It always makes me sad, though I never know why."

"What sound makes you happy?" He glanced over to her, and she brushed wisps of flying hair from her face.

"Popping corn," she answered instantly then laughed at herself.

Leaning her head back, Cassidy looked up at the sky. It was piercingly blue. How many cities could have tumbling fog and blue skies? she wondered. When Colin pulled to the curb, her gaze traveled down until it encountered the huge expanse of the hotel. Her lips parted in surprise as she recognized the area. Nob Hill. She had paid no attention to their direction.

Her door was opened by a uniformed doorman who offered his hand to help her alight. She waited while Colin passed him a bill then joined her.

"Do you like seafood?" He took her hand and moved toward the entrance.

"Why, yes, I—"

"Good. They have rather exceptional seafood here."

"So I've heard," Cassidy murmured.

In a few steps she walked from a world she knew into one she had only read of.

The restaurant was huge and sumptuous. High, iridescent glass ceilings crowned a room dripping with chandeliers. The carpet was rich, the tables many and elegantly white clothed. The maître d' was immediately attentive, and as Colin called him by name Cassidy realized the artist was no stranger there.

The secluded corner table set them apart from the

vastness of the restaurant yet left Cassidy with a full view of the splendor. Jeff's cheeseburger seemed light-years away. Having gawked as much as she deemed proper, Cassidy turned to Colin.

"It seems I'm going to do better than tacos after all."

"I'm a man of my word," he informed her. "That's why I give it as seldom as possible. Wine?" he asked and smiled at her in his masterfully charming fashion. "You don't look the cocktail type."

"Oh?" Her head tilted. "Why not?"

"Too much innocence in those big violet eyes." He brushed her hair behind her shoulder. "It almost makes me consider doing something bourgeois like cutting the wine with water."

A black-coated waiter stood respectfully at Colin's elbow. "A bottle of Château Haut-Brion blanc," he ordered, keeping his eyes on Cassidy. With a slight bow the waiter drifted backward and away. She watched him then took another long look around the room, trying to absorb every detail. "I noticed by your desk that you've been working. Is it going well?"

Cassidy studied Colin with some surprise. Perhaps he saw more than she assumed he did. "Yes, actually, I think it is. I'm having one of those periods when everything falls into place. They don't last long, but they're productive. Does it work like that with painting?"

"Yes. Times when everything seems to flow without effort, and times when you scrape the canvas down again and again." He smiled at her, and his long fingers traced her wrist. "Somewhat like you tearing up pages, I imagine."

The waiter returned with their wine, and the ritual of opening and tasting began. Gratefully, Cassidy remained silent. The pulse in her wrist had leapt at Colin's casual touch, and she used the time to quiet its skittish rhythm. When her glass was filled, she was able to lift it with complete composure. The wine was lightly chilled and exquisite.

"To your taste?" Colin asked as he watched her sip.

Cassidy's eyes smiled into his. "It could become a habit."

"Tell me what you're writing about." He, too, lifted his glass, but his free hand covered hers.

"It's about two people and their life together and apart from each other."

"A love story?"

"Yes, a complex one." She frowned a moment at their joined hands then brought her eyes to Colin's again. The flame of the candle threw gold among the violet. She reminded herself to enjoy the moment, not to think of tomorrow. A smile lifted her lips as she touched the glass to them. "They both seem to be volatile characters and get away from me sometimes. There's a fierce determination in them both to stand separate, yet they're drawn together. I'd like to think love allows them to remain separate in some aspects."

"Love makes its own rules, depending on who's playing." His finger trailed over her knuckles then down to her nails before they traveled back. The simple gesture quickened her heartbeat. "Will they have a happy ending?"

Cassidy allowed herself to absorb the pure blue of his eyes. "Perhaps they will," she murmured. "Their destinies are in my hands."

Watching her, Colin brought her hand to his lips. "And for tonight, Cass," he said softly, "is yours in mine?"

Her eyes were dark and steady on his. "For tonight."

He smiled then, with the flash of the pirate. Lifting his glass, he toasted her. "To the long evening ahead."

It was a luxuriously lengthy meal. Wine sparkled in crystal. Even after endless courses, they lingered long over coffee. Cassidy savored each moment. If she was to have only one evening with the man she loved, she would relish each morsel of time. Perhaps by the force of her own will, she could slow the hands of the clock.

The candle flickered low when they rose from the table. Her hand slipped into his. Just as they reached the lobby Cassidy heard Colin's name called. Looking up, she saw a round, balding man in an impeccably cut suit coming toward them. He had a full smile and an extended hand. On reaching Colin, he pumped it enthusiastically while his other thumped on Colin's shoulder. Cassidy saw a large diamond flash from the ring on his hand.

"Sullivan, you rascal, it's good to see you."

"Jack." An easy grin spread over Colin's face. "How've you been?"

"Getting by, getting by. Have a little job in town." His eyes drifted to Cassidy and lingered.

"Cass, this is Jack Swanson, a perfect reprobate. Jack, Cassidy St. John, a perfect treasure."

Cassidy was torn between pleasure at Colin's description and astonishment as she put Swanson's face and name together. Over the past twenty-five years he had produced some of the finest motion pictures in the industry. As he took her hand and squeezed it, she struggled to conceal her feelings.

"Reprobate?" Swanson snorted and kept possession

of Cassidy's hand. "You can't believe half the things this Irishman says. I'm a pillar of the community."

"There's a plaque in his den that says so," Colin added.

"Never did have an ounce of respect. Still…" Swanson's eyes roamed over Cassidy's face. There was appreciation in the look. "His taste is flawless. Not an actress, are you?"

"Not unless you count being a mushroom in the fourth-grade pageant." Cassidy smiled.

Swanson chuckled and nodded. "I've dealt with actresses who had lesser credits."

"Cassidy's a writer," Colin put in. He draped an arm around her shoulders, running his hand lightly down her arm. "You warned me to stay away from actresses."

"Since when have you listened to my sage advice?" Swanson scoffed. He pursed his lips as he studied Cassidy. Appreciation became speculation. "A writer. What sort of writer are you?"

"Why, a brilliant one, of course," she told him. "Without a scrap of ego or temperament."

Swanson patted her hand. "I've a late meeting or I'd steal you away from this young scamp now. We'll have dinner before I leave town." He cast an eye at Colin. "You can bring him along if you like." With another slap for Colin's shoulder, he lumbered away.

"Quite a character, isn't he?" Colin asked as he steered Cassidy toward the door again.

"Marvelous." It occurred to her that since meeting Colin, she had held hands with an Italian duke and one of Hollywood's reigning monarchs.

They stepped outside into the soft light of evening. The sun was gone, but some of its light still lingered.

Cassidy slipped into the Ferrari with a contented sigh. She watched the first star flicker into life. With surprise she noted that Colin was headed away from the direction of her apartment.

"Where are we going?"

"There's this little place I know." He turned a corner and eased into traffic. "I thought you'd enjoy it." He shot her a glance and a smile. "Not tired, are you?"

Cassidy's lips curved. "No, I'm not tired."

The nightclub was dimly lit and smoky. Tables were small and crowded together. Jeans sat next to elegant evening dresses and splashy designer outfits. Brassy music blared from a band near a postage-stamp dance floor. Couples swayed together as they moved to the beat.

Colin escorted Cassidy to a dark table at the side of the room. His name was called now and again, but he only made a gesture of acknowledgment and continued until they were seated.

"This is wonderful! I'm certain it's a front for gun running or jewel smuggling," Cassidy exclaimed.

Colin laughed, taking both her hands. "You'd like that, would you?"

"Of course." She grinned, and her eyes lit with mischief.

A waitress had pushed her way over to them and stood, impatient, with her weight on one hip. "The lady needs champagne," Colin told her.

"Who doesn't," she mumbled and shoved her way back through the tables.

Cassidy laughed with unbridled delight. "No deferential bows for Mr. Sullivan in here," she commented.

"It's all a matter of atmosphere. I'm rather fond of

sassy waitresses in the right setting. And," he added softly, turning her hand over and kissing the inside of her wrist, "crowded tables that require very close contact. Poor lighting," he continued, pressing his lips to her palm. "Where I can enjoy the taste of your skin in relative privacy." With a slight movement of his head, he kissed the sensitive skin behind her ear.

"Colin," she said breathlessly and lifted her hand to his lips in defense. He merely took it in his and kissed her fingers.

The bottle of champagne came down on the table with a bang. Colin pulled out a bill and handed it to the waitress. Shoving it in her pocket, she stalked away.

"Annoyingly speedy service tonight," he murmured as he opened the bottle. The pop was drowned out by the loud horns of the band. Cassidy accepted the wine and took a long, slow sip in the hope of stabilizing her pulse.

They drank champagne in quiet companionship, watching the raucous nightlife revolve around them. Cassidy's mood grew mellow and dreamy. Reality and make-believe became too difficult to separate. When Colin stood and took her hand, she rose to go with him to the dance floor.

The music had turned low and bluesy. He slipped both arms around her waist, and in response she lifted hers to circle his neck. Their bodies came together. The air was thick with smoke and clashing perfumes. Other couples were little more than shadows in the dim light. Their movement was only a slow swaying with their bodies pressed close.

Cassidy tilted back her head to look at him. Their eyes joined, their lips tarried less than a whisper apart.

She felt a quick surge of desire. If they had been on an island without a trace of humanity, she could not have felt more alone with him. The music ended on a haunted bass note.

Silently Colin took her hand and led her from the crowd.

The moon was a white slice. Cooler air blew some of the heat from Cassidy's blood and some of the clouds from her brain. The Ferrari climbed a hill then descended. Cassidy smiled to herself. There was nothing in the evening she would have changed. No regrets.

Fog curled in twisting fingers on the road ahead. As she glanced to the side Cassidy saw the solid mass of clouds over the bay below them. Again she turned to Colin.

"To my houseboat," he told her before she could form the question. "I have something for you."

Warning lights flashed on and off in her brain. The bittersweet taste of danger was in her mouth. Cassidy looked out on the fog-choked bay and told herself she should ask Colin to take her home. But the night isn't over, she reminded herself. I promised myself tonight.

Fog swirled more thickly as they drove toward sea level. Now and again, from somewhere deep in the mist, came the low warning horns. She'd lost all sense of time when Colin stopped the car. Once again she was in a make-believe world. This one had drifting mists and the sigh of lapping water. Colin led her toward a shrouded shape. The high, maniacal call of a loon speared the silence. A narrow rope bridge swayed lightly under her feet as they crossed it. A breeze blew aside a curtain of fog, and the houseboat jumped into the opening.

"Oh, Colin." She stopped to stare at it with delight and surprise. "It's wonderful."

She saw a wide structure of aged wood in two levels with a high deck on the bow. Fog misted over again as they approached.

Inside Cassidy shook the dampness from her hair as Colin switched on a light. They walked down two steps and into the living room. It was a large square room with a low, inviting couch and tables scattered for convenience. To the right another short set of stairs led to the galley.

"How marvelous to live on the water." Cassidy spun to Colin and smiled.

"On a clear night the city's all prisms and crystals. In the fog it's brooding and wrapped in mystery." He came to her and, with a habitual gesture, brushed her hair behind her shoulder. His fingers lingered. "Your hair's damp," he murmured. "Do you know how many shades of gold and brown I used to paint your hair? It changes in every light, daring someone to define its color." Colin frowned suddenly and dropped his hand. "You should have a brandy to ward off the chill."

He turned away and walked to a cabinet. Cassidy watched him pour brandy into snifters while she dealt with the effect the intimate tone of his voice and the touch of his hand had had on her.

After accepting the brandy she turned to wander around the room. On a far wall was a painting of the bay at sunrise. The sky was molten with color, reds and golds at their most intense. There was a feeling of frenzied motion and brilliance. Even before she looked for the signature, Cassidy knew it was a Kingsley.

"She's immensely talented," Colin commented from behind.

"Yes," Cassidy agreed with sincerity. The painting gripped her. "It makes the start of a day demand your attention. A sunrise like this would be exciting, but I don't think I could begin each morning with such violence, however beautiful."

"Are you speaking of the painting or of the artist?"

Realizing his question had followed her thoughts, Cassidy shrugged and stepped away. "Strange," she began again. "One would think an artist would cover his walls with paintings. You have relatively few." She began to examine his collection, moving slowly from one to the next. Abruptly she stopped, staring at a small canvas. It was the Irish landscape she had told him of that morning.

"I wondered if you'd remember it." He stood behind her again, but this time his hands came to her shoulders. There was something casually possessive in the gesture.

"Yes, of course I do."

"I was twenty when I painted that. On my first trip back to Ireland."

"How odd that I should have spoken of it just this morning," Cassidy murmured.

"Destiny, Cass," Colin claimed and kissed the top of her head. Stepping around her, he took the canvas from the wall. "I want you to have it."

Cassidy's eyes flew to his. "No, Colin, I couldn't." Distress and amazement mingled in her voice.

"No?" His brow arched under his fall of hair. "You appeared to like it."

"Oh, Colin, you know I do. It's beautiful, it's wonderful." Her distress deepened, reflecting clearly on her face. "I can't just take one of your paintings."

"You're not taking it, I'm giving it to you," he countered. "That's one of the privileges of the artist."

"Colin." Her eyes went back to the painting then lifted to his. "You wouldn't have kept it all this time if it hadn't meant something special to you. You'd have sold it."

"Some things you don't sell. Some things you give." He held the small canvas out to her. "Please."

Tears thickened in her throat. "I've never heard you say 'please' before."

"I save it for special occasions."

Cassidy looked back at him. He had given her more than the painting; it was a bond—between herself and a woman she had never known. Her smile came slowly. "Thank you."

Colin traced her lips with a fingertip. "This is one of the loveliest things about you," he murmured. "Come," he said abruptly. "Sit down and drink your brandy." He took the canvas and set it aside, then led Cassidy to the sofa.

"Do you paint here, too?" she asked as she sipped her brandy.

"Sometimes."

"I remember the night I met you, your wanting me to come back here for sketches."

"And you threatened me with a husband in a football helmet."

"It was the best I could think up on the spur of the moment." She turned her head to grin at him and found his face dangerously close. His fingers tangled in her hair before she could ease away. Slowly he leaned closer until his lips brushed her cheek. Feather light, the kiss moved to her other cheek, lingering over her lips without touching. Still, she could taste the kiss on them.

"Colin," Cassidy whispered. She put a hand to his chest as his lips moved to her temple. She knew the warmth she felt was not from the brandy.

"Cassidy." He trailed his mouth down to her jawline then drew away. His eyes were grave as he looked down at her, his hand light on her shoulder. "The last time I kissed you, I hurt you. I regret that."

"Please, Colin." Cassidy shook her head to halt his words. "We were both angry."

"You've already forgiven me, because it's your nature to do so. But I remember the look on your face." He ran his hand down her arm until it linked with hers. "I want to kiss you again, Cass, the way you should be kissed." He took his hand and gently circled her neck. "But I need you to tell me it's what you want."

It would be so easy to refuse. She had only to form the word "no," and she knew he'd let her go. But she was as truly his prisoner now as if she were chained to him. "Yes," she said and closed her eyes. "Yes."

His mouth touched hers lightly, and her lips parted. His kisses were soft and gentle, lingering before one ended and another began. She felt him slip the light jacket from her shoulders and enjoyed the warmth of his hands on her skin. Slowly the kisses grew deeper. Her arms found their way around him. The languor that spread through her went far beyond the effects of the wine. Her limbs were pliant, her mind clouded as her senses grew sharper.

When their lips parted, Colin loosened his hold. "Cass."

With a sigh she snuggled against him, brushing his neck with a kiss. She ran a hand experimentally up the silk of his shirt. "Yes?" she murmured, lifting her face to his. Her eyes were slumberous, her lips a temptation. Colin swore under his breath before he crushed his mouth to hers.

Cassidy's response was instantaneous. Her passion went from languid to flaming in the space of a heartbeat. Blood pounded thickly in her brain as she found herself falling backward onto the cushions of the sofa. Colin's body was taut. His hands caressed the bare skin of her shoulders as the kiss deepened. At the base of her throat he found more pleasure, and his mouth lingered there as her pulse beat wildly beneath it.

The elastic of her bodice slid down at his insistence, freeing her breasts to his searching hands. Unbridled, her passion raced through her, bringing a moan that spoke of longing and delight. His mouth trailed down through the valley between her breasts, devouring her heated skin. His fingers brushed over the peak of her breasts, exploring, learning, until his mouth replaced them. Cassidy gave a shuddering moan as he brought his lips back to hers, accepting the fierce, final urgency that flared before he ended the kiss. Her eyes opened to meet the dark fire of his.

Seeing the tumble of his hair over his brow, she lifted a hand to push it back. She murmured his name. Colin caught her hand in his as she took it to his cheek. Carefully he drew the bodice of her dress into place then pulled her with him to a sitting position.

"I make few noble gestures, Cassidy." His voice was husky, and under her palm she could feel the rapid beat of his heart. "This is one of them." Rising, he drew her to her feet then draped her jacket over her shoulders. "I'll take you home."

"Colin," she began, knowing only that she wanted to be his.

"No, don't say anything." He dropped his hands from her shoulders and put them in his pockets. "You put your destiny in my hands for tonight. I'll take you home. Next time the decision will be in your hands."

Chapter 8

The sun was high and bright. Cassidy watched it spear through her window as she lay in bed. It fell in a patch on the floor and shimmered. Her eyes drifted to the painting that hung to her left. It had hung there for only two days, but she knew every minute detail of the canvas. She knew the very texture of the brush strokes. Sighing, she stared up at the ceiling.

She remembered every moment of her evening with Colin, from the instant she had looked up from her hands and knees by her couch to the brief good-bye at the door.

When she had returned to the studio the morning after their date, Colin had fallen into his work pattern with apparent ease. Whatever had been between them, Cassidy decided, had been for that night. For him, it was over. For me, she thought, studying the painting again, it's forever.

I should be grateful to him for taking me home when he did. If I had stayed… If I had stayed, she repeated after a long breath, I would have become one of his lovers. And then he would have picked up his life exactly where he left off, and I would be even more alone than I am now. As it is, I have one exceptional evening to remember. Wine and candlelight and music.

"Romantic fool," she muttered abruptly then rolled over and punched her pillow.

"Cassidy." The knock sounded as a brief concession before Jeff burst through the door. "Hey, Cassidy." He stopped and gave her a look of disgust. "Still in bed? It's eleven o'clock."

Cassidy pulled the sheet up to her chin and scrambled to sit up. "Yes, I'm still in bed. I worked till three-thirty." She frowned past him. "I thought I'd remembered to lock that door."

"Uh-uh." Jeff hurried over and plopped on the bed while she flushed with embarrassed amusement.

"Make yourself at home," she said with a grand gesture of her free arm. "Don't mind me."

"Take a look at this! You got yourself in the paper."

"What?" Cassidy glanced down at the newspaper Jeff had clutched in his hand. "What are you talking about?"

"I splurged on a Sunday paper," he began then his lips spread in a grin. He touched her nose with a fingertip. "And who do I see when I take a look at the society section, but my friend and neighbor, Cassidy St. John."

"You're making that up," Cassidy accused and tossed back her sleep-tumbled hair. "What would I be doing on the society page?"

"Dancing with Colin Sullivan," Jeff informed her as he waved the paper under her nose.

Cassidy grabbed his wrist to stop the movement, then her mouth fell open in astonishment. She stared, unbelievingly, at the picture. In two quick moves she had dropped the sheet and grabbed the paper from Jeff's hand. "Let me see that."

"Help yourself," he said amiably. He settled back on one elbow to watch myriad expressions cross her face. The flush sleep had put into her cheeks grew deeper. "Seems you were seen together in some hot spot. A picture gets snapped, and they add a bit of interesting speculation of who Sullivan's latest flame is." He pulled on his beard and chuckled. "Little do they know she's sitting right here in a number fifty-three football jersey that looks a lot better on her than it would on a right tackle." He chuckled again then peered down at the newspaper. "You look real good in there, too."

"This is all—all drivel!" Cassidy slammed down the paper then scrambled to her knees. Pushing Jeff aside she stepped over him to the floor. "Did you read that story?" she demanded and kicked a stray tennis shoe into a corner. "How dare they imply such things?"

Jeff sat back up, watching her spin around the room. "Hey, Cassidy, it's just a story, nothing to get all worked up about. Besides…" He picked up the discarded paper and smoothed it out. "They're really pretty complimentary where you're concerned. Listen, they call you a…" He paused while he searched down the phrase. "Oh, yeah, here it is. A 'nubile young beauty.' Sounds pretty good."

Cassidy made a low sound in her throat then kicked the mate to the tennis shoe into an opposing corner. "That's just like a man," she stormed back at him. Turning away, she pulled open a drawer and yanked out a pair of cutoffs; then, spinning around, she waved them at him. "Toss out a few compliments and it makes everything all right." Cassidy dove back into the drawer and came up with a crimson scoop-necked T-shirt. "Well, it's not, it's absolutely not." She pushed her hair out of her face and drew in a deep breath. "Can I keep that?" she asked in more controlled tones.

"Sure." Warily, Jeff rose and handed her the paper. He cleared his throat. "Well, I guess I'll just go read the rest of the paper," he told her, but she was already scowling down at the picture again. Taking advantage of her preoccupation, he slipped out the door.

Less than an hour later Cassidy was stalking down the pier toward Colin's houseboat. Gripped in her hand was the folded page of the Sunday paper. Filled with righteous indignation, she crossed the narrow swaying bridge then pounded on the door. There was silence and the lapping of waves. She glanced around then scowled at the Ferrari.

"Oh, you're home all right, Sullivan," she muttered darkly then pounded again.

"What the devil are you banging about?" Colin's voice boomed over her head. Cassidy backed away from the door, looked up and was blinded by the sun. Furious, she flung up a hand to shade her eyes.

She saw him leaning over the rail of the top deck. He was bare-chested, his cutoffs a slight concession to modesty. He held a paint brush tipped in blue in his hand.

"I've got to talk to you!" Cassidy shouted and waved the paper at him.

"All right then, come up, but stop that idiotic banging." He disappeared from the rail before she could speak again. Cassidy walked toward the bow until she spotted a steep set of stairs. After climbing them, she stood on the upper deck with her hands on her hips. She scowled at his back.

He was on a three-legged stool in front of a canvas, painting with sure, rapid strokes. Glancing over, she saw the sailboats he was recreating. They skimmed over the bay with spinnakers billowing in a riot of color.

"Well, what brings you rapping at my door, Cass?" His voice was muffled as he held the stem of a brush between his teeth like a pirate's saber. Another glided over the canvas. Cassidy stomped over and fearlessly waved the paper in front of his face.

"This!"

With surprising calm, Colin put down both of his brushes, cast her a raised-brow look, then took the paper from her. "It's a good likeness," he said after a moment.

"Colin!"

"Ssh. I'm reading." He lapsed into silence, eyes on the paper, while Cassidy ground her teeth and stalked around the deck. Once he laughed outright but held up a hand when she started to speak. She shut her mouth on something like a growl and turned her back on him. "Well," he said at length. "That was highly entertaining."

Cassidy whirled around. "Entertaining? *Entertaining?!* Is that all you have to say about this—this trash?"

Colin shrugged. "It could be better written, I suppose. Do you want coffee?"

"Did you *read* that?" she demanded and stormed forward until she stood in front of him. The wind tugged at her hair, and she pushed it back, annoyed. "Did you read the things it said, the things…" Cassidy sputtered to a halt, stomped her foot in frustration then gave him a firm rap on the chest with her fist. "I am not your latest flame, Sullivan."

"Ah."

Her eyes kindled. "Don't you use that significant 'ah' on me. I am *not* your latest flame, or your flame of any sort, and I resent the term. I resent all the little insinuations and innuendos in that article. I resent the unstated fact that you and I are lovers." She tossed back her head. "What sort of logic is it that because we dance together, we have to be lovers?"

"You have to admit the idea is appealing." He chuckled at her smoldering glare. The breeze rolling in from the bay continued to blow her hair around her face. Absently Colin brushed it back then laid a hand on her shoulder. "Would you like to sue the paper?"

She heard the soft amusement in his voice and stuck her hands in her pockets. "I want a retraction," she said stubbornly.

"For what?" he countered. "For snapping a picture? For writing a bit of gossip? My dear child, the picture's enough all by itself." He held it out, drawing her eyes to it. "These two people appear to be totally absorbed in each other."

Cassidy turned away and walked to the rail. She knew it had been the picture that had set her off. Their bodies were close, her arms around his neck, their eyes locked. The dark, smoky nightclub was a backdrop. No words were needed to complete the picture. She remembered the moment, the feeling that had rushed through her, the utter intimacy they had shared.

The picture was an invasion of her private self, and

she hated it. She detested the chatty little column beside it that linked her so casually with Colin. Without even having learned her name, they had titled her his woman, his woman of the moment…until the next one. Cassidy frowned out at the water, watching the gulls swoop.

"I don't like it," she muttered. "I don't like being splashed in print for speculation over cornflakes and coffee. I don't like being made into something I'm not by someone's lively imagination. And I don't like being described as a…"

"'Nubile young beauty'?" Colin provided.

"I see nothing funny in that grand little phrase. It makes me feel absurd." She folded her arms over her chest. "It's not a compliment, whatever you and Jeff might think."

"Who the devil is Jeff?"

"He thought the article was just peachy," she continued, working up to a high temper again. "He sat on my bed this morning, telling me I should be flattered, that I should—"

"Perhaps," Colin interrupted and walked to her, "you'd tell me who Jeff is and why he was in your bed this morning?"

"Not in, *on*," Cassidy corrected impatiently. "And stick to the point, Sullivan."

"I'd like this matter cleared up first." He took a final step toward her then captured her chin. His fingers were surprisingly firm. "In fact, I insist."

"Will you stop it?" she demanded and jerked away. "How can I get anywhere when you're constantly badgering and belittling me."

"Badgering and belittling?" Colin repeated then

tossed back his head and roared with laughter. "Now *that's* a grand little phrase. Now, about Jeff."

"Oh, leave him out of it, would you?" Cassidy blew out a frustrated breath, making a wide sweep with her arms. Her eyes began to glitter again. "He brought me the article this morning, that's all. I'm telling you, Colin, I won't be lumped in with all your former and future flames. And I won't be used to sustain the romantic mystique of the artist."

His brows drew together. "Now what precisely is the meaning of that last sentence, for those of us who missed the first installment?"

"I think it's clear, a simple declarative sentence in the first person. I mean it, Colin."

"Yes." He studied her curiously. "I can see you do."

They watched each other in silence. She was painfully aware of the lean attraction of his build, of the bronzed skin left bare but for low-slung cutoffs. Thrown off balance by her own thoughts, Cassidy turned away again and leaned over the rail. For a moment she listened to the gentle slap of water against the wood of the boat. Her shoulders moved with her sigh.

"I'm basically a simple person, Colin. I've never been out of the state and scarcely been more than a hundred miles from the city. I don't have a fascinating background. I'm not a woman of mystery." Composed again, she turned back to him. The breeze picked up her hair and tossed it behind her. "I don't like being misrepresented." She lifted her hands a moment then dropped them to her sides. "I'm not the sort of woman they made me seem in that paper."

Colin folded the paper then tucked it in his back pocket before he crossed to her. "You are infinitely more fascinating than the sort of woman they made you seem in that paper."

Cassidy shook her head. "I wasn't fishing for a compliment."

"A simple statement of fact." He kissed her before she could decide whether to accept or evade him. "Feel better now?"

Cassidy frowned at him. "I'm not a child having a temper tantrum."

His brow lifted. "A nubile young beauty, then."

Cassidy narrowed her eyes at him then glanced down at herself. "I'm nubile enough, I should think."

"And certainly young."

Bringing her eyes back up, she gave him a provocative look. "Don't you think I'm beautiful?"

"No."

"Oh."

Colin laughed then captured her face with his hands. "That face," he said as his eyes roamed over her, "has superb bones, exquisite skin. There's strength and frailty and vivacity, and you're totally unaware of it. A unique, expressive face. *Beautiful* is far too ordinary a word."

Color warmed Cassidy's cheeks. She wondered why, after so many close examinations, her blood still churned when he studied her face. "A charming way to make up for an insult," she said lightly. "It must be the Irish in you."

"I've a much better way."

The kiss was so quickly insistent, Cassidy had no time for thought, only response. A sound of pleasure escaped her she moved her hands up the taut, bare skin of his chest. She felt the heat of the sun and her own instant need. Her mouth became avid. Desire swirled through her blood, causing her to demand rather than surrender. The passion he released in her ruled her, changing submission to aggression. She felt Colin's arms tighten around her and heard his low moan of approval.

"Cassidy," he murmured as his lips roamed over her face. "You bewitch me."

With a curiosity of their own, her hands explored the long line of his torso, the wiry muscles of his arms and back. His heart hammered against hers as she touched him. Here was a whole new world, and her mouth searched his ravenously as she tested it.

"Oh, dear, I seem to be interrupting."

Startled, Cassidy pulled her mouth from Colin's but was unable to break his hold. Twisting her head, she stared at Gail Kingsley. She stood just at the top of the stairs, one hand poised on the railing. An emerald silk scarf rippled at her throat and trailed in the breeze.

"That seems obvious enough," Colin returned evenly. Flushing to the roots of her hair, Cassidy wriggled for freedom.

"I do apologize, Colin darling. I had no idea you had company. So rare for you on a Sunday, after all." She gave him a smile that established her knowledge of his habits. "I needed to pick up those Rothchild canvases, you remember? And we do have one or two things to discuss. I'll just wait downstairs." She crossed the deck as she spoke and opened a door that led inside. "Shall I make coffee for three?" she added then disappeared without waiting for an answer.

Cassidy twisted her head back to Colin, pressing her

hands against his chest. "Let me go," she demanded between her teeth. "Let me go this minute."

"Why? You seemed happy enough to be held a moment ago."

She threw back her head as she shoved against him. The muscles she had just tested made her movements useless. "A moment ago I was blinded by animal lust. I see perfectly now."

"Animal lust?" Colin repeated. He grinned widely in appreciation. "How interesting. Does it come over you often?"

"Don't you grin at me, Sullivan. Don't you dare!"

Colin released her without sobering his features. "At times it's difficult not to."

"I won't have you holding me while Gail stands there with her superior little smile." With a sniff, she brushed at her T-shirt and shorts.

"Why, Cass, are you jealous?" His grin grew yet wider. "How flattering."

Her head snapped up, her breathing grew rapid. "Why you smug, insufferable—"

"You were perfectly willing to suffer me when you were blinded by animal lust."

A sound of temper came low in her throat. Tested past her limit, Cassidy took an enthusiastic swing at him that carried her in a complete circle. He dodged it, catching her neatly by the waist.

"Women are supposed to slap," he instructed. "Not punch."

"I never read the rules," she snapped then jerked away. Cassidy turned, intending to leave in the same manner she had arrived. Colin caught her hand and spun her back until she collided with his chest. He smiled then kissed the tip of her nose.

"What's your hurry?"

"There's an old Irish saying," she told him as she pushed away again. "Three's a crowd."

He chuckled, patting her cheek. "Cass, don't be a fool."

She rolled her eyes to the sky and prayed for willpower. Screaming wouldn't solve anything. She took several deep breaths. "Oh, go…go paint your spinnakers," she suggested and stalked down the steps to the lower deck.

"Sure and it's a fine-looking woman you are, Cassidy St. John," Colin called after her in an exaggerated brogue. She glanced back over her shoulder with eyes blazing. He leaned companionably over the rail. "And it's the truth it's no more hardship watching your temper walking away than it is watching it coming ahead. Next time I'll be wanting to paint you in a pose that shows your more charming end."

"When pigs fly," she called back and doubled her pace. His laughter raced after her.

Chapter 9

Cassidy knew the painting was nearly finished. She had the frantic, hollow sensation of one living on borrowed time. Though she sensed the end would be almost a relief, a release from the tension of waiting, she tried to hold it off by sheer force of will. As she held the pose, she sensed Colin was perfecting, polishing, rather than creating fresh. His quick impatience had relaxed.

He made no mention of her Sunday visit, and she was grateful. In retrospect, with her temper at a reasoning degree, she knew she had overreacted. She was also forced to admit that she had made a fool of herself. A complete fool.

It's not the first time, she mused. And perhaps, in a way, excusable. All I could see was a very public picture revealing my very private feelings. Then that silly little article... Then remembering Gail's spouting off about romantic press and Colin's image. Cassidy caught herself before she scowled. *Well, I won't have to listen to her much longer. I'd better start picking up the pieces. It's time to start thinking about tomorrow. A new job,* she concluded dismally. *A new start,* she corrected. *New experiences, new people. Empty nights.*

"Fortunately, I finished the face yesterday," Colin commented. "Your expression's altered a dozen times in the last ten minutes. Amazing what a range you have."

"I'm sorry. I was…" She searched for a word and settled on an inanity. "Thinking."

"Yes, I could see." His eyes caught hers. "Unhappy thoughts."

"No, I was working out a scene."

"Mmm," Colin commented noncommittally then stepped back from the easel. "Not a particularly joyful one."

"No. They can't all be." She swallowed. "It's finished, isn't it?"

"Yes. Quite finished." Cassidy let out a quiet sigh as she watched his critical study. "Come, have a look," he invited. He held out his hand, but his eyes remained on the canvas.

It surprised her that she was afraid. Colin glanced up at her and lifted a brow.

"Come on, then."

Her fingers tightened around the nosegay, but she walked toward him. Obediently she slipped her hand into his extended one. She turned and looked.

Cassidy had tried to imagine it a hundred times, but it was nothing like what she'd thought. The background was dark and shadowy, playing on shading and depth. In its midst, she stood highlighted in the oyster-white dress. Her nosegay was a surprising splash of color calling attention to the frailty of her hands. Pride was in the stance, in the tilt of her head. Her hair was thick and gloriously tumbled, offsetting the quiet innocence of the dress. It was hair that invited passion. There was a delicacy in the bones of her face she had been unaware of, a fragility competing with the strength of the features. She had been right in thinking he would see her as she had never seen herself.

Her lips were parted, unsmiling but waiting to smile. The smile would be to welcome a lover. The knowledge was in her expression, along with the anticipation of something yet to come. The eyes told everything. They were the eyes of a woman consumed by love…the eyes of innocence waiting to be surrendered. No one could look at it and remain unaware that the woman in the painting had loved the man who painted it.

"So silent, Cass?" Colin murmured and slipped an arm around her shoulders.

"I can't find the word," she whispered then drew a trembling breath. "Nothing's adequate, and anything less would sound platitudinous." She leaned against him a moment. "Colin." Cassidy tried to forget for a moment that the eyes in the painting were naked with love. She tried to see the whole and not the revelation of her emotions. Secrets, he had said. Dreams.

Colin kissed her neck above the silk of the dress then released her. "Rarely, an artist steps back from his work and is astonished that his hands have created something extraordinary." She could hear the excitement in his voice, a wonder she had not expected him to be capable of feeling. "This is the finest thing I've ever done." He turned to her then. "I'm grateful to you, Cassidy. You're the soul of it."

Unable to bear his words, Cassidy turned away. She had to cling to some rags of pride. Desperately she kept her voice calm. "I've always felt the artist is the soul of a painting." Cassidy dropped the nosegay on the worktable then continued to wander around the room. The silk whispered over her legs. "It's your—your imagination, your talent. How much of me is really in that painting?"

There was silence for a long moment, but Cassidy didn't turn back to him. "Don't you know?" Cassidy moistened her lips and struggled to keep her tone light as she turned around.

"My face," she agreed; then, gesturing down the dress, she added, "My body. The rest is yours, Colin, I can't take credit for it. You set the mood, you drew out of me what you already saw. You had the vision. It was a wish you asked me to be, and that's what you've made. It's your illusion." Saying the words caused her more pain than she had believed possible. Still, she felt they had to be said.

"Is that how you see it?" Colin's look was speculative, but she sensed the anger just beneath the surface. "You stood, and I pulled the strings."

"You're the artist, Colin." She shrugged and answered lightly. "I'm just an unemployed writer."

After a long, silent study, he crossed to her. There was a steady calculation about the way his hands took her shoulders. She had felt that seeking, probing look before and stiffened her defenses against it. His fingers tightened on her skin. "Has the woman in that portrait anything to do with you?" He asked the question slowly.

Cassidy swallowed the knot in her throat. "Why, of course, Colin, I've just told you—"

He shook her so quickly, the words slid back down her throat. She saw the fury on his face, the vivid temper she knew could turn violent. "Do you think it was only your face I wanted? Just the shell? Is there nothing that's inside you in that painting?"

"Must you have everything?" she demanded in despair and anger. "Must you have it all?" Her voice thickened with emotion. "You've drained me, Colin. That's drained me." She flung a hand toward the canvas. "I've given you everything, how much more do you want?"

She pushed him away as a tidal wave of anguish engulfed her. "You never looked at me, thought of me, unless it was because of that painting." She pushed her hair back with both hands, pressing her fingers against her temples. "I won't give you anymore. I can't, there isn't any. It's all there!" She gestured again, and her voice shook. "Thank God it's over."

With a quick jerk, she was out of his hold and running from the studio.

Cassidy spent the next two weeks in the apartment of vacationing friends. Leaving a brief note for Jeff, she packed up her typewriter and buried herself in work. She unplugged the phone, bolted the door and shut herself in. For two weeks she tried to forget there was a world outside the people and places of her imagination. She lost herself in her characters in an attempt to forget Cassidy St. John. If she didn't exist, she couldn't feel pain. At the end of the interlude, she'd shed five pounds, produced a hundred pages of fresh copy and nearly balanced her nerves.

As she returned, hauling her typewriter back up the steps to her apartment, she heard Jeff's guitar playing through his door. For a moment she hesitated, thinking to stop and tell him she was back, but she passed into her own apartment. She wasn't ready to answer questions. She considered calling Colin at The Gallery to apologize, then decided against that as well. It was best that their break had been complete. If they parted on good terms, he might be tempted to get in touch with her from time to time. Cassidy knew she could never bear the casual friendliness.

She packed up the dress she had worn on her flight from the studio. Her fingers lingered on the material as she placed it back in the dress box. So much had happened since she had first put it on. Quickly she smoothed the tissue over it and closed the lid. That part of her life was over. Turning, she went to the phone to call The Gallery. The clerk who answered referred her immediately to Gail.

"Why, hello, Cassidy. Where did you run off to?"

"I have the dress from the portrait and the key to the studio," Cassidy told her. "I'd like someone to come pick them up."

"I see." There was a brief hesitation before Gail continued. "I'm afraid we're just terribly busy right now, dear. I know Colin particularly wanted that dress. Be sweet and drop it by? You can just let yourself into the studio and leave everything there. Colin's away, and we're just swamped."

"I'd rather not—"

"Thank you, darling. I must run." The phone clicked. With a quick oath of annoyance, Cassidy hung up.

Colin's away, she thought as she picked up the dress box. Now's the time to finish it completely.

A short time later Cassidy pushed open the back door of Colin's studio. The familiar scents reached out and brought him vividly to her mind. Resolutely she pushed him away. Now is not the time, she told herself and walked briskly to his worktable to set down the dress and key.

For a moment she stood in the room's center and looked about her. She had spent hours there, days. Every detail was already etched with clarity on her memory. Yet she wanted to see it all again. A part of her was afraid she would forget something, something small and insignificant and vital. It surprised her that the portrait still stood on the easel. Forgetting her promise to leave quickly, Cassidy walked over to study it one last time.

How could he look at that, she wondered as she gazed into her own eyes, and believe the things I said? I can only be grateful that he did. I can only be grateful he believed what I said rather than what he saw. Reaching out a hand, she touched the painted violets.

When the door of the studio opened, Cassidy jerked her hand from the painting and whirled. Her heart flew to her throat.

"Cassidy?" Vince strolled into the room with a wide smile. "What a surprise." In seconds, her hands were enveloped by his.

"Hello." Her voice was a trifle unsteady, but she managed to smile at him.

He heard the breathlessness in her voice and saw there was little color in her face. "Did you know Colin has been looking for you?"

"No." She felt a moment's panic and glanced at the

door. "No, I didn't. I've been away, I've been working. I just…" She drew her hands away and clasped them together as she heard herself ramble. "I just brought back the dress I wore for the portrait."

Vince's dark eyes became shrewd. "Were you hiding, madonna?"

"No." Cassidy turned and walked to a window. "No, of course not, I was working." She saw the sparrow, busily feeding three babies with gaping mouths. "I didn't realize you were going to be in America this long." Say anything, she told herself, but don't think until you're out of here.

"I have stayed a bit longer in order to convince Colin to sell me a painting he was reluctant to part with."

Cassidy gripped the windowsill tightly. *You knew he would sell it.* You knew from the beginning all that would be left would be dollars and cents. Did you expect him to keep it and think of you? Shaking her head, she made a quiet sound of despair.

"Cassidy." Vince's hand pressed lightly on her shoulder.

"I shouldn't have come here," she whispered, shaking her head again. "I should've known better." She started to flee, but he tightened his grip and turned her to face him. As he studied her, he lifted a hand to brush her cheek. "Please…" She closed her eyes. "Please don't be kind to me. I'm not as strong as I thought I was."

"And you love him very much."

Cassidy's eyes flew open. "No, it's only that I—"

"Madonna." Vince stopped her with a finger to her lips. There was a wealth of understanding in his eyes. "I've seen the portrait. It speaks louder than your words."

Lowering her head, Cassidy pressed the heel of her hand between her brows. "I don't want to... I'm trying so very hard not to. I have to go," she said quickly.

"Cassidy." Vince held her shoulders. His voice was gentle. "You must see him...speak to him."

"I can't." She placed her hands on his chest, shaking her head in desperation. "Please, don't tell him. Please, just take the portrait and let it be over." Her voice broke, and when she found herself cradled against Vince's chest she made no protest. "I always knew it was going to be over." She closed her eyes on the tears, but allowed herself to be held until the need to release them faded. He stroked her hair and kept silent until he felt her breathing steady. Gently he kissed the top of her head then tilted her face to his.

"Cassidy, Colin is my friend—"

"Interesting." Cassidy's eyes darted to the doorway... and to Colin. "I'd thought so myself." His voice was quiet. "It appears I've been mistaken about more than one person recently." Even before he crossed the room, Cassidy felt the danger. "Gail told me I'd find you up here," he said when he stood directly in front of them. "With my *friend*."

"Colin..." Vince began, only to be cut off with a fierce look.

"Take your hands off her, and keep out of this. When I've finished, you can pick up where you left off."

Hearing the fury in his words, Cassidy nudged out of Vince's hold. "Please," she murmured, not wanting to cause any trouble between them. "Leave us alone for a moment." When Vince's hand stayed on her arm, she turned her eyes to him. "Please," she repeated.

Reluctantly Vince dropped his hand. "Very well,

cara." He turned briefly to Colin. "I've never known you to be mistaken about anyone, my friend." He walked across the room then closed the door quietly behind him. Cassidy waited an extra moment before she spoke.

"I came to return the dress and the key." She moistened her lips when he only stared down at her. "Gail told me you were away."

"How convenient the studio was available for you and Vince."

"Colin, don't."

"Setting yourself up as a duchess?" he asked coldly. "I should warn you, Vince is known for his generosity, but not his constancy." His eyes raked her face. "Still, a woman like you should do very well for herself in a week or two."

"That's beneath you, Colin." She turned and took a step away, but he grabbed a handful of her hair. With a small sound of surprise and pain, she stared up at him.

His eyes were shadowed and dark, as was his chin with at least a day's growth of beard. It occurred to her suddenly that he looked exhausted. Thinking back, she knew he had never shown fatigue after hours of painting. His fingers tightened in her hair.

"Colin." In defense, she lifted a hand to his.

"Such innocence," he said softly. "Such innocence. You're a clever woman, Cassidy." His hands came to her shoulders, quickly, ruthlessly. She stared up at him in silence, tasting fear. "It's one thing to lie with words, but another to lie with a look, to lie with the eyes day after day. That takes a special kind of cheat."

"No." She shook her head as his words brought back the tears she had stemmed. "No, Colin, please." She wanted to tell him she had never lied to him, but she couldn't. She had lied the very last time they had been together. She could only shake her head and helplessly let the tears come.

"What is it you want from me?" he demanded. His voice became more infuriated as tears slipped down her cheeks. The sun fell through the skylight and set them glinting. "Do you want me to forget that I looked at you day after day and saw something that was never there?"

"I gave you what you wanted." Tears became sobs and she struggled against him. "Please, let me go now. I gave you what you wanted. It's finished."

"You gave me a shell, a mask. Isn't that what you told me?" He pulled her closer, forcing her head back until she looked at him. "The rest was my imagination. Finished, Cass? How can something be finished when it never was?" His hand went back to her hair as she tried to lower her head. "You said that I'd drained you. Have you any idea what these past weeks have done to me?" He shook her, and her sobs grew wilder.

"You were right when you told me that painting was nothing more than your face and body. There's no warmth in you. I created the woman in that painting."

"Please, Colin. Enough." She pressed her hands over her ears to shut out his words.

"Do you cringe from the truth, Cassidy?" He tore her hands away, forcing her face back to his again. "Only you and I will know the painting's a lie, that the woman there doesn't exist. We served each other's needs after all, didn't we?" He pushed her aside with a whispered oath. "Get out."

Freed, Cassidy ran blindly for escape.

Chapter 10

It was late afternoon when Cassidy approached her apartment building. She had walked for a long time after her tears had dried. The city had been jammed with people, and she had sought the crowd while remaining separate. The pain had become numbed with fatigue. She was two blocks from home when the rain started, but she didn't increase her pace. It was cool and soft.

Inside her building she began an automatic search for her mailbox key. Her movements were mechanical, but she forced herself to perform the routine task. She would not crawl into a hole of despair. She would function. She would survive. These things she had promised herself during the long afternoon walk.

With the key at last in the lock, Cassidy lifted the cover on the narrow slot and pulled out her mail. She riffled through the advertisements and bills automatically as she started for the stairs. Her feet came to an abrupt halt as she spotted the return address on one of the envelopes. *New York.*

For several minutes she merely studied it, turning it over then back again. Walking back to her mailbox, she pushed the rest of her mail back inside then leaned against the wall. A rejection slip? she reflected, nibbling her bottom lip. Then where was the manuscript? She turned the envelope over again and swallowed.

"Oh, the devil with it," she muttered and ripped it open. She read the letter twice in absolute silence. "Oh, why now?" she asked and hated herself for weeping again. "I'm not ready for it now." She forced back the tears and shook her head. "No, it's the perfect time," she corrected then made herself read the letter again. There couldn't be a better time.

She stuffed the letter into her pocket and ran back into the rain. In ten minutes she was banging on Jeff's door.

Guitar in hand, he pulled open the door. "Cassidy, you're back! Where've you been? We were ready to call out the marines." Stopping, he took his eyes from the top of her head to her feet. "Hey…you're drenched."

"I am not drenched," Cassidy corrected as she dripped on the hall floor. She hoisted up a bottle of champagne. "I'm much too extraordinary to be drenched. I've been accepted into the annals of literature. I shall be copywritten and printed and posted in your public library."

"You sold your book!" Jeff let out a whoop and hugged her. His guitar pressed into her back.

Laughing, Cassidy pulled away. "Is that any way to express such a momentous occurrence? Peasant."

She pushed back her sopping hair with her free hand. "However, I'm a superior person, and will share my bottle of champagne with you in my parlor. No dinner jacket required." Turning, she walked to her own door, pushed it open then gestured. Grinning, Jeff set down his guitar and followed her.

"Here," he said after he had closed the door and taken the bottle from her. "I'll open it, you go get a towel and dry off or else you'll die of pneumonia before the first copy hits the stands."

When she came back from the bathroom wrapped in a terry-cloth robe and rubbing a towel over her hair, Jeff was just releasing the cork. Champagne squirted out in a jet.

"It's good for the carpet," he claimed and poured. "I could only find jelly glasses."

"My crystal's been smashed," Cassidy told him as she picked up her glass. "To a very wise man," she said solemnly.

"Who?" Jeff raised his glass.

"My publisher," she announced, then grinned and drank. "An excellent year," she mused, gazing critically into the glass. The wine fizzed gently.

"What year is it?" Jeff lifted the bottle curiously.

"This one." Cassidy laughed and drank again. "I only buy new champagne."

They drank again then Jeff leaned over and kissed her. "Congratulations, babe." He pulled the damp towel from her shoulders. "How does it feel?"

"I don't know." She threw her head back and closed her eyes. "I feel like someone else." Quickly she filled her glass again. She knew she had to keep moving, had to keep talking. She couldn't think seriously about what she had won that day or she would remember what she had lost. "I should've bought two bottles," she said, spinning a circle. "This is definitely a two-bottle occasion." She drank, feeling the wine rise to her head. "The last time I had champagne..." Cassidy stopped, remembering, then shook her head. Jeff eyed her in puzzlement. "No, no." She gestured with her hand as if to wipe the thought away. "I had champagne at Barbara Seabright's wedding in Sausalito. One of the ushers propositioned me in the cloakroom."

Jeff laughed and took another sip. A knock sounded. Cassidy called out, "Come in, there's enough for—" Her words were cut off as Colin opened the door.

Cassidy's color drained slowly. Her eyes darkened. Jeff looked quickly from one to the other, then set down his glass.

"Well, I gotta be going. Thanks for the champagne, babe. We'll talk later."

"No, Jeff," Cassidy began. "You don't have to—"

"I've got a gig," he announced, lifting her restraining hand from her arm. She saw him exchange one long look with Colin before he slipped through the door.

"Cass." Colin stepped forward.

"Colin, please go." Shutting her eyes, she pressed her fingers between her brows. There was a pressure in her chest and behind her lids. Don't cry. Don't cry, she ordered herself.

"I know I haven't any right to be here." There was a low harshness in his tone. "I know I haven't the right to ask you to listen to me. I'm asking anyway."

"There isn't anything to say." Cassidy forced herself to stand straight and face him. "I don't want you here," she said flatly.

He flinched. "I understand, Cassidy, but I feel you have a right to an apology…an explanation."

Her hands were clenched, and slowly she spread her fingers and stared down at them. "I appreciate the offer, Colin, but it isn't necessary. Now—" she lifted her eyes to his "—if that's all…"

"Oh, Cass, for pity's sake, show more mercy than I did. At least let me apologize before you shut me out of your life."

Unable to respond, Cassidy merely stared at him. He stooped to pick up the bottle of champagne. "I seem to have interrupted a celebration." He set the bottle back and looked at her. "Yours?"

"Yes." Cassidy swallowed and tried to speak lightly. "Yes, mine. My manuscript was accepted for publication. I had a letter today."

"Cass." He moved toward her, lifting a hand to touch her cheek.

Cassidy stiffened and took a quick step back. Catching the look that crossed his face, she knew she had hurt him. Colin slowly dropped his hand.

"I'm sorry," Cassidy began.

"Don't be." His voice had a quiet, final quality. "I can hardly expect you to welcome my touch. I hurt you." He paused, looking down at his hand a moment before bringing his gaze back to her face. His eyes searched hers. "Because I know you as well as I know myself, I'm aware of how badly I hurt you. I have to live with that. I haven't the right to ask you to forgive me, but I'll ask you to hear me out."

"All right, Colin, I'm listening," Cassidy said wearily. She drew a deep breath and tried to speak calmly. "Why don't you sit down."

He shook his head and, turning, moved back to the window and looked out, resting his hands in the sill. "The rain's stopped and there's fog. I still remember how you looked that night, standing in the fog looking up at the sky. I thought you were a mirage." He murmured the last sentence, as if to himself. "I had an image in my mind of a woman. My own idea of perfection, a balance of qualities. When I saw you, I knew I had found her. I had to paint you."

For a moment he lapsed into silence, brooding out at the gloom. "After we'd started, I found everything in you I'd ever looked for—goodness, spirit, intelligence, strength, passion. The longer I painted you, the more you fascinated me. I told you once you bewitched me; I almost believe it. I've never known a woman I've wanted more than I've wanted you."

He turned then and faced her. The play of the light threw his features into shadows. "Each time I touched you, I wanted more. I didn't make love to you that night on the houseboat because I wouldn't have you think of yourself as just one of my lovers. I couldn't take advantage of your being in love with me."

At his words, Cassidy's eyes closed. She made a soft sound of despair.

"Please, don't turn away. Let me finish. The day the painting was finished, you denied everything. You said the things I'd seen had been in my own imagination. You were so cool and dispassionate. You very nearly destroyed me.... I had no idea anyone had such power over me," he continued softly. "It was a revelation, and it hurt a great deal. I wanted more from you, I needed more, but you told me you had nothing left. I was angry when you ran away, and I let you go. When I came here later, you were gone.

"I've been out of my mind for over two weeks, not knowing where you were or when—worse, *if*—you were coming back. Your friend next door had your cryptic little note and nothing else."

"You saw Jeff?" she asked.

"Cassidy, don't you understand? You disappeared. The last time I saw you, you were running away from me, and then you were gone. I didn't know where you were, or how to find you, if something had happened to you. I've been going slowly mad."

She took a step toward him. "Colin, I'm sorry. I had no idea you'd be concerned...."

"Concerned?" he repeated. "I was frantic! Two weeks, Cassidy. Two weeks without a word. Do you know what a helpless feeling it is to simply have to wait? Not to know. I've haunted Fisherman's Wharf, been everywhere in the city. Where in heaven's name were you?" he demanded furiously then held up a hand before she could answer. She watched him take a deep breath before turning away from her. "I'm sorry. I haven't had much sleep lately, and I'm not completely in control."

His movements became restless again. He stopped and lifted Cassidy's discarded glass of champagne. Thoughtfully, he studied the etchings on the side. "An interesting concept in a wineglass," he murmured. Turning back, he toasted her. "To you, Cass. To only you." He drank then set down the empty glass.

Cassidy dropped her eyes. "Colin, I am sorry you were worried. I was working, and—"

"Don't." The word stopped her, and her eyes shot back to his. "Don't explain to me," he said in more controlled tones. "Just listen. When I walked into the studio today and saw you with Vince, something snapped. I can give you excuses—pressure, exhaustion, madness, take your pick. None of them make up for the things I said to you." His eyes were eloquent on hers. "I despise myself for making you cry. I hated the things I said to you even as I said them. Finding you there, with Vince, after looking for you everywhere for days..." He stopped, shaking his head, then moved back to the window.

"Gail arranged the timing very well," he said. "She knew what I'd been through the past two weeks and knows me well enough to predict how I'd react finding you alone with Vince. She sent him up to the studio on a fictitious errand before I got back to The Gallery. She told me the two of you were meeting up there. She made the suggestion, but I grabbed on to it with both hands." He rubbed his fingers over the back of his neck as if to release some tension.

"We'd been occasional lovers up until about a year ago when things got a bit complicated. I should have remembered whom I was dealing with, but I wasn't thinking too clearly. Gail's decided to take a long—perhaps permanent—sabbatical on the East Coast." He paused a moment then turned to study her. "I'd like to think you could understand why I behaved so abominably."

In the silence Cassidy could just hear Jeff's guitar through the thin walls of the apartment. "Colin." Her eyes searched his face then softened. "You look so tired."

His expression altered, and for a moment she thought he would cross to her. He stood still, however, keeping the distance between them. "I don't know when I fell in love with you. Perhaps it was that first night in the fog. Perhaps it was when you first wore that dress. Perhaps it was years before I met you. I suppose it doesn't matter when."

Cassidy stared at him, robbed of speech. "I'm not an easy man, Cassidy, you told me that once."

"Yes," she managed. "I remember."

"I'm selfish and given to temper and black moods. I have little patience except with my work. I can promise to hurt you, to infuriate you, to be unreasonable and impatient, but no one will love you more. No one." He paused, but still she could only stare at him, transfixed. "I'm asking you to forget what makes sense and be my wife and my lover and mother my children. I'm asking that you share your life with me, taking me as I am." He paused again, and his voice softened. "I love you, Cass. This time, my destiny's in your hands."

She watched him as he spoke, heard the cadence of his native land grow stronger in his speech. Still he made no move toward her, but stood across the room with shadows playing over his face. Cassidy remembered how he had looked when she had flinched away from his touch.

Slowly she walked to him. Reaching up, she circled his neck with her arms then buried her face against his shoulder. "Hold me." His arms came gently around her as his cheek lowered to the top of her head. "Hold me, Sullivan," she ordered again, pressing hard against him. She turned her head until her mouth found his.

His arms drew tight around her, and she murmured in pleasure at their strength. "I love you," she whispered as their lips parted then clung again. "I've needed to tell you for so long."

"You told me every time you looked at me." Colin buried his face in her hair. "I refused to believe I'd fallen in love with you, that it could have happened so quickly, so effortlessly. The painting was nearly finished when I admitted to myself I'd never be able to live without you."

His voice lowered, and he drew her closer. "I've been crazy these last two weeks, staring at your portrait and not knowing where you were or if I'd ever see you again."

"Now you have me," she murmured, making no objection when his hands slipped under the terry cloth to roam her skin. "And Vince will have the portrait."

"No, I told you once some things can't be sold. The portrait has too much of both of us in it." He shook his head, breathing in the rain-fresh fragrance of her hair. "Not even for Vince."

"But I thought..." She realized that she had only assumed Vince had been speaking of her portrait. There was a new wealth of happiness in the knowledge that Colin had not intended to sell what was to her a revelation of their love.

"What did you think?"

"No, it's nothing." She pressed her lips against his neck. "I love you." Her mouth roamed slowly up his jawline, savoring what she knew now was hers.

"Cass." She felt his heart thud desperately against hers as his fingers tightened in her hair. "Do you know what you do to me?"

"Show me," she whispered against his ear.

With a groan, Colin kissed her again. She could taste his need for her and wondered at the strength of it. Her answer was to offer everything.

"We'll get married quickly," Colin murmured then took her lips again, urgently. Inside her robe, his hands ran in one long stroke down her sides, then roamed to her back to bring her closer. "Very quickly."

"Yes." Cassidy closed her eyes in contentment as his cheek rested against hers. "I already have the perfect dress." She sighed and nestled against him. "What will you title the painting, Colin?"

"I've already titled it." He smiled into her eyes. *"Sullivan's Woman."*

* * * * *

LESS OF A STRANGER

For my friend Joanne.

Chapter 1

He watched her coming. Though she wore jeans and a jacket, with a concealing helmet over her head, Katch recognized her femininity. She rode a small Honda motorcycle. He drew on his thin cigar and appreciated the competent way she swung into the market's parking lot.

Settling the bike, she dismounted. She was tall, Katch noted, perhaps five feet eight, and slender. He leaned back on the soda machine and continued to watch her out of idle curiosity. Then she removed the helmet. Instantly, his curiosity was intensified. She was a stunner.

Her hair was loose and straight, swinging nearly to her shoulders, with a fringe of bangs sweeping over her forehead. It was a deep, rich brunette that showed glints of red and gold from the sun. Her face was narrow, the features sharp and distinct. He'd known models who'd

starved themselves to get the angles and shadows that
were in this woman's face. Her mouth, however, was
full and generous.

Katch recognized the subtleties of cosmetics and
knew that none had been used to add interest to the
woman's features. She didn't need them. Her eyes were
large, and even with the distance of the parking lot between them, he caught the depth of dark brown. They
reminded him of a colt's eyes—deep and wide and
aware. Her movements were unaffected. They had an
unrefined grace that was as coltish as her eyes. She was
young, he decided, barely twenty. He drew on the cigar
again. She was definitely a stunner.

"Hey, Megan!"

Megan turned at the call, brushing the bangs from
her eyes as she moved. Seeing the Bailey twins pull to
the curb in their Jeep, she smiled.

"Hi." Clipping the helmet onto a strap on her bike,
Megan walked to the Jeep. She was very fond of the
Bailey twins.

Like herself, they were twenty-three and had golden,
beach-town complexions, but they were petite, blue-
eyed and pertly blond. The long, baby-fine hair they
shared had been tossed into confusion by the wind.
Both pairs of blue eyes drifted past Megan to focus on
the man who leaned against the soda machine. In re-
flex, both women straightened and tucked strands of
hair behind their ears. Tacitly, they agreed their right
profile was the most comely.

"We haven't seen you in a while." Teri Bailey kept
one eye cocked on Katch as she spoke to Megan.

"I've been trying to get some things finished before

the season starts." Megan's voice was low, with the gentle flow of coastal South Carolina. "How've you been?"

"Terrific!" Jeri answered, shifting in the driver's seat. "We've got the afternoon off. Why don't you come shopping with us?" She, too, kept Katch in her peripheral vision.

"I'd like to—" Megan was already shaking her head "—but I've got to pick up a few things here."

"Like the guy over there with terrific gray eyes?" Jeri demanded.

"What?" Megan laughed.

"And shoulders," Teri remarked.

"He hasn't taken those eyes off her, has he, Teri?" Jeri remarked. "And we spent twelve-fifty for this blouse." She fingered the thin strap of the pink camisole top which matched her twin's.

"What," Megan asked, totally bewildered, "are you talking about?"

"Behind you," Teri said with a faint inclination of her fair head. "The hunk by the soda machine. Absolutely gorgeous." But as Megan began to turn her head, Teri continued in a desperate whisper, "Don't turn around, for goodness sake!"

"How can I see if I don't look?" Megan pointed out reasonably as she turned.

His hair was blond, not pale like the twins', but dusky and sun-streaked. It was thick and curled loosely and carelessly around his face. He was lean, and the jeans he wore were well faded from wear. His stance was negligent, completely relaxed as he leaned back against the machine and drank from a can. But his face wasn't lazy, Megan thought as he met her stare without a blink. It was sharply aware. He needed a shave, certainly, but his bone structure was superb. There was the faintest of clefts in his chin, and his mouth was long and thin.

Normally, Megan would have found the face fascinating—strongly sculpted, even handsome in a rough-and-ready fashion. But the eyes were insolent. They were gray, as the twins had stated, dark and smoky. And, Megan decided with a frown, rude. She'd seen his type before—drifters, loners, looking for the sun and some fleeting female companionship. Under her bangs, her eyebrows drew together. He was openly staring at her. As the can touched his lips, he sent Megan a slow wink.

Hearing one of the twins giggle, Megan whipped her head back around.

"He's adorable," Jeri decided.

"Don't be an idiot." Megan swung her hair back with a toss of her head. "He's typical."

The twins exchanged a look as Jeri started the Jeep's engine. "Too choosy," she stated. They gave Megan mirror smiles as they pulled away from the curb. "Bye!"

Megan wrinkled her nose at them, but waved before she turned away. Purposefully ignoring the man who loitered beside the concessions, Megan walked into the market.

She acknowledged the salute from the clerk behind the counter. Megan had grown up in Myrtle Beach. She knew all the small merchants in the five-mile radius around her grandfather's amusement park.

After choosing a basket, she began to push it down the first aisle. Just a few things, she decided, plucking a quart of milk from a shelf. She had only the saddlebags on the bike for transporting. If the truck hadn't been acting up... She let her thoughts drift away from that particular problem. Nothing could be done about it at the moment.

Megan paused in the cookie section. She'd missed lunch and the bags and boxes looked tempting. Maybe the oatmeal...

"These are better."

Megan started as a hand reached in front of her to choose a bag of cookies promising a double dose of chocolate chips. Twisting her head, she looked up into the insolent gray eyes.

"Want the cookies?" He grinned much as he had outside.

"No," she said, giving a meaningful glance at his hand on her basket. Shrugging, he took his hand away but, to Megan's irritation, he strolled along beside her.

"What's on the list, Meg?" he asked companionably as he tore open the bag of cookies.

"I can handle it alone, thanks." She started down the next aisle, grabbing a can of tuna. He walked, Megan noted, like a gunslinger—long, lanky strides with just a hint of swagger.

"You've got a nice bike." He bit into a cookie as he strolled along beside her. "Live around here?"

Megan chose a box of tea bags. She gave it a critical glance before tossing it into the basket. "It lives with me," she told him as she moved on.

"Cute," he decided and offered her a cookie. Megan ignored him and moved down the next aisle. When she reached for a loaf of bread, however, he laid a hand on top of hers. "Whole wheat's better for you." His palm was hard and firm on the back of her hand. Megan met his eyes indignantly and tried to pull away.

"Listen, I have…"

"No rings," he commented, lacing his fingers through hers and lifting her hand for a closer study. "No entanglements. How about dinner?"

"No way." She shook her hand but found it firmly locked in his.

"Don't be unfriendly, Meg. You have fantastic eyes." He smiled into them, looking at her as though they were the only two people on earth. Someone reached around her, with an annoyed mutter, to get a loaf of rye.

"Will you go away?" she demanded in an undertone. It amazed her that his smile was having an effect on her even though she knew what was behind it. "I'll make a scene if you don't."

"That's all right," he said genially, "I don't mind scenes."

He wouldn't, she thought, eyeing him. He'd thrive on them. "Look," she began angrily, "I don't know who you are, but…"

"David Katcherton," he volunteered with another easy smile. "Katch. What time should I pick you up?"

"You're not going to pick me up," she said distinctly. "Not now, not later." Megan cast a quick look around. The market was all but empty. She couldn't cause a decent scene if she'd wanted to. "Let go of my hand," she ordered firmly.

"The Chamber of Commerce claims Myrtle Beach is a friendly town, Meg." Katch released her hand. "You're going to give them a bad name."

"And stop calling me Meg," she said furiously. "I don't know you."

She stomped off, wheeling the basket in front of her.

"You will." He made the claim quietly, but she heard him.

Their eyes met again, hers dark with temper, his assured. Turning away, she quickened her pace to the check-out counter.

"You wouldn't believe what happened at the market." Megan set the bag on the kitchen table with a thump.

Her grandfather sat at the table, on one of the four matching maple chairs, earnestly tying a fly. He grunted in acknowledgment but didn't glance up. Wires and feathers and weights were neatly piled in front of him.

"This man," she began, pulling the bread from the top bag. "This incredibly rude man tried to pick me up. Right in the cookie section." Megan frowned as she stored tea bags in a canister. "He wanted me to go to dinner with him."

"Hmm." Her grandfather meticulously attached a yellow feather to the fly. "Have a nice time."

"Pop!" Megan shook her head in frustration, but a smile tugged at her mouth.

Timothy Miller was a small, spare man in his mid-sixties. His round, lined face was tanned, surrounded by a shock of white hair and a full beard. The beard was soft as a cloud and carefully tended. His blue eyes, unfaded by the years, were settled deeply into the folds and lines of his face. They missed little. Megan could see he was focused on his lures. That he had heard her at all was a tribute to his affection for his granddaughter.

Moving over, she dropped a kiss on the crown of his head. "Going fishing tomorrow?"

"Yessiree, bright and early." Pop counted out his assortment of lures and mentally reviewed his strategy. Fishing was a serious business. "The truck should be fixed this evening. I'll be back before supper."

Megan nodded, giving him a second kiss. He needed his fishing days. The amusement parks opened for business on weekends in the spring and fall. In the three summer months they worked seven days a week. The summer kept the town alive; it drew tourists, and tourists meant business. For one-fourth of the year, the town swelled from a population of thirteen or fourteen thousand to three hundred thousand. The bulk of those three hundred thousand people had come to the small coastal town to have fun.

To provide it, and make his living, her grandfather worked hard. He always had, Megan mused. It would have been a trial if he hadn't loved the park so much. It had been part of her life for as long as she could remember.

Megan had been barely five when she had lost her parents. Over the years, Pop had been mother, father and friend to her. And Joyland was home to her as much as the beach-side cottage they lived in. Years before, they had turned to each other in grief. Now, their love was bedrock firm. With the exclusion of her grandfather, Megan was careful with her emotions, for once involved, they were intense. When she loved, she loved totally.

"Trout would be nice," she murmured, as she gave him a last, quick hug. "We'll have to settle for tuna casserole tonight."

"Thought you were going out."

"Pop!" Megan leaned back against the stove and pushed her hair from her face with both hands. "Do you think I'd spend the evening with a man who tried to pick me up with a bag of chocolate chip cookies?" With a jerk of her wrist, she flicked on the burner under the teakettle.

"Depends on the man." She saw the twinkle in his eye as he glanced up at her. Megan knew she finally had his full attention. "What'd he look like?"

"A beach bum," she retorted, although she knew the answer wasn't precisely true. "With a bit of cowboy thrown in." She smiled then in response to Pop's grin. "Actually, he had a great face. Lean and strong, very attractive in an unscrupulous sort of way. He'd do well in bronze."

"Sounds interesting. Where'd you meet him again?"

"In the cookie section."

"And you're going to fix tuna casserole instead of having dinner out?" Pop gave a heavy sigh and shook his head. "I don't know what's the matter with this girl," he addressed a favored lure.

"He was cocky," Megan claimed and folded her arms. "And he *leered* at me. Aren't grandfathers supposed to tote shotguns around for the purpose of discouraging leerers?"

"Want to borrow one and go hunting for him?"

The shrill whistling of the kettle drowned out her response. Pop watched Megan as she rose to fix the tea.

She was a good girl, he mused. A bit too serious about things at times, but a good girl. And a beauty, too. It didn't surprise him that a stranger had tried to make a date with her. He was more surprised that it hadn't happened more often. But Megan could discourage a man without opening her mouth, he recalled. All she had to do was aim one of her "I beg your pardon" looks and most of them backed off. That seemed to be the way she wanted it.

Between the amusement park and her art, she never seemed to have time for much socializing. Or didn't make time, Pop amended thoughtfully. Still, he wasn't certain that he didn't detect more than just annoyance in her attitude toward the man in the market. Unless he missed his guess, she had been amused and perhaps a touch attracted. Because he knew his granddaughter well, he decided to let the subject ride for the time being.

"The weather's supposed to hold all weekend," he commented as he carefully placed his lures in his fishing box. "There should be a good crowd in the park. Are you going to work in the arcade?"

"Of course." Megan set two cups of tea on the table and sat again. "Have those seats been adjusted on the Ferris wheel?"

"Saw to it myself this morning." Pop blew on his tea to cool it, then sipped.

He was relaxed, Megan saw. Pop was a simple man. She'd always admired his unassuming manner, his quiet humor, his lack of pretensions. He loved to watch people enjoy. More, she added with a sigh, than he liked to charge them for doing so. Joyland never made more than a modest profit. He was, Megan concluded, a much better grandfather than businessman.

To a large extent, it was she who handled the profit-and-loss aspect of the park. Though the responsibility took time away from her art, she knew it was the park that supported them. And, more important, it was the park that Pop loved.

At the moment, the books were teetering a bit too steeply into the red for comfort. Neither of them spoke of it at any length with the other. They mentioned improvements during the busy season, talked vaguely about promoting business during the Easter break and over Memorial Day weekend.

Megan sipped at her tea and half listened to Pop's rambling about hiring summer help. She would see to it when the time came. Pop was a whiz in dealing with cranky machines and sunburned tourists, but he tended to overpay and underwork his employees. Megan was more practical. She had to be.

I'll have to work full-time myself this summer, she reflected. She thought fleetingly of the half-completed sculpture in her studio over the garage. It'll just have to wait for December, she told herself and tried not to sigh. There's no other way until things are on a more even keel again. Maybe next year…it was always next year. There were things to do, always things to do. With a small shrug, she turned back to Pop's monologue.

"So, I figure we'll get some of the usual college kids and drifters to run the rides."

"I don't imagine that'll be a problem," Megan murmured. Pop's mention of drifters had led her thoughts back to David Katcherton.

Katch, she mused, letting his face form in her mind again. Ordinarily, she'd have cast his type as a drifter, but there had been something more than that. Megan prided herself on her observations, her characterizations of people. It annoyed her that she wasn't able to make a conclusive profile on this man. It annoyed her further that she was again thinking of a silly encounter with a rude stranger.

"Want some more tea?" Pop was already making his way to the stove when Megan shook herself back.

"Ah...yeah, sure." She scolded herself for dwelling on the insignificant when there were things to do. "I guess I'd better start dinner. You'll want an early night if you're going fishing in the morning."

"That's my girl." Pop turned the flame back on under the kettle as he glanced out the window. He cast a quick look at his unsuspecting granddaughter. "I hope you've got enough for three," he said casually. "It looks like your beach-cowboy found his way to the ranch."

"What?" Megan's brows drew together as she stood up.

"A perfect description, as usual, Megan," Pop complimented her as he watched the man approach, loose-limbed with a touch of a swashbuckler, a strong, good-looking face. Pop liked his looks. He turned with a grin as Megan walked to the window to stare out. Pop suppressed a chuckle at her expression.

"It *is* him," she whispered, hardly believing her eyes as she watched Katch approach her kitchen door.

"I thought it might be," Pop said mildly.

"Of all the nerve," she muttered darkly. "Of all the *incredible* nerve!"

Chapter 2

Before her grandfather could comment, Megan took the few strides necessary to bring her to the kitchen door. She swung it open just as Katch stepped up on the stoop. There was a flicker, only a flicker, of surprise in the gray eyes.

"You have a nerve," she said coolly.

"So I've been told," he agreed easily. "You're prettier than you were an hour ago." He ran a finger down her cheek. "There's a bit of rose under the honey now. Very becoming." He traced the line of her chin before dropping his hand. "Do you live here?"

"You know very well I do," she retorted. "You followed me."

Katch grinned. "Sorry to disappoint you, Meg. Finding you here's just a bonus. I'm looking for Timothy Miller. Friend of yours?"

"He's my grandfather." She moved, almost imperceptibly, positioning herself between Katch and the doorway. "What do you want with him?"

Katch recognized the protective move, but before he could comment, Pop spoke from behind her.

"Why don't you let the man in, Megan? He can tell me himself."

"I'm basically human, Meg," Katch said quietly. The tone of his voice had her looking at him more closely.

She glanced briefly over her shoulder, then turned back to Katch. The look she gave him was a warning. Don't do anything to upset him.

She noticed something in his eyes she hadn't expected—gentleness. It was more disconcerting than his earlier arrogance. Megan backed into the kitchen, holding open the door in silent invitation.

Katch smiled at her, casually brushing a strand of hair from her cheek as he walked by and into the kitchen. Megan stood for a moment, wondering why she should be so moved by a stranger's touch.

"Mr. Miller?" She heard the unaffected friendliness in Katch's voice and glanced over as he held out a hand to her grandfather. "I'm David Katcherton."

Pop nodded in approval. "You're the fellow who called me a couple of hours ago." He shot a look past Katch's shoulder to Megan. "I see you've already met my granddaughter."

His eyes smiled in response. "Yes. Charming."

Pop chuckled and moved toward the stove. "I was just about to make some more tea. How about a cup?"

Megan noticed the faint lift of his brow. Tea, she thought, was probably not his first choice.

"That'd be nice. Thanks." He walked to the table

and sat, Megan decided, as if his acquaintance were long-standing and personal. Half reluctant, half defiant, she sat next to him. Her eyes asked him questions behind Pop's back.

"Did I tell you before that you have fabulous eyes?" he murmured. Without waiting for her answer, he turned his attention to Pop's tackle box. "You've got some great lures here," he observed to Pop, picking up a bone squid, then a wood plug painted to simulate a small frog. "Do you make any of your own?"

"That's half the sport," Pop stated, bringing a fresh cup to the table. "Have you done much fishing?"

"Here and there. I'd guess you'd know the best spots along the Grand Strand."

"A few of them," Pop said modestly.

Megan scowled into her tea. Once the subject of fishing had been brought up, Pop could go on for hours. And hours.

"I thought I'd do some surf casting while I'm here," Katch mentioned offhandedly. Megan was surprised to catch a shrewdly measuring expression in his eyes.

"Well now—" Pop warmed to the theme "—I might just be able to show you a spot or two. Do you have your own gear?"

"Not with me, no."

Pop brushed this off as inconsequential. "Where are you from, Mr. Katcherton?"

"Katch," he corrected, leaning back in his chair. "California originally."

That, Megan decided, explained the beachboy look. She drank her cooling tea with a casual air while studying him over the rim.

"You're a long way from home," Pop commented. He

shifted comfortably, then brought out a pipe he saved for interesting conversations. "Do you plan to be in Myrtle Beach long?"

"Depends. I'd like to talk with you about your amusement park."

Pop puffed rapidly on his pipe while holding a match to the bowl. The tobacco caught, sending out cherry-scented smoke. "So you said on the phone. Funny, Megan and I were just talking about hiring on help for the summer. Only about six weeks before the season starts." He puffed and let the smoke waft lazily. "Less than three until Easter. Ever worked rides or a booth?"

"No." Katch sampled his tea.

"Well…" Pop shrugged his inexperience away. "It's simple enough to learn. You look smart." Again, Megan caught the flash of Katch's grin. She set down her cup.

"We can't pay more than minimum to a novice," she said dampeningly.

He made her nervous, she was forced to admit. With any luck, she could discourage him from Joyland so that he'd try his luck elsewhere. But something nagged at her. He didn't look the type to take a job running a roller coaster or hawking a pitch-and-toss for a summer. There were hints of authority in his face, touches of casual power in his stance. Yet there was something not altogether respectable in his raffish charm.

He met her stare with a complete lack of self-consciousness. "That seems reasonable. Do you work in the park, Meg?"

She bit back a retort to his familiarity. "Often," she said succinctly.

"Megan's got a good business head," Pop interjected. "She keeps me straight."

"Funny," Katch said speculatively. "Somehow I thought you might be a model. You've the face for it." There was no flirtatiousness in his tone.

"Megan's an artist," Pop said, puffing contentedly at his pipe.

"Oh?"

She watched Katch's eyes narrow and focus on her. Uncomfortable, she shifted in her chair. "We seem to be drifting away from the subject," she said crisply. "If you've come about a job—"

"No."

"But…didn't you say—"

"I don't think so," he cut her off again and added a smile. He turned to Pop now, and Megan recognized a subtle change in his manner. "I don't want a job in your park, Mr. Miller. I want to buy it."

Both men were intent on each other. Pop was surprised, unmistakably so, but there was also a look of consideration in his eyes. Neither of them noticed Megan. She stared at Katch, her face open and young, and just a little frightened. She wanted to laugh and say he was making a foolish joke, but she knew better. Katch said exactly what he meant.

She'd recognized the understated authority and power beneath the glib exterior. This was business, pure and simple. She could see it on his face. There was a flutter of panic in her stomach as she looked at her grandfather.

"Pop?" Her voice was very small, and he made no sign that he heard her.

"You're a surprise," the old man said eventually. Then he began to puff on his pipe again. "Why my park?"

"I've done some research on the amusements here." Katch shrugged off the details. "I like yours."

Pop sighed and blew smoke at the ceiling. "I can't say I'm interested in selling out, son. A man gets used to a certain way of life."

"With the offer I'm prepared to make, you might find it easy to get used to another."

Pop gave a quiet laugh. "How old are you, Katch?"

"Thirty-one."

"That's just about how long I've been in this business. How much do you know about running a park?"

"Not as much as you do." Katch grinned and leaned back again. "But I could learn fast with the right teacher."

Megan saw that her grandfather was studying Katch carefully. She felt excluded from the conversation and resented it. Her grandfather was capable of doing this very subtly. She recognized that David Katcherton had the same talent. Megan sat silently; natural courtesy forbade her interrupting private conversation.

"Why do you want to own an amusement park?" Pop asked suddenly. Megan could tell he was interested in David Katcherton. A warning bell began to ring in her head. The last thing she wanted was for her grandfather to become too involved with Katch. He was trouble, Megan was sure of it.

"It's good business," Katch answered Pop's question after a moment. "And fun." He smiled. "I like things that put fun into life."

He knows how to say the right thing, Megan acknowledged grudgingly, noting Pop's expression.

"I'd appreciate it if you'd think about it, Mr. Miller,"

Katch continued. "We could talk about it again in a few days."

And how to advance and retreat, she thought.

"I can't refuse to think about it," Pop agreed, but shook his head. "Still, you might take another look around. Megan and I've run Joyland for a good many years. It's home to us." He looked to his granddaughter teasingly. "Weren't you two going out to dinner?"

"No!" She flashed him a scowl.

"Exactly what I had in mind," Katch said smoothly. "Come on, Meg, I'll buy you a hamburger." As he rose, he took her hand, pulling her to her feet. Feeling her temper rise with her, Megan attempted to control it.

"I can't tell you how I hate to refuse such a charming invitation," she began.

"Then don't," Katch cut her off before turning to Pop. "Would you like to join us?"

Pop chuckled and motioned them away with the back of his hand. "Go on. I've got to get my gear together for the morning."

"Want company?"

Pop studied Katch over the bowl of his pipe. "I'm leaving at five-thirty," he said after a moment. "I have extra gear."

"I'll be here."

Megan was so astonished that she allowed Katch to lead her outside without making another protest. Pop never invited anyone along on his fishing mornings. They were his relaxation, and he enjoyed his solitude too much to share it.

"He never takes anyone with him," she murmured, thinking aloud.

"Then I'm flattered."

Megan noticed that Katch still had her hand, his fingers comfortably laced with hers.

"I'm not going out with you," she said positively and stopped walking. "You might be able to charm Pop into taking you fishing, but—"

"So you think I'm charming?" His smile was audacious as he took her other hand.

"Not in the least," she said firmly, repressing an answering smile.

"Why won't you have dinner with me?"

"Because," she said, meeting his eyes directly, "I don't like you."

His smile broadened. "I'd like the chance to change your mind."

"You couldn't." Megan started to draw her hands away, but he tightened his fingers.

"Wanna bet?" Again, she squashed the desire to smile. "If I change your mind, you'll go to the park with me Friday night."

"And if I don't change my mind?" she asked. "What then?"

"I won't bother you anymore." He grinned, as persuasive, she noted, as he was confident.

Her brow lifted in speculation. It might, she reflected, it just might be worth it.

"All you have to do is have dinner with me tonight," Katch continued, watching Megan's face. "Just a couple of hours."

"All right," she agreed impulsively. "It's a deal." She wriggled her fingers, but he didn't release them. "We could shake on it," she said, "but you still have my hands."

"So I do," he agreed. "We'll seal it my way then."

With a quick tug, he had her colliding against his chest. She felt a strength there which wasn't apparent in the lean, somewhat lanky frame. Before she could express annoyance, his mouth had taken hers.

He was skillful and thorough. She never knew whether she had parted her lips instinctively or if he had urged her to do so with the gently probing tip of his tongue.

From the instant of contact, Megan's mind had emptied, to be filled only with thoughts she couldn't center on. Her body dominated, taking command in simple surrender. She was melted against him, aware of his chest hard against her breasts...aware of his mouth quietly savaging hers. There was nothing else. She found there was nothing to hold on to. No anchor to keep her from veering off into wild water. Megan gave a small, protesting moan and drew away.

His eyes were darker than she'd thought, and too smoky to read clearly. Why had she thought them so decipherable? Why had she thought him so manageable? Nothing was as she had thought it had been minutes before. Her breath trembled as she fought to collect herself.

"You're very warm," Katch said softly. "It's a pity you struggle so hard to be remote."

"I'm not. I don't..." Megan shook her head, wishing desperately for her heartbeat to slow.

"You are," he corrected, "and you do." Katch gave her hands a companionable squeeze before releasing one of them. The other he kept snugly in his as he turned toward his car.

Panic was welling up inside Megan, and she tried to suppress it. *You've been kissed before,* she reminded herself. This was just unexpected. It just caught you off guard. Even as the excuse ran through her mind, she knew it for a lie. She'd never been kissed like that before. And the situation was no longer under her control.

"I don't think I'll go after all," she told him in calmer tones.

Katch turned, smiling at her as he opened the car door. "A bet's a bet, Meg."

Chapter 3

Katch drove a black Porsche. Megan wasn't surprised. She wouldn't have expected him to drive anything ordinary. It wasn't difficult to deduce that David Katcherton could afford the best of everything.

He'd probably inherited his money, she decided as she settled back against the silver gray seat cushion. He'd probably never worked a day in his life. She remembered the hard, unpampered feel of his palm. Probably a whiz at sports, she thought. Plays tennis, squash, sails his own yacht. Never does anything worthwhile. Only looks for pleasure. *And finds it,* she thought.

Megan turned to him, pushing her swinging hair back behind her shoulders. His profile was sharply attractive, with the dusky blond hair curling negligently over his ear.

"See something you like?"

Megan flushed in annoyance, aware that she'd been caught staring.

"You need a shave," she said primly.

Katch turned the rearview mirror toward him as if to check her analysis. "Guess I do." He smiled as they merged into the traffic. "On our next date I'll be sure to remember. Don't say anything," he added, feeling her stiffen at his side. "Didn't your mother ever tell you not to say anything if you couldn't say something pleasant?"

Megan stifled a retort.

Katch smiled as he merged into traffic. "How long have you lived here?"

"Always." With the windows down, Megan could hear the outdoor noises. The music from a variety of car radios competed against each other and merged into a strange sort of harmony. Megan liked the cluttered, indefinable sound. She felt herself relaxing and straightened her shoulders and faced Katch again.

"And what do you do?"

He caught the thread of disdain in the question, but merely lifted a brow. "I own things."

"Really? What sort of things?"

Katch stopped at a red light, then turned, giving her a long, direct look. "Anything I want." The light changed and he deftly slid the car into the parking lot.

"We can't go in there," Megan told him with a glance at the exclusive restaurant.

"Why not?" Katch switched off the ignition. "The food's good here."

"I know, but we're not dressed properly, and—"

"Do you like doing things properly all the time, Meg?"

The question stopped her. She searched his face

carefully, wondering if he was laughing at her, and unsure of the answer.

"Tell you what." He eased himself out of the car, then leaned back in the window. "Think about it for a few minutes. I'll be back."

Megan watched him slide through the elegant doors of the restaurant and shook her head. They'll boot him out, she thought. Still, she couldn't help admiring his confidence. There was something rather elusive about it. She crossed her arms over. "Still, I don't really *like* him," she muttered.

Fifteen minutes later, she decided she liked him even less. How impossibly rude! she fumed as she slammed out of his car. Keeping me waiting out here all this time!

She decided to find the nearest phone booth and call her grandfather to ask him to come pick her up. She searched the pockets in her jeans and her jacket. Not a dime, she thought furiously. Not one thin dime to my name. Taking a deep breath, she stared at the doors of the restaurant. She'd have to borrow change, or beg their permission to use the house phone. Anything was better than waiting in the car. Just as she pulled open the door of the restaurant, Katch strolled out.

"Thanks," he said casually and moved past her.

Megan stared after him. He was carrying the biggest picnic basket she'd ever seen. After he'd opened the trunk and settled it inside, he glanced back up at her.

"Well come on." He slammed the lid. "I'm starving."

"What's in there?" she asked suspiciously.

"Dinner." He motioned for her to get in the car. Megan stood beside the closed door on the passenger side.

"How did you get them to do that?"

"I asked. Are you hungry?"

"Well, yes… But how—"

"Then let's go." Katch dropped into the driver's seat and started the engine. The moment she sat beside him, he swung out of the parking lot. "Where's your favorite place?" he demanded.

"My favorite place?" she repeated dumbly.

"You can't tell me you've lived here all your life and don't have a favorite place." Katch turned the car toward the ocean. "Where is it?"

"Toward the north end of the beach," she said. "Not many people go there, except at the height of the season."

"Good. I want to be alone with you."

The simple directness had butterflies dancing in her stomach. Slowly, she turned to look at him again.

"Anything wrong with that?" The smile was back, irreverent and engaging. Megan sighed, feeling like she was just climbing the first hill of a roller coaster.

"Probably," she murmured.

The beach was deserted but for the crying gulls. She stood for a moment facing west, enjoying the rich glow of the dying sun.

"I love this time of day," she said softly. "Everything seems so still. As if the day's holding its breath." She jumped when Katch's hands came to her shoulders.

"Easy," he murmured, kneading the suddenly tense muscles as he stood behind her. He looked over her head to the sunset. "I like it just before dawn, when the birds first start to sing and the light's still soft.

"You should relax more often," he told her. He slid his fingers lazily up her neck and down again. The pleasure became less quiet and more demanding. When she would have slipped away, Katch turned her to face him.

"No," she said immediately, "don't." Megan placed both her hands on his chest. "Don't."

"All right." He relaxed his hold, but didn't release her for a moment. Then he stooped for the picnic basket and pulled out a white tablecloth saying briskly, "Besides, it's time to eat." Megan took it from him, marveling that the restaurant had given him their best linen.

"Here you go." With his head still bent over the basket, he handed her the glasses.

And they're crystal, she thought, dazed as she accepted the elegant wineglasses. There was china next, then silver.

"Why did they give you all this?"

"They were low on paper plates."

"Champagne?" She glanced at the label as he poured. "You must be crazy!"

"What's the matter?" he returned mildly. "Don't you like champagne?"

"Actually I do, though I've only had American."

"Here's to the French." Katch held out a glass to her.

Megan sipped. "It's wonderful," she said before experimenting with another sip. "But you didn't have to…" she gestured expansively.

"I decided I wasn't in the mood for a hamburger." Katch screwed the bottle down into the sand. He placed a small container on the cloth, then dived back into the basket.

"What's this?" Megan demanded as she opened it. She frowned at the shiny black mass inside. He placed toast points on a plate. "Is it…" She paused in disbelief and glanced at him. "Is this caviar?"

"Yeah. Let me have some, will you? I'm starving."
Katch took it from her and spread a generous amount
on a piece of toast. "Don't you want any?" he asked her
as he took a bite.

"I don't know." Megan examined it critically. "I've
never tasted it before."

"No?" He offered her his piece. "Taste it." When she
hesitated, Katch grinned and held it closer to her mouth.
"Go on, Meg, have a bite."

"It's salty," she said with surprise. She plucked the
toast from his hand and took another bite. "And it's
good," she decided, swallowing.

"You might've left me some," he complained when
Megan finished off the toast. She laughed and, heaping
caviar onto another piece, handed it to him. "I wondered
how it would sound." Katch took the offering, but his
attention was on Megan.

"What?" Still smiling, she licked a bit of caviar from
her thumb.

"Your laugh. I wondered if it would be as appealing as your face." He took a bite now, still watching
her. "It is."

Megan tried to calm her fluttering pulse. "You
didn't have to feed me caviar and champagne to hear
me laugh." With a casual shrug, she moved out of his
reach. "I laugh quite a bit."

"Not often enough."

She looked back at him in surprise. "Why do you
say that?"

"Your eyes are so serious. So's your mouth." His
glance swept over her face. "Perhaps that's why I feel
compelled to make you smile."

"How extraordinary." Megan sat back on her heels and stared at him. "You barely know me."

"Does it matter?"

"I always thought it should," she murmured as he reached into the hamper again. Megan watched, no longer surprised as he drew out lobster tails and fresh strawberries. She laughed again and, pushing back her hair, moved closer to him.

"Here," she said. "Let me help."

The sun sank as they ate. The moon rose. It shot a shimmering white line across the sea. Megan thought it was like a dream—the china and silver gleaming in the moonlight, the exotic tastes on her tongue, the familiar sound of surf and the stranger beside her, who was becoming less of a stranger every minute.

Already Megan knew the exact movement of his face when he smiled, the precise tonal quality of his voice. She knew the exact pattern of the curls over his ear. More than once, bewitched by moonlight and champagne, she had to restrain her fingers from reaching for them, experimenting with them.

"Aren't you going to eat any cheesecake?" Katch gestured with a forkful, then slid it into his mouth.

"I can't." Megan brought her knees up to her chest and rested her chin on them. She watched his obvious enjoyment with dessert. "How do you do it?"

"Dedication." Katch took the last bite. "I try to see every project through to the finish."

"I've never had a picnic like this," she told him with a contented sigh. Leaning back on her elbows, she stretched out her legs and looked up at the stars. "I've never tasted anything so wonderful."

"I'll give Ricardo your compliments." Katch moved

to sit beside her. His eyes moved from the crown of her head down the slender arch of her neck. Her face was thrown up to the stars.

"Who's Ricardo?" she asked absently. There was no thought of objection when Katch tucked her hair behind her ear with his fingertip.

"The chef. He loves compliments."

Megan smiled, liking the way the sound of his voice mixed with the sound of the sea. "How do you know?"

"That's how I lured him away from Chicago."

"Lured him away? What do you mean?" It took only an instant for the answer to come to her. "You own that restaurant?"

"Yes." He smiled at the incredulity in her face. "I bought it a couple of years ago."

Megan glanced at the white linen cloth scattered with fine china and heavy silver. She recalled that a little more than two years before, the restaurant had been ready to go under. The food had been overpriced and the service slack. Then it had received a face-lift. The interior had been redesigned, boasting, she was told, a mirrored ceiling. Since its reopening, it had maintained the highest of reputations in a town which prided itself on its quality and variety of restaurants.

She shifted her attention back to him. "*You* bought it?"

"That's right." Katch smiled at her. He sat Indian-style, facing her as she leaned back on her elbows. "Does that surprise you?"

Megan looked at him carefully: the careless toss of curls, the white knees of his jeans, the frayed sneakers. He was not her conception of a successful businessman. Where was the three-piece suit, the careful hairstyling?

And yet…she had to admit there was something in his face.

"No," she said at length. "No, I suppose it doesn't." Megan frowned as he shifted his position. In a moment he was close, facing the sea as she did. "You bought it the same way you want to buy Joyland."

"I told you, that's what I do."

"But it's more than owning things, isn't it?" she insisted, not satisfied with his offhand answers. "It's making a success of them."

"That's the idea," he agreed. "There's a certain satisfaction in succeeding, don't you think?"

Megan sat up and turned to him. "But you can't have Joyland, it's Pop's whole life. You don't understand…"

"Maybe not," he said easily. "You can explain it to me later. Not tonight." He covered her hand with his. "This isn't a night for business."

"Katch, you have to—"

"Look at the stars, Meg," he suggested as he did so himself. "Have you ever tried to count them?"

Her eyes were irresistibly drawn upward. "When I was little. But—"

"Star counting isn't just for kids," he instructed in a voice warm and laced with humor. "Do you come here at night?"

The stars were brilliant and low over the sea. "Sometimes," she murmured. "When a project isn't going well and I need to clear my head, or just be alone."

"What sort of artist are you?" His fingers trailed over her knuckles. "Do you paint seascapes? Portraits?"

She smiled and shook her head. "No, I sculpt."

"Ah." He lifted her hand, then examined it—one side, then the other—while she watched him. "Yes, I can see that. Your hands are strong and capable." When he pressed his lips to the center of her palm, she felt the jolt shoot through her entire body.

Carefully, Megan drew her hand away; then, bringing her knees up to her chest, wrapped her arms around them. She could feel Katch smile without seeing it.

"What do you work in? Clay, wood, stone?"

"All three." Turning her head, she smiled again.

"Where did you study?"

"I took courses in college." With a shrug, she passed this off. "There hasn't been much time for it." She looked up at the sky again. "The moon's so white tonight. I like to come here when it's full like this, so that the light's silvery."

When his lips brushed her ear, she would have jerked away, but he slipped an arm around her shoulders. "Relax, Meg." His voice was a whisper at her cheek. "There's a moon and the ocean. That's all there is besides us."

With his lips tingling on her skin, she could almost believe him. Her limbs were heavy, drugged with wine and the magic of his touch. Katch trailed his mouth down to her throat so that she moaned with the leap of her pulse.

"Katch, I'd better go." He was tracing her jaw with light kisses. "Please," she said weakly.

"Later," he murmured, going back to nuzzle her ear. "Much, much later."

"No, I…" Megan turned her head, and the words died.

Her lips were no more than a breath from his. She stared at him, eyes wide and aware as he bent closer. Still his mouth didn't touch hers. It hovered, offering, promising. She moaned again, lids lowering as he teased the corners of her lips. His hands never touched her. He had moved his arm so that their only contact was his mouth and tongue on her skin and the mingling of their breath.

Megan felt her resistance peel away, layer by layer until there was only need. She forgot to question the dangers, the consequences. She could only feel. Her mouth sought his. There was no hesitation or shyness now but demand, impatient demand, as she hungered to feel what she had felt before—the delicious confusion, the dark awareness.

When he still didn't touch her, Megan slipped her arms around him. She pulled him close, enjoying his soft sound of pleasure as the kiss deepened. Still, he let her lead, touching her now, but lightly, his fingers in her hair. She could barely hear the hissing of the surf over the pounding of her heart. Finally, she drew away, pulling in a deep breath as their lips separated.

But he wouldn't let her go. "Again?" The question was quiet and seemed to shout through the still night.

Refusal trembled on Megan's tongue. She knew the ground beneath her was far from solid. His hand on the back of her neck brought her a whisper closer.

"Yes," she said, and went into his arms.

This time he was less passive. He showed her there were many ways to kiss. Short and light, long and deep. Tongue and teeth and lips could all bring pleasure. Together, they lowered themselves to the sand.

It was a rough blanket, but she felt only the excitement of his lips on her skin as they wandered to her throat. She ran her fingers through his hair. His mouth returned to hers, harder now, more insistent. She was ready for it, answering it. Craving it.

When his hand took the naked skin of her breast, she murmured in resistance. She hadn't felt him release the zipper of her jacket or the buttons of her shirt. But his hand was gentle, persuasive. He let his fingers trail over her, a whispering touch. Resistance melted into surrender, then heated into passion. It was smoldering just under her skin, threatening to explode into something out of her control. She moved under him and his hands became less gentle.

There was a hunger in the kiss now. She could taste it, a flavor sharper than any she'd known. It was more seductive than soft words or champagne, and more frightening.

"I want you." Katch spoke against her mouth, but the words were not in his easygoing tone. "I want to make love with you."

Megan felt control slipping from her grasp. Her need for him was overpowering, her appetite ravenous. She struggled to climb back to reality, to remember who they were. Names, places, responsibilities. There was more than the moon and the sea. And he was a stranger, a man she barely knew.

"No." Megan managed to free her mouth from his. She struggled to her feet. "No." The repetition was shaky. Quickly, she began to fumble with the buttons of her shirt.

Katch stood and gathered the shirttail in his hands. Surprised, Megan looked up at him. His eyes were no longer calm, but his voice was deadly so. "Why not?"

Megan swallowed. There wasn't lazy arrogance here,

but a hint of ruthlessness. She had sensed it, but seeing it was much more potent. "I don't want to."

"Liar," he said simply.

"All right." She nodded, conceding his point. "I don't know you."

Katch inclined his head in agreement but tugged on the tails of her shirt to bring her closer. "You will," he assured her. He kissed her then, searingly. "But we'll wait until you do."

She fought to steady her breathing and stabilize her pulse. "Do you think you should always get what you want?" she demanded. The defiance was back, calming her.

"Yes," he said and grinned. "Of course."

"You're going to be disappointed." She smacked his hands from her shirt and began doing the buttons. Her fingers were unfaltering. "You can't have Joyland and you can't have me. Neither of us is for sale."

The roughness with which he took her arm had her eyes flying back to his face. "I don't buy women." He was angry, his eyes dark with it. The appealing voice had hardened like flint. The artist in her was fascinated by the planes of his face, the woman was uneasy with his harsh tone. "I don't have to. We're both aware that with a bit more persuasion I'd have had you tonight."

Megan pulled out of his hold. "What happened tonight doesn't mean I find you irresistible, you know." She zipped up her jacket with one quick jerk. "I can only repeat, you can't have Joyland and you can't have me."

Katch watched her a moment as she stood in the moonlight, her back to the sea. The smile came again, slowly, arrogantly. "I'll have you both, Meg," he promised quietly. "Before the season begins."

Chapter 4

The afternoon sun poured into Megan's studio. She was oblivious to it, and to the birdsong outside the windows. Her mind was focused on the clay her hands worked with, or, more precisely, on what she saw in the partially formed mound.

She had put her current project aside, something she rarely did, to begin a new one. The new subject had haunted her throughout the night. She would exorcise David Katcherton by doing a bust of him.

Megan could see it clearly, knew precisely what she wanted to capture: strength and determination behind a surface affability.

Though she had yet to admit it, Katch had frightened her the night before. Not physically—he was too intelligent to use brute force, she acknowledged—but by the force of his personality. Angrily, she stabbed at the clay.

Obviously, this was a man who got what he wanted. But she was determined that this time he would not have his way. He would soon find out that she couldn't be pushed around any more than Pop could. Slowly and meticulously, her fingers worked to mold the planes of his face. It gave her a certain satisfaction to have control over him—if only vicariously with the clay.

Almost without thinking, she shaped a careless curl over the high brow. She stepped back to survey it. Somehow, she had caught a facet of his nature. He was a rogue, she decided. The old-fashioned word suited him. She could picture him with boots and six-guns, dealing cards for stud poker in a Tucson saloon; with a saber, captaining a ship into the Barbary Coast. Her fingers absently caressed the clay curls. He would laugh in the face of the wind, take treasure and women where he found them. *Women.* Megan's thoughts zeroed in on the night before.... On the feel of his lips on hers, the touch of his hand on her skin. She could remember the texture of the sand as they had lain together, the scent and sounds of the sea. And she remembered how the moonlight had fallen on his hair, how her hands had sought it while his lips had wandered over her. How thick and soft it had felt. How...

Megan stopped, appalled. She glanced down to see her fingers in the clay replica of Katch's hair. She swore, and nearly, very nearly, reduced the clay to a formless mass. Controlling herself, she rose, backing away from the forming bust. I should never allow myself to be distracted from my work by petty annoyances, she thought. Her evening with Katch belonged in that category. Just a petty annoyance. Not important.

But it was difficult for Megan to convince herself

this was true. Both her intuition and her emotions told her that Katch was important, far more important than a stranger should be to a sensible woman.

And I *am* sensible, she reminded herself. Taking a long breath, she moved to the basin to rinse the clay from her hands. She had to be sensible. Pop needed someone around to remind him that bills had to be paid. A smile crept across her mouth as she dried her hands. Megan thought, as she did from time to time, that she had been almost as much of a savior to her grandfather as he had been to her.

In the beginning, she'd been so young, so dependent upon him. And he hadn't let her down. Then, as she had grown older, Megan had helped by assuming the duties her grandfather had found tiresome: accounts and bank reconciliations. Often, Megan suppressed her own desires in order to fulfill what she thought of as her duty. She dealt with figures, the unromantic process of adding and subtracting. But she also dealt with the illusionary world of art. There were times, when she was deep in her work, that she forgot the rules she had set up for day-to-day living. Often she felt pulled in two directions. She had enough to think about without David Katcherton.

Why a man virtually unknown to her should so successfully upset the delicate balance of her world, she didn't know. She shook her head. Instead of dwelling on it, she decided, she would work out her frustration by finishing the bust. When it was done, perhaps she would be able to see more clearly exactly how she perceived him. She returned to her work.

The next hour passed quickly. She forgot her irritation with Katch for going fishing with her grandfather. How annoying to have seen him so eager and well rested when she had peeked through her bedroom curtain at five-thirty that morning! She'd fallen back into her rumpled bed to spend another hour staring, heavy-eyed, at the ceiling. She refused to remember how appealing his laugh had sounded in the hush of dawn.

The planes of his face were just taking shape under her hands when she heard a car drive up. Katch's laugh was followed by the more gravelly tones of her grandfather's.

Because her studio was above the garage, Megan had a bird's-eye view of the house and drive. She watched as Katch lifted their fishing cooler from the back of the pickup. A grin was on his face, but whatever he said was too low for Megan to hear. Pop threw back his head, his dramatic mane of white flying back as he roared his appreciation. He gave Katch a companionable slap on the back. Unaccountably, Megan was miffed. They seemed to be getting along entirely too well.

She continued to watch the men as they unloaded tackle boxes and gear. Katch was dressed much as he had been the day before. The pale blue T-shirt had lettering across the chest, but the words were faded and the distance was too great for Megan to read them. He wore Pop's fishing cap, another source of annoyance for Megan. She was forced to admit the two of them looked good together. There was the contrast between their ages and their builds, but both seemed to her to be extraordinarily masculine men. Their looks were neither smooth nor pampered. She became engrossed with the similarities and differences between them. When Katch looked up, spotting her at the window, Megan continued to stare down, oblivious, absorbed with what she saw in them.

Katch grinned, pushing the fishing cap back so that he had a clearer view. The window was long, the sill coming low at her knees. It had the effect of making Megan seem to be standing in a full-size picture frame. As was her habit when working, she had pulled her hair back in a ribbon. Her face seemed younger and more vulnerable, her eyes wider. The ancient shirt of Pop's she used as a smock dwarfed her.

Her eyes locked on Katch's, and for a moment she thought she saw something flash in them—something she'd seen briefly the night before in the moonlight. A response trembled along her skin. Then his grin was arrogant again, his eyes amused.

"Come on down, Meg." He gestured before he bent to lift the cooler again. "We brought you a present." He turned to carry the cooler around the side of the house.

"I'd rather have emeralds," she called back.

"Next time," Katch promised carelessly, before turning to carry the cooler around the side of the house.

She found Katch alone, setting up for the cleaning of the catch. He smiled when he saw her and set down the knife he held, then pulled her into his arms and kissed her thoroughly, to her utter astonishment. It was a kiss of casual ownership rather than passion, but it elicited a response that surprised her with its force. More than a little shaken, Megan pushed away.

"You can't just…"

"I already did," he pointed out. "You've been working," Katch stated as if the searing kiss had never taken place. "I'd like to see your studio."

It was better, Megan decided, to follow his lead and keep the conversation light. "Where's my grandfather?" she asked as she moved to the cooler and prepared to lift the lid.

"Pop's inside stowing the gear."

Though it was the habit of everyone who knew him to refer to Timothy Miller as Pop, Megan frowned at Katch.

"You work fast, don't you?"

"Yes, I do. I like your grandfather, Meg. You of all people should understand how easy that is to do."

Megan regarded him steadily. She took a step closer, as if testing the air between them. "I don't know if I should trust you."

"You shouldn't." Katch grinned again and ran a finger down the bridge of her nose. "Not for a second." He tossed open the lid of the cooler, then gestured to the fish inside. "Hungry?"

Megan smiled, letting herself be charmed despite the warnings of her sensible self. "I wasn't. But I could be. Especially if I don't have to clean them."

"Pop told me you were squeamish."

"Oh, he *did,* did he?" Megan cast a long, baleful look over her shoulder toward the house. "What else did he tell you?"

"That you like daffodils and used to have a stuffed elephant named Henry."

Megan's mouth dropped open. "He told you that?"

"And that you watch horror movies, then sleep with the blankets over your head."

Megan narrowed her eyes as Katch's grin widened. "Excuse me," she said crossly, pushing Katch aside before racing through the kitchen door. She could hear Katch's laughter behind her.

"Pop!" She found him in the narrow room off the kitchen where he stored his fishing paraphernalia. He gave her an affectionate smile as she stood, hands on hips, in the doorway.

"Hi, Megan. Let me tell you, that boy knows how to fish. Yessiree, he knows how to fish."

His obvious delight with Katch caused Megan to clench her teeth. "That's the best news I've had all day," she said, stepping into the room. "But exactly why did you feel it necessary to tell *that boy* that I had a stuffed elephant and slept with the covers over my head?"

Pop lifted a hand, ostensibly to scratch his head. It wasn't in time, however, to conceal the grin. Megan's brows drew together.

"Pop, really," she said in exasperation. "Must you babble about me as if I were a little girl?"

"You'll always be my little girl," he said maddeningly, and kissed her cheek. "Did you see those trout? We'll have a heck of a fish fry tonight."

"I suppose," Megan began and folded her arms, "*he's* going to eat with us."

"Well, of course." Pop blinked his eyes. "After all, Meg, he caught half the fish."

"That's just peachy."

"We thought you might whip up some of your special blueberry tarts." He smiled ingenuously.

Megan sighed, recognizing defeat.

Within minutes, Pop heard the thumping and banging of pans. He grinned, then slipped out of the room, moving noiselessly through the house and out the front door.

"Whip up some tarts," Megan muttered later as she cut shortening into the flour. *"Men."*

She was bending over to slip the pastry shells into the oven when the screen door slammed shut behind her. Turning, she brushed at the seat of her pants and met the predictable grin.

"I've heard about your tarts," Katch commented, setting the cleaned, filleted fish on the counter. "Pop said he had a few things to see to in the garage and to call him when dinner's ready."

Megan glared through the screen door at the adjoining building. "Oh, he did, did he?" She turned back to Katch. "Well, if you think you can just sit back and be waited on, then you're in for a disappointment."

"You didn't think I'd allow you to cook my fish, did you?" he interrupted.

She stared at his unperturbed face.

"I always cook my own fish. Where's the frying pan?"

Silently, still eyeing him, Megan pointed out the cabinet. She watched as he squatted down to rummage for it.

"It's not that I don't think you're a good cook," he went on as he stood again with the cast-iron skillet in his hand. "It's that I know I am."

"Are you implying I couldn't cook those pathetic little sardines properly?"

"Let's just say I just don't like to take chances with my dinner." He began poking into cupboards. "Why don't you make a salad," he suggested mildly, "and leave the fish to me?" There was a grunt of approval as he located the cracker meal.

Megan watched him casually going through her

kitchen cupboards. "Why don't you," she began, "take your trout and…"

Her suggestion was interrupted by the rude buzz of the oven timer.

"Your tarts." Katch walked to the refrigerator for eggs and milk.

With supreme effort, Megan controlled herself enough to deal with the pastry shells. Setting them on the rack to cool, she decided to create the salad of the decade. It would put his pan-fried trout to shame.

For a time there were no words. The hot oil hissed as Katch added his coated trout. Megan tore the lettuce. She sliced raw vegetables. The scent from the pan was enticing. Megan peeled a carrot and sighed. Hearing her, Katch raised a questioning eyebrow.

"You had to be good at it, didn't you?" Megan's smile was reluctant. "You had to do it right."

He shrugged, then snatched the peeled carrot from her hand. "You'd like it better if I didn't?" Katch took a bite of the carrot before Megan could retrieve it. Shaking her head, she selected another.

"It would have been more gratifying if you'd fumbled around and made a mess of things."

Katch tilted his head as he poked at the sizzling fish with a spatula. "Is that a compliment?"

Megan diced the carrot, frowning at it thoughtfully. "I don't know. It might be easier to deal with you if you didn't seem so capable."

He caught her off guard by taking her shoulders and turning her around to face him. "Is that what you want to do?" His fingers gently massaged her flesh. "Deal with me?" When she felt herself being drawn closer, she placed her hands on his chest. "Do I make you nervous?"

"No." Megan shook her head with the denial. "No, of course not." Katch only lifted a brow and drew her closer. "Yes," she admitted in a rush, and pulled away. "Yes, blast it, you do." Stalking to the refrigerator, she yanked out the blueberry filling she had prepared. "You needn't look so pleased about it," she told him, wishing she could work up the annoyance she thought she should feel.

"Several things make me nervous." Megan moved to the pastry shells and began to spoon in the filling. "Snakes, tooth decay, large unfriendly dogs." When she heard him chuckle, Megan turned her head and found herself grinning at him. "It's difficult to actively dislike you when you make me laugh."

"Do you have to actively dislike me?" Katch flipped the fish expertly and sent oil sizzling.

"That was my plan," Megan admitted. "It seemed like a good idea."

"Why don't we work on a different plan?" Katch suggested, searching through a cupboard again for a platter. "What do you like? Besides daffodils?"

"Soft ice cream," Megan responded spontaneously. "Oscar Wilde, walking barefoot."

"How about baseball?" Katch demanded.

Megan paused in the act of filling the shells. "What about it?"

"Do you like it?"

"Yes," she considered, smiling. "As a matter of fact, I do."

"I knew we had something in common." Katch

grinned. He turned the flame off under the pan. "Why don't you call Pop? The fish is done."

There was something altogether too cozy about the three of them sitting around the kitchen table eating a meal each of them had a part in providing, Megan thought. She could sense the growing affection between the two men and it worried her. She was sure that Katch was still as determined as ever to buy Joyland. Yet Pop was so obviously happy in his company. Megan decided that, while she couldn't trust Katch unreservedly, neither could she maintain her original plan. She couldn't dislike him or keep him from touching their lives. She thought it best not to dwell on precisely how he was touching hers.

"Tell you what." Pop sighed over his empty plate and leaned back in his chair. "Since the pair of you cooked dinner, I'll do the dishes." His eyes passed over Megan to Katch. "Why don't you two go for a walk? Megan likes to walk on the beach."

"Pop!"

"I know you young people like to be alone," he continued shamelessly.

Megan opened her mouth to protest, but Katch spoke first. "I'm always willing to take a walk with a beautiful woman, especially if it means getting out of KP," he said.

"You have such a gracious way of putting things," Megan began.

"Actually, I'd really like to see your studio."

"Take Katch up, Megan," Pop insisted. "I've been bragging about your pieces all day. Let him see for himself."

After a moment's hesitation, Megan decided it was simpler to agree. Certainly she didn't mind showing Katch her work. And, there was little doubt that it was safer to let him putter around her studio than to walk with him on the beach.

"All right." She rose. "I'll take you up."

As they passed through the screen door, Katch slipped his arm over her shoulders. "This is a nice place," he commented. He looked around the small trim yard lined with azalea shrubs. "Very quiet and settled."

The weight of his arm was pleasant. Megan allowed it to remain as they walked toward the garage. "I wouldn't think you'd find something quiet and settled terribly appealing."

"There's a time for porch swings and a time for roller coasters." Katch glanced down at her as she paused at the foot of the steps. "I'd think you'd know that."

"I do," she said, knowing her involvement with him was beginning to slip beyond her control. "I wasn't aware you did." Thoughtfully, Megan climbed the stairs. "It's rather a small-scale studio, I suppose, and not very impressive. It's really just a place to work where I won't disturb Pop and he won't disturb me."

Megan opened the door, flicking on the light as the sun was growing dim.

There was much less order here than she permitted herself in other areas of her life. The room was hers, personally, more exclusively than her bedroom in the house next door. There were tools—calipers, chisels, gouges, and an assortment of knives and files. There was the smock she'd carelessly thrown over a chair when Katch had called her downstairs. Future projects sat waiting inside, untouched slabs of limestone and chunks of wood. There was a precious piece of marble she hoarded like a miser. Everywhere, on shelves, tables and even the floor, were samples of her work.

Katch moved past her into the room. Strangely, Megan felt a flutter of nerves. She found herself wondering how to react if he spoke critically, or worse, offered some trite compliment. Her work was important to her and very personal. To her surprise she realized that she cared about his opinion. Quietly, she closed the door behind her, then stood with her back against it.

Katch had gone directly to a small walnut study of a young girl building a sand castle. She was particularly pleased with the piece, as she had achieved exactly the mood she had sought. There was more than youth and innocence in the child's face. The girl saw herself as the princess in the castle tower. The half-smile on her face made the onlooker believe in happy endings.

It was painstakingly detailed, the beginnings of a crenellated roof and the turrets of the castle, the slender fingers of the girl as she sculpted the sand. Her hair was long, falling over her shoulders and wisping into her face as though a breeze teased it. Megan had felt successful when the study had been complete, but now, watching Katch turn it over in his hands, his mouth oddly grave, his eyes intent, she felt a twinge of doubt.

"This is your work?" Because the silence had seemed so permanent, Megan jerked when Katch spoke.

"Well, yes." While she was still searching for something more to say, Katch turned away to prowl the room.

He picked up piece after piece, examining, saying nothing. As the silence dragged on, minute upon minute, Megan became more and more tense. If he'd just say something, she thought. She picked up the discarded smock and folded it, nervously smoothing creases as she listened to the soft sound of his tennis shoes on the wood floor.

"What are you doing here?"

She whirled, eyes wide. Whatever reaction she had expected, it certainly hadn't been anger. And there was anger on his face, a sharp, penetrating anger which caused her to grip the worn material of the smock tighter.

"I don't know what you mean." Megan's voice was calm, but her heart had begun to beat faster.

"Why are you hiding?" he demanded. "What are you afraid of?"

She shook her head in bewilderment. "I'm not hiding, Katch. You're not making any sense."

"I'm not making sense?" He took a step toward her, then stopped, turning away to pace again. She watched in fascination. "Do you think it makes sense to create things like this and lock them up in a room over a garage?" He lifted polished limestone which had been formed into a head-and-shoulders study of a man and a woman in each other's arms. "When you've been given talent like this, you have an obligation. What are you going to do, continue to stack them in here until there isn't any more room?"

His reaction had thrown Megan completely off-balance. She looked around the room. "No, I… I take pieces into an art gallery downtown now and then. They sell fairly well, especially during the season, and—"

Katch's pungent oath cut her off. Megan gave her full attention back to him. Was this furious, disapproving man the same one who had amiably prepared trout in her kitchen a short time ago?

"I don't understand why you're so mad." Annoyed with herself for nervously pleating the material of the smock, Megan tossed it down.

"Waste," he said tersely, placing the limestone back on the shelf. "Waste infuriates me." He came to her, taking her deliberately by the shoulders. "Why haven't you done anything with your work?" His eyes were direct on hers, demanding answers, not evasions.

"It's not as simple as that," she began. "I have responsibilities."

"Your responsibilities are to yourself, to your talent."

"You make it sound as though I've done something wrong." Confused, Megan searched his face. "I've done what I know how to do. I don't understand why you're angry. There are things, like time and money, to be considered," she went on. "A business to run. And reality to face." Megan shook her head. "I can hardly cart my work to a Charleston art gallery and demand a showing."

"That would make more sense than cloistering it up here." He released her abruptly, then paced again.

He was, Megan discovered, much more volatile than her first impression had allowed. She glanced at the clay wrapped in the damp towel. Her fingertips itched to work while fresh impressions were streaming through her brain.

"When's the last time you've been to New York?" Katch demanded, facing her again. "Chicago, L.A.?"

"We can't all be globetrotters," she told him. "Some are born to other things."

He picked up the sand-castle girl again, then strode over to the limestone couple. "I want these two," he stated. "Will you sell them to me?"

They were two of her favorites, though totally opposite in tone. "Yes, I suppose. If you want them."

"I'll give you five hundred." Megan's eyes widened. "Apiece."

"Oh, no, they're not worth—"

"They're worth a lot more, I imagine." Katch lifted the limestone. "Have you got a box I can carry them in?"

"Yes, but, Katch." Megan paused and pushed the bangs from her eyes. "A thousand dollars?"

He set down both pieces and came back to her. He was still angry; she could feel it vibrating from him. "Do you think it's safer to underestimate yourself than to face up to your own worth?"

Megan started to make a furious denial, then stopped. Uncertain, she made a helpless gesture with her hands. Katch turned away again to search for a box himself. She watched him as he wrapped the sculptures in old newspapers. The frown was still on his face, the temper in his eyes.

"I'll bring you a check," he stated, and was gone without another word.

Chapter 5

There was a long, high-pitched scream. The roller coaster rumbled along the track as it whipped around another curve and tilted its passengers. Lights along the midway were twinkling, and there was noise. Such noise. There was the whirl and whine of machinery, the electronic buzz and beeps from video games, the pop of arcade rifles and the call of concessionaires.

Tinny music floated all over, but for the most part, there was the sound of people. They were laughing, calling, talking, shouting. There were smells: popcorn, peanuts, grilled hot dogs, machine oil.

Megan loaded another clip into the scaled-down rifle and handed it to a would-be Wyatt Earp. "Rabbits are five points, ducks ten, deer twenty-five and the bears fifty."

The sixteen-year-old sharpshooter aimed and managed to bag a duck and a rabbit. He chose a rubber snake as his prize, to the ensuing screams and disgust of his girl.

Shaking her head, Megan watched them walk away. The boy slipped his arm around the girl's shoulders, then pursued the romance by dangling the snake in front of her face. He earned a quick jab in the ribs.

The crowd was thin tonight, but that was to be expected in the off-season. Particularly, Megan knew, when there were so many other parks with more rides, live entertainment and a more sophisticated selection of video games. She didn't mind the slack. Megan was preoccupied, as she had been since the evening Katch had seen her studio. In three days, she hadn't heard a word from him. At first, she had wanted badly to see him, to talk about the things he'd said to her. He had made her think, made her consider a part of herself she had ignored or submerged most of her life.

Her desire to speak with Katch had faded as the days had passed, however. After all, what right did he have to criticize her lifestyle? What right did he have to make her feel as if she'd committed a crime? He'd accused, tried and condemned her in the space of minutes. Then, he'd disappeared.

Three days, Megan mused, handing another hopeful deadeye a rifle. Three days without a word. And she'd watched for him—much to her self-disgust. She'd waited for him. As the days had passed, Megan had taken refuge in anger. Not only had he criticized and scolded her, she remembered, but he'd walked out with two of her favorite sculptures. A thousand dollars my foot, she mused, frowning fiercely as she slid a fresh clip into an empty rifle. Just talk, that's all. Talk. He does that very well. It was probably all a line, owning that restaurant. *But why?* Men like that don't need logical reasons, she decided. It's all ego.

"Men," she muttered as she handed a rifle to a new customer.

"I know what you mean, honey." The plump blond woman took the rifle from Megan with a wink.

Megan pushed her bangs back and frowned deeper. "Who needs them?" she demanded.

The woman shouldered the rifle. "We do, honey. That's the problem."

Megan let out a long sigh as the woman earned 125 points. "Nice shooting," she congratulated. "Your choice on the second row."

"Let me have the hippo, sweetie. It looks a little like my second husband."

Laughing, Megan plucked it from the shelf and handed it over. "Here you go." With another wink, the woman tucked the hippo under her arm and waddled off.

Megan settled back while two kids tried their luck. The exchange had been typical of the informality enjoyed by people in amusement parks. She smiled, feeling less grim, if not entirely mollified by the woman's remarks. But she doesn't know Katch, Megan reflected, again exchanging a rifle for a quarter. And neither, she reminded herself, do I.

Automatically, Megan made change when a dollar bill was placed on the counter. "Ten shots for a quarter," she began the spiel. "Rabbits are five, ducks ten…" Megan pushed three quarters back as she reached for a rifle. The moment the fingers pushed the change back to her, she recognized them.

"I'll take a dollar's worth," Katch told her as she looked up in surprise. He grinned, then leaned over to press a quick kiss to her lips. "For luck," he claimed when she jerked away.

Before Megan had pocketed the quarters, Katch had bull's-eyed every one of the bears.

"Wow!" The two boys standing next to Katch were suitably impressed. "Hey, mister, can you do it again?" one asked.

"Maybe." Katch turned to Megan. "Let's have a reload." Without speaking, she handed him the rifle.

"I like the perfume you're wearing," he commented as he sighed. "What is it?"

"Gun oil."

He laughed, then blasted the hapless bears one by one. The two boys gave simultaneous yelps of appreciation. A crowd began to gather.

"Hey, Megan." She glanced up to see the Bailey twins leaning over the counter. Both pairs of eyes drifted meaningfully to Katch. "Isn't he the…"

"Yes," Megan said shortly, not wanting to explain.

"Delicious," Teri decided quietly, giving Katch a flirtatious smile when he straightened.

"Mmm-hmm," Jeri agreed with a twin smile.

Katch gave them a long, appreciative look.

"Here." Megan shoved the rifle at him. "This is your last quarter."

Katch accepted the rifle. "Thanks." He hefted it again. "Going to wish me luck?"

Megan met his eyes levelly. "Why not?"

"Meg, I'm crazy about you."

She dealt with the surge his careless words brought her as he picked off his fourth set of bears. Bystanders broke into raucous applause. Katch set the rifle on the counter, then gave his full attention to Meg.

"What'd I win?"

"Anything you want."

His grin was a flash, and his eyes never left her face. She blushed instantly, hating herself. Deliberately, she stepped to the side and gestured toward the prizes.

"I'll take Henry," he told her. When she gave him a puzzled look, he pointed. "The elephant." Glancing up, Megan spotted the three-foot lavender elephant. She lifted it down from its perch. Even as she set it on the counter for him, Katch took her hands. "And you."

She made her voice prim. "Only the items on display are eligible prizes."

"I love it when you talk that way," he commented.

"Stop it!" she hissed, flushing as she heard the Bailey twins giggle.

"We had a bet, remember?" Katch smiled at her. "It's Friday night."

Megan tried to tug her hands away, but his fingers interlocked with hers. "Who says I lost the bet?" she demanded. The crowd was still milling around the stand so she spoke in an undertone, but Katch didn't bother.

"Come on, Meg, I won fair and square. You're not going to welch, are you?"

"Shh!" She glanced behind him at the curious crowd. "I never welch," she whispered furiously. "And even if I did lose, which I never said I did, I can't leave the stand. I'm sure you can find somebody else to keep you company."

"I want you."

She struggled to keep her eyes steady on his. "Well, I can't leave. Someone has to run the booth."

"Megan." One of the part-timers slipped under the counter. "Pop sent me to relieve you." He smiled innocently when she gave him a disgusted look.

"Perfect timing," she mumbled, then stripped off the change apron and stuffed it in his hands. "Thanks a lot."

"Sure, Megan."

"Hey, keep this back there for me, will you?" Katch dumped the elephant into his arms and captured Megan's hands again as she ducked under the counter. As she straightened, he tugged, tumbling her into his arms.

The kiss was long and demanding. When Katch drew her away, her arms were around his neck. She left them there, staring up into his face with eyes newly aware and darkened.

"I've wanted to do that for three days," he murmured, and rubbed her nose lightly with his.

"Why didn't you?"

He lifted a brow at that, then grinned when her blush betrayed the impetuousness of her words.

"I didn't mean that the way it sounded," Megan began, dropping her arms and trying to wriggle away.

"Yes you did," he countered. Katch released her but dropped a friendly arm over her shoulder. "It was nice, don't spoil it." He took a sweeping glance of the park. "How about a tour?"

"I don't know why you want one. We're not selling."

"We'll see about that," he said, as maddeningly confident as ever. "But in any case, I'm interested. Do you know why people come here? To a place like this?" He gestured with his free arm to encompass the park.

"To be entertained," Megan told him as she followed the movement of his arm.

"You left out two of the most important reasons," he added. "To fantasize and to show off."

They stopped to watch a middle-aged man strip out of his jacket and attempt to ring the bell. The hammer came down with a loud thump, but the ball rose only halfway up the pole. He rubbed his hands together and prepared to try again.

"Yes, you're right." Megan tossed her hair back with a move of her head, then smiled at Katch. "You ought to know."

He tilted his head and shot her a grin. "Want me to ring the bell?"

"Muscles don't impress me," she said firmly.

"No?" He guided her away with his arm still around her. "What does?"

"Poetry," Megan decided all at once.

"Hmm." Katch rubbed his chin and avoided a trio of teenagers. "How about a limerick? I know some great limericks."

"I bet you do." Megan shook her head. "I think I'll pass."

"Coward."

"Oh? Let's ride the roller coaster, then we'll see who's a coward."

"You're on." Taking her hand, he set off in a sprint. He stopped at the ticket booth, and gratefully she caught her breath.

I might as well face it, she reflected as she studied his face. I enjoy him. There isn't any use in pretending I don't.

"What are you thinking?" Katch demanded as he paid for their ride.

"That I could learn to like you—in three or four years. For short periods of time," she added, still smiling.

Katch took both her hands and kissed them, surprising Megan with the shock that raced up her arms. "Flatterer," he murmured, and his eyes laughed at her over their joined hands.

Distressed by the power she felt rushing through her system, Megan tried to tug her hands from his. It was imperative, for reasons only half-formed in her brain, that she keep their relationship casual.

"You have to hold my hand." Katch jerked his head toward the roller coaster. "I'm afraid of heights."

Megan laughed. She let herself forget the tempestuous instant and the hint of danger. She kept her hand in his.

Katch wasn't satisfied with only the roller coaster. He pulled Megan to ride after ride. They were scrambled on the Mind Maze, spooked in the Haunted Castle and spun lazily on the Ferris wheel.

From the top of the wheel, they watched the colored lights of the park, and the sea stretching out to the right. The wind tossed her hair into her face. Katch took it in his hand as they rose toward the top again. When he kissed her, it felt natural and right...a shared thing, a moment which belonged only to them. The noise and people below were of another world. Theirs was only the gentle movement of the wheel and the dance of the breeze. And the touch of mouth on mouth. There was no demand, only an offering of pleasure.

Megan relaxed against him, finding her head fit naturally in the curve of his shoulder. Held close beside him, she watched the world revolve. Above, the stars were scattered and few. A waning moon shifted in and out of the clouds. The air was cool with a hint of the sea. She sighed, utterly content.

"When's the last time you did this?"

"Did what?" Megan tilted her head to look at him. Their faces were close, but she felt no danger now, only satisfaction.

"Enjoyed this park." Katch had caught the confusion on her face. "Just enjoyed it, Megan, for the fun."

"I…" The Ferris wheel slowed, then stopped. The carts rocked gently as old passengers were exchanged for new. She remembered times when she had been very young. When had they stopped? "I don't know." Megan rose when the attendant lifted the safety bar.

This time, as she walked with Katch, she looked around thoughtfully. She saw several people she knew; locals out for an evening's entertainment mixed with tourists taking a preseason vacation.

"You need to do this more often," Katch commented, steering her toward the east end of the park. "Laugh," he continued as she turned her head to him. "Unbend, relax those restrictions you put on yourself."

Megan's spine stiffened. "For somebody who barely knows me, you seem remarkably certain of what's good for me."

"It isn't difficult." He stopped at a concession wagon and ordered two ice-cream cones. "You haven't any mysteries, Meg."

"Thank you very much."

With a laugh, Katch handed her a cone. "Don't get huffy, I meant that as a compliment."

"I suppose you've known a lot of sophisticated women."

Katch smiled, then his arm came around her as they

began to walk again. "There's one, her name's Jessica. She's one of the most beautiful women I know."

"Really?" Megan licked at the soft swirl of vanilla.

"That blond, classical look. You know, fair skin, finely chiseled features, blue eyes. Terrific blue eyes."

"How interesting."

"Oh, she's all of that," he continued. "And more: intelligent, a sense of humor."

"You sound very fond of her." Megan gave the ice cream her undivided attention.

"A bit more than that actually. Jessica and I lived together for a number of years." He dropped the bomb matter-of-factly. "She's married now and has a couple of kids, but still manage to see each other now and again. Maybe she can make it down for a few days, then you can meet her."

"Oh, really!" Megan stopped, incensed. "Flaunt your relationship somewhere else. If you think I want to meet your—your…"

"Sister," Katch supplied, then crunched into his cone. "You'd like her. Your ice cream's dripping, Meg."

They walked to the entrance gates of the park.

"It's a very nice park," Katch murmured. "Small but well set up. No bored-faced attendants." He reached absently in his pocket and pulled out a slip of paper. "I forgot to give you your check."

Megan stuffed it into her pocket without even glancing at it. Her eyes were on Katch's face. She was all too aware of the direction his thoughts had taken. "My grandfather's devoted his life to this park," she reminded him.

"So have you," Katch said.

"Why do you want to buy it?" she asked. "To make money?"

Katch was silent for a long moment. By mutual consent, they cut across the boardwalk and moved down the sloping sand toward the water. "Is that such a bad reason, Megan? Do you object to making money?"

"No, of course not. That would be ridiculous."

"I wondered if that was why you haven't done anything with your sculpting."

"No. I do what I'm capable of doing, and what I have time for. There are priorities."

"Perhaps you have them wrong." Before she could comment, he spoke again. "How would it affect the park's business if it had some updated rides and an expanded arcade?"

"We can't afford…"

"That wasn't my question." He took her by the shoulders and his eyes were serious.

"Business would improve, naturally," Megan answered. "People come here to be entertained. The more entertainment provided, the slicker, the faster the entertainment, the happier they are. And the more money they spend."

Katch nodded as he searched her face. "Those were my thoughts."

"It's academic because we simply haven't the sort of money necessary for an overhaul."

"Hmm?" Though he was looking directly at her, Megan saw that his attention had wandered. She watched it refocus.

"What are you thinking?" she demanded.

The grip on her shoulder altered to a caress. "That you're extraordinarily beautiful."

Megan pulled away. "No, you weren't."

"It's what I'm thinking now." The gleam was back in his eyes as he put his hands to her waist. "It's what I was thinking the first time I saw you."

"You're ridiculous." She made an attempt to pull away, but he caught her closer.

"I've never denied that. But you can't call me ridiculous for finding you beautiful." The wind blew her hair back, leaving her face unframed. He laid a soft, unexpected kiss on her forehead. Megan felt her knees turn to water. She placed her hands on his chest both for support and in protest. "You're an artist." He drew her fractionally closer, and his voice lowered. "You recognize beauty when you see it."

"Don't!" The protest was feeble as she made no attempt to struggle out of his gentle hold.

"Don't what? Don't kiss you?" Slowly, luxuriously, his mouth journeyed over her skin. "But I have to, Meg." His lips touched hers softly, then withdrew, and her heart seemed to stop. The flavor of his lips as they brushed against hers overwhelmed her. They tempted, then ruled. With a moan of pleasure, Megan drew him close against her.

Something seemed to explode inside her as the kiss deepened. She clung to him a moment, dazed, then terrified by the power of it. Needs, emotions and new sensations tumbled together too quickly for her to control them. As panic swamped her, Megan struggled in his arms. She would have run, blindly, without direction, but Katch took her arms and held her still.

"What is it? You're trembling." Gently, he tilted her chin until their eyes met. Hers were wide, his serious. "I didn't mean to frighten you. I'm sorry."

The gentleness was nearly her undoing. Love, so newly discovered, hammered for release. She shook her head, knowing her voice would be thick with tears if she spoke. Swallowing, Megan prayed she could steady it.

"No, it's... I have to get back. They're closing." Behind him, she could see the lights flickering off.

"Meg." The tone halted her. It was not a demand this time, but a request. "Have dinner with me."

"No—"

"I haven't even suggested an evening," he pointed out mildly. "How about Monday?"

Megan stood firm. "No."

"Please."

Her resolution dissolved on a sigh. "You don't play fair," she murmured.

"Never. How about seven?"

"No picnics on the beach," she compromised.

"We'll eat inside, I promise."

"All right, but just dinner." She stepped away from him. "Now, I have to go."

"I'll walk you back." Katch took her hand and kissed it before she could stop him. "I have to get my elephant."

Chapter 6

Megan held Katch's face in her hands. With totally focused absorption, she formed his cheekbones. She had thought when she had first begun to work on this bust that morning that it would be good therapy. To an extent, she'd been right. The hours had passed peacefully, without the restless worry of the past two nights. Her mind was centered on her work, leaving no spaces for the disturbing thoughts that had plagued her all weekend.

She opened and closed her hands slowly, using the muscles until the cramping was a dull ache. A glance at her watch told her she had worked for longer than she'd intended. Late afternoon sun poured through the windows. Critically, as she pulled on each finger to soothe it, Megan studied her work.

The model was good, she decided, with just the

proper touches of roughness and intelligence she had aimed for. The mouth was strong and sensuous, the eyes perceptive and far too aware. The mobility of the face which Megan found fascinating could only be suggested. It was a face that urged one to trust against better judgment and common sense.

Narrowing her eyes, she studied the clay replica of Katch's face. There are certain men, she thought, who make a career out of women—winning them, making love to them, leaving them. There are other men who settle down and marry, raise families. How could she doubt what category Katch fell into?

Megan rose to wash her hands. Infatuation, she reflected. It's simply infatuation. He's different, and I can't deny he's exciting. I wouldn't be human if I weren't flattered that he's attracted to me. I've overreacted, that's all. She dried her hands on a towel and tried to convince herself. A person doesn't fall in love this quickly. And if they do, it's just a surface thing, nothing lasting. Megan's eyes were drawn to the clay model. Katch's smile seemed to mock all her sensible arguments. She hurled the towel to the floor.

"It can't happen this fast!" she told him furiously. "Not this way. Not to me." She swung away from his assured expression. "I won't let it."

It's only the park he wants, she reminded herself. Once he's finally convinced he can't have it, he'll go away. The ache was unexpected, and unwelcome. That's what I want, she thought. For him to go away and leave us alone. She tried not to remember the new frontiers she had glimpsed while being held in his arms.

With a brisk shake of her head, Megan pulled the tie from her hair so that it tumbled back to brush her shoulders. I'll start in wood tomorrow, she decided, and covered the clay model. Tonight, I'll simply enjoy a dinner date with an attractive man. It's that simple.

With a great deal more ease than she was feeling, Megan took off her work smock and left her studio.

"Hi, sweetheart." Pop pulled the truck into the driveway just as Megan reached the bottom step.

She noticed the weariness the moment he climbed from the cab. Knowing he hated fussing, she said nothing, but walked over and slipped an arm around his waist.

"Hi, yourself. You've been gone a long time."

"A problem or two at the park," he told her as they moved together toward the house.

That explained the weariness, Megan thought as she pushed open the back door. "What sort of problem?" Megan waited for him to settle himself at the kitchen table before she walked to the stove to brew tea.

"Repairs, Megan, just repairs. The coaster and the Octopus and a few of the smaller rides." He leaned back in his chair as Megan turned to face him.

"How bad?"

Pop sighed, knowing it was better to tell her outright than to hedge. "Ten thousand, maybe fifteen."

Megan let out a long, steady breath. "Ten thousand dollars." She ran a hand under her bangs to rub her brow. There was no purpose in asking if he was sure. If he'd had any doubt, he'd have kept the matter to himself.

"Well, we can come up with five," she began, lumping the check she had just received from Katch into their savings. "We'll have to have a more exact amount so we can decide how big a loan we'll need."

"Banks take a dim view of lending great lumps of money to people my age," Pop murmured.

Because she saw he was tired and discouraged, she spoke briskly. "Don't be silly." She walked back to the stove to set on the kettle. "In any case, they'd be lending it to the park, wouldn't they?" She tried not to think of tight money and high interest rates.

"I'll go see a few people tomorrow," he promised, reaching for his pipe as if to indicate their business talk was over. "You're having dinner with Katch tonight?"

"Yes." Megan took out cups and saucers.

"Fine young man." He puffed pleasantly on his pipe. "I like him. Has style."

"He has style all right," she grumbled as the kettle began to sing. Carefully, she poured boiling water into cups.

"Knows how to fish," Pop pointed out.

"Which, of course, makes him a paragon of virtue."

"Well, it doesn't make me think any less of him." He spoke genially, smiling into Megan's face. "I couldn't help noticing the two of you on the wheel the other night. You looked real pretty together."

"Pop, really." Feeling her cheeks warm, Megan walked back to fiddle with the dishes in the sink.

"You seemed to like him well enough then," he pointed out before he tested his tea. "I didn't notice any objections when he kissed you." Pop sipped, enjoying. "In fact, you seemed to like it."

"Pop!" Megan turned back, astonished.

"Now, Meg, I wasn't spying," he said soothingly, and coughed to mask a chuckle. "You were right out in public, you know. I'd wager a lot of people noticed. Like I said, you looked real pretty together."

Megan came back to sit at the table without any idea of what she should say. "It was just a kiss," she managed at length. "It didn't mean anything."

Pop nodded twice and drank his tea.

"It didn't," Megan insisted.

He gave her one of his angelic smiles. "But you do like him, don't you?"

Megan dropped her eyes. "Sometimes," she murmured. "Sometimes I do."

Pop covered her hand with his and waited until she looked at him again. "Caring for someone is the easiest thing in the world if you let it be."

"I hardly know him," she said quickly.

"I trust him," Pop said simply.

Megan searched his face. "Why?"

After a shrug, Pop drew on his pipe again. "A feeling I have, a look in his eyes. In a people business like mine, you get to be a good judge of character. He has integrity. He wants his way, all right, but he doesn't cheat. That's important."

Megan sat silently for a moment, not touching her cooling tea. "He wants the park," she said quietly.

Pop looked at her through a nimbus of pipe smoke. "Yes, I know. He said so up front. He doesn't sneak around either." Pop's expression softened a bit as he looked into Megan's eyes. "Things don't always stay the same in life, Megan. That's what makes it work."

"I don't know what you mean. Do you…are you thinking of selling him the park?"

Pop heard the underlying hint of panic and patted her hand again. "Let's not worry about that now. The first problem is getting the rides repaired for the Easter break. Why don't you wear the yellow dress I like tonight, Meg? The one with the little jacket. It makes me think of spring."

Megan considered questioning him further, then subsided. There was no harder nut to crack than her grandfather when he had made up his mind to close a subject. "All right. I think I'll go up and have a bath."

"Megan." She turned at the door and looked back at him. "Enjoy yourself. Sometimes it's best to roll with the punches."

When she walked away, he looked at the empty doorway and thoughtfully stroked his beard.

An hour later, Megan looked at herself in the yellow dress. The shade hinted at apricot and warmed against her skin. The lines were simple, suiting her willow-slim figure and height. Without the jacket, her arms and shoulders were bare but for wispy straps. She ran a brush through her hair in long, steady strokes. The tiny gold hoops in her ears were her only jewelry.

"Hey, Megan!"

The brush paused in midair as she watched her own eyes widen in the mirror. He wasn't really standing outside shouting for her!

"Meg!"

Shaking her head in disbelief, Megan went to the window. Katch stood two stories down. He lifted a hand in salute when she appeared in the window.

"What are you doing?" she demanded.

"Open the screen."

"Why?"

"Open it," he repeated.

"If you expect me to jump, you can forget it." Out of curiosity, she leaned out the window.

"Catch!"

Her reflexes responded before she could think. Megan reached for the bundle he tossed up to her, and found her hands full of daffodils. She buried her face in the bouquet.

"They're beautiful." Her eyes smiled over the blooms and down at him. "Thank you."

"You're welcome," he returned. "Are you coming down?"

"Yes." She tossed her hair behind her shoulder. "Yes, yes, in a minute."

Katch drove quickly and competently, but not toward Restaurant Row as Megan had anticipated. He turned toward the ocean and headed north. She relaxed, enjoying the quieting light of dusk and his effortless driving.

She recognized the area. The houses there were larger, more elaborate than those in and on the very outskirts of town. There were tall hedges to assure privacy both from other houses and the public beaches. There were neatly trimmed lawns, willows, blossoming crepe myrtle, and asphalt drives. Katch pulled into one set well away from the other homes and bordered by purplish shrubbery.

The house was small by the neighborhood standards, and done in the weathered wood Megan invariably found attractive. It was a split-level building, with an observation deck crowning the upper story.

"What's this?" she asked, liking the house immediately.

"This is where I live." Katch leaned across her to unlatch her door, then slid out his own side.

"You live here?"

Katch smiled at the surprised doubt in her voice. "I have to live somewhere, Meg."

She wandered farther along the stone path that led to the house. "I suppose I really didn't think about you buying a house here. It suggests roots."

"I have them," he told her. "I just transplant them easily."

She looked at the house, the widespread yard. "You've picked the perfect spot."

Katch took her hand, interlocking fingers. "Come inside," he invited.

"When did you buy this?" she asked as they climbed the front steps.

"Oh, a few months ago when I came through. I moved in last week and haven't had a lot of time to look for furniture." The key shot into the lock. "I've picked up a few things here and there, and had others sent down from my apartment in New York."

It was scantily furnished, but with style. There was a low, sectional sofa in biscuit with a hodgepodge of colored pillows and a wicker throne chair coupled with a large hanging ivy in a pottery dish. A pair of étagères in brass and glass held a collection of shells; on the oak planked floor lay a large sisal rug.

The room was open, with stairs to the right leading to the second level, and a stone fireplace on the left wall. The quick survey showed Megan he had not placed her sculptures in the main room. She wondered fleetingly what he had done with them.

"It's wonderful, Katch." She wandered to a window. The lawn sloped downward and ended in tall hedges that gave the house comfortable privacy. "Can you see the ocean from the top level?"

When he didn't answer, she turned back to him. Her smile faded against the intensity of his gaze. Her heart beat faster. This was the part of him she had to fear, not the amiable gallant who had tossed her daffodils.

She tilted her head back, afraid, but wanting to meet him equally. He brought his hands to her face, and she felt the hardness of his palms on her skin. He brushed her hair back from her face as he brought her closer. He lowered his mouth, pausing only briefly before it claimed hers, as if to ascertain the need mirrored in her eyes. The kiss was instantly deep, instantly seeking.

She had been a fool—a fool to believe she could talk herself out of being in love with him. A fool to think that reason had anything to do with the heart.

When Katch drew her away, Megan pressed her cheek against his chest, letting her arms wind their way around his waist. His hesitation was almost too brief to measure before he gathered her close. She felt his lips in her hair and sighed from the sheer joy of it. His heartbeat was quick and steady in her ear.

"Did you say something?" he murmured.

"Hmm? When?"

"Before." His fingers came up to massage the back of her neck. Megan shivered with pleasure as she tried to remember the world before she had been in his arms.

"I think I asked if I could see the ocean from the top level."

"Yes." Again he took his hands to her face to tilt it back for one long, searing kiss. "You can."

"Will you show me?"

The grip on her skin tightened and her eyes closed in anticipation of the next kiss. But he drew her away until only their hands were touching. "After dinner."

Megan, content with looking at him, smiled. "Are we eating here?"

"I hate restaurants," Katch said, leading her toward the kitchen.

"An odd sentiment from a man who owns one."

"Let's say there are times when I prefer more intimate surroundings."

"I see." He pushed open the door to the kitchen and Megan glanced around at efficiency in wood and stainless steel. "And who's doing the cooking this time?"

"We are," he said easily, and grinned at her. "How do you like your steak?"

There was a rich, red wine to accompany the meal they ate at a smoked-glass table. A dozen candles flickered on a sideboard behind them, held in small brass holders. Megan's mood was as mellow as the wine that waltzed in her head. The man across from her held her in the palm of his hand. When she rose to stack the dishes, he took her hand. "Not now. There's a moon tonight."

Without hesitation, she went with him.

They climbed the stairs together, wide, uncarpeted stairs which were split into two sections by a landing. He led her through the main bedroom, a room dominated by a large bed with brass head- and footboards. There were long glass doors which led to a walkway. From there, stairs ascended to the observation deck.

Megan could hear the breakers before she moved to the rail. Beyond the hedgerow, the surf was turbulent. White water frothed against the dark. The moon's light was thin, but was aided by the power of uncountable stars.

She took a long breath and leaned on the rail. "It's

lovely here. I never tire of looking at the ocean." There was a click from his lighter, then tobacco mixed pleasantly with the scent of the sea.

"Do you ever think about traveling?"

Megan moved her shoulders, a sudden, restless gesture. "Of course, sometimes. It isn't possible right now."

Katch drew on the thin cigar. "Where would you go?"

"Where would I go?" she repeated.

"Yes, where would you go if you could?" The smoke from his cigar wafted upward and vanished. "Pretend, Meg. You like to pretend, don't you?"

She closed her eyes a moment, letting the wine swim with her thoughts. "New Orleans," she murmured. "I've always wanted to see New Orleans. And Paris. When I was young I used to dream about studying in Paris like the great artists." She opened her eyes again. "You've been there, I suppose. To New Orleans and to Paris?"

"Yes, I've been there."

"What are they like?"

Katch traced the line of her jaw with a fingertip before answering. "New Orleans smells of the river and swelters in the summer. There's music at all hours from open nightclubs and street musicians. It moves constantly, like New York, but at a more civilized pace."

"And Paris?" Megan insisted, wanting to see her wishes through his eyes. "Tell me about Paris."

"It's ancient and elegant, like a grand old woman. It's not very clean, but it never seems to matter. It's best in the spring; nothing smells like Paris in the spring. I'd like to take you there." Unexpectedly he took her hair in his hand. His eyes were intense again and direct on hers. "I'd like to see the emotions you control break loose. You'd never restrict them in Paris."

"I don't do that." Something more than wine began to swim in her head.

He tossed the cigar over the rail, then his free hand came to her waist to press her body against his. "Don't you?" There was a hint of impatience in his voice as he began to slide the jacket from her shoulders. "You've passion, but you bank it down. It escapes into your work, but even that's kept closed up in a studio. When I kiss you, I can taste it struggling to the surface."

He freed her arms from the confines of the jacket and laid it over the rail. Slowly, deliberately, he ran his fingers over the naked skin, feeling the warmth of response. "One day it's going to break loose. I intend to be there when it does."

Katch pushed the straps from her shoulders and replaced them with his lips. Megan made no protest as the kisses trailed to her throat. His tongue played lightly with the pulse as his hand came up to cup her breast. But when his mouth came to hers, the gentleness fled, and with it her passivity. Hunger incited hunger.

When he nipped her bottom lip, she gasped with pleasure. His tongue was avid, searching while his hands began a quest of their own. He slipped the bodice of her dress to her waist, murmuring with approval as he found her naked breasts taut with desire. Megan allowed him his freedom, riding on the crest of the wave that rose inside her. She had no knowledge to guide her, no experience. Desire ruled and instinct followed.

She trailed her fingers along the back of his neck, kneading the warm skin, thrilling to the response she felt to her touch. Here was a power she had never explored. She slipped her hands under the back of his sweater. Their journey was slow, exploring. She felt the muscles of his shoulders tense as her hands played over them.

The quality of the kiss changed from demanding to urgent. His passion swamped her, mixing with her own until the combined power was more than she could bear. The ache came from nowhere and spread through her with impossible rapidity. She hurt for him. Desire was a pain as sharp as it was irresistible. In surrender, in anticipation, Megan swayed against him.

"Katch." Her voice was husky. "I want to stay with you tonight."

She was crushed against him for a moment, held so tightly, so strongly, there was no room for breath. Then, slowly, she felt him loosen his hold. Taking her by the shoulders, Katch looked down at her, his eyes dark, spearing into hers. Her breath was uneven; shivers raced along her skin. Slowly, with hands that barely touched her skin, he slipped her dress back into place.

"I'll take you home now."

The shock of rejection struck her like a blow. Her mouth trembled open, then shut again. Quickly, fighting against the tears that were pressing for release, she fumbled for her jacket.

"Meg." He reached out to touch her shoulders, but she backed away.

"No. No, don't touch me." The tears were thickening her voice. She swallowed. "I won't be patted on the head. It appears I misunderstood."

"You didn't misunderstand anything," he tossed back. "And don't cry, damn it."

"I have no intention of crying," she said. "I'd like to

go home." The hurt was in her eyes, shimmering behind the tears she denied.

"We'll talk." Katch took her hand, but she jerked
it away.

"Oh, no. No, we won't." Megan straightened her
shoulders and looked at him squarely. "We had dinner—
things got a bit beyond what they should have. It's as
simple as that, and it's over."

"It's not simple or over, Meg." Katch took another
long look into her eyes. "But we'll drop it for now."

Megan turned away and walked back down the stairs.

Chapter 7

Amusement parks lose their mystique in the light of day. Dirt, scratched paint and dents show up. What is shiny and bright under artificial light is ordinary in the sunshine. Only the very young or the very young hearted can believe in magic when faced with reality.

Megan knew her grandfather was perennially young. She loved him for it. Fondly, she watched him supervising repairs on the Haunted Castle. His ghosts, she thought with a smile, are important to him. She walked beside the track, avoiding her own ghost along the way. It had been ten days since Pop had told her of the repair problems. Ten days since she had seen Katch. Megan pushed thoughts of him from her mind and concentrated on her own reality—her grandfather and their park. She was old enough to know what was real and what was fantasy.

"Hi," she called out from behind him. "How are things going?"

Pop turned at the sound of her voice, and his grin was expansive. "Just fine, Megan." The sound of repairs echoed around his words. "Quicker than I thought they would. We'll be rolling before the Easter rush." He swung an arm around her shoulder and squeezed. "The smaller rides are already back in order. How about you?"

She made no objection when he began to steer her outside. The noise made it difficult to hear. "What about me?" she replied. The sudden flash of sunlight made her blink. The spring day had all the heat of midsummer.

"You've that unhappy look in your eyes. Have had, for more than a week." Pop rubbed his palm against her shoulder as if to warm her despite the strength of the sun. "You know you don't hide things from me, Megan. I know you too well."

She was silent a moment, wanting to choose her words carefully. "I wasn't trying to hide anything, Pop." Megan shrugged, turning to watch the crew working on the roller coaster. "It's just not important enough to talk about, that's all. How long before the coaster's fixed?"

"Important enough to make you unhappy," he countered, ignoring her evasion. "That's plenty important to me. You haven't gotten too old to talk to me about your problems now, have you?"

She turned dark apologetic eyes on him. "Oh no, Pop, I can always talk to you."

"Well," he said simply, "I'm listening."

"I made a mistake, that's all." She shook her head and would have walked closer to inspect the work crew had he not held her to him with a firm hand.

"Megan." Pop placed both hands on her shoulders and looked into her eyes. As they were nearly the same height, their eyes were level. "I'm going to ask you straight," he continued. "Are you in love with him?"

"No," she denied quickly.

Pop raised an eyebrow. "I didn't have to mention any names, I see."

Megan paused a moment. She had forgotten how shrewd her grandfather could be. "I thought I was," she said more carefully. "I was wrong."

"Then why are you so unhappy?"

"Pop, please." She tried to back away, but again his broad hands held her steady.

"You've always given me straight answers, Meg, even when I've had to drag them out of you."

She sighed, knowing evasions and half-truths were useless when he was in this mood. "All right. Yes, I'm in love with him, but it doesn't matter."

"Not a very bright statement from a bright girl like you," he said with a gentle hint of disapproval. Megan shrugged. "Why don't you explain why being in love doesn't matter," he invited.

"Well, it certainly doesn't work if you're not loved back," Megan murmured.

"Who says you're not?" Pop wanted to know. His voice was so indignant, she felt some of the ache subside.

"Pop." Her expression softened. "Just because you love me doesn't mean everyone else does."

"What makes you so sure he doesn't?" her grandfather argued. "Did you ask him?"

"No!" Megan was so astonished, she nearly laughed at the thought.

"Why not? Things are simpler that way."

Megan took a deep breath, hoping to make him understand. "David Katcherton isn't a man who falls in love with a woman, not seriously. And certainly not with someone like me." The broad gesture she made was an attempt to enhance an explanation she knew was far from adequate. "He's been to Paris, he lives in New York. He has a sister named Jessica."

"That clears things up," Pop agreed, and Megan made a quick sound of frustration.

"I've never been anywhere." She dragged a hand through her hair. "In the summer I see millions, literally millions of people, but they're all transient. I don't know who they are. The only people I really know are ones who live right here. The farthest I've been away from the beach is Charleston."

Pop brushed a hand over her hair to smooth it. "I've kept you too close," he murmured. "I always told myself there'd be other times."

"Oh no, Pop, I didn't mean it that way." She threw her arms around him, burying her face in his shoulder. "I didn't mean to sound that way. I love you, I love it here. I wouldn't change anything. That was hateful of me."

He laughed and patted her back. The subtle scent of her perfume reminded him forcefully that she was no longer a girl but a woman. The years had been incredibly quick. "You've never done a hateful thing in your life. We both know you've wanted to see a bit of the world, and I know you've stuck close to keep an eye on me. Oh yes," he said, anticipating her objection. "And I was selfish enough to let you."

"You've never done anything selfish," she retorted and drew away. "I only meant that Katch and I have so little common ground. He's bound to see things differently than I do. I'm out of my depth with him."

"You're a strong swimmer, as I recall." Pop shook his head at her expression and sighed. "All right, we'll let it lie awhile. You're also stubborn."

"Adamant," she corrected, smiling again. "It's a nicer word."

"Just a fancy way of saying pigheaded," Pop said bluntly, but his eyes smiled back at her. "Why aren't you back in your studio instead of hanging around an amusement park in the middle of the day?"

"It wasn't going very well," she confessed, thinking of the half-carved face that haunted her. "Besides, I've always had a thing for amusement parks." She tucked her arm in his as they began to walk again.

"Well, this one'll be in apple-pie order in another week," Pop said, looking around in satisfaction. "With luck, we'll have a good season and be able to pay back a healthy chunk of that ten thousand."

"Maybe the bank will send us some customers so they'll get their money faster," Megan suggested, half listening to the sound of hammer against wood as they drew closer to the roller coaster.

"Oh, I didn't get the money from the bank, I got it from—" Pop cut himself off abruptly. With a cough and a wheeze, he bent down to tie his shoe.

"You didn't get the money from the bank?" Megan frowned at the snowy white head in puzzlement. "Well, where in the world did you get it then?"

His answer was an unintelligible grunt.

"You don't know anybody with that kind of money," she began with a half-smile. "Where…" The smile flew away. "No. No, you didn't." Even as she denied it, Megan knew it had to be the truth. "You didn't get it from him?"

"Oh now, Megan, you weren't to know." Distress showed in his eyes and seemed to weaken his voice. "He especially didn't want you to know."

"Why?" she demanded. "Why did you do it?"

"It just sort of happened, Meg." Pop reached out to pat her hand in his old, soothing fashion. "He was here, I was telling him about the repairs and getting a loan, and he offered. It seemed like the perfect solution." He fiddled with his shoestrings. "Banks poke around and take all that time for paperwork, and he isn't charging me nearly as much interest. I thought you'd be happy about that…" He trailed off.

"Is everything in writing?" she asked, deadly calm.

"Of course." Pop assumed a vaguely injured air. "Katch said it didn't matter, but I know how fussy you are, so I had papers drawn up, nice and legal."

"Didn't matter," she repeated softly. "And what did you use as collateral?"

"The park, naturally."

"Naturally," she repeated. Fury bubbled in the single word. "I bet he loved that."

"Now, don't you worry, Megan. Everything's coming along just fine. The repairs are going well, and we'll be opening right on schedule. Besides," he added with a sigh, "you weren't even supposed to know. Katch wanted it that way."

"Oh, I'm sure he did," she said bitterly. "I'm sure he did."

Turning, she darted away. Pop watched her streak out of sight, then hauled himself to his feet. She had the devil's own temper when she cut loose, that girl.

Brushing his hands together, he grinned. That, he decided, pleased with his own maneuvering, should stir up something.

Megan brought the bike to a halt at the crest of Katch's drive, then killed the engine. She took off her helmet and clipped it on the seat. He was not, she determined, going to get away with it.

Cutting across the lawn, she marched to the front door. The knock was closer to a pound but still brought no response. Megan stuffed her hands into her pockets and scowled. Her bike sat behind his black Porsche. Ignoring amenities, she tried the knob. When it turned, she didn't hesitate. She opened the door and walked inside.

The house was quiet. Instinct told her immediately that no one was inside. Still, she walked through the living room looking for signs of him.

A watch, wafer-thin and gold, was tossed on the glass shelves of the étagère. A Nikon camera sat on the coffee table, its back open and empty of film. A pair of disreputable tennis shoes were half under the couch. A volume of John Cheever lay beside them.

Abruptly, she realized what she had done. She'd intruded where she had no right. She was both uncomfortable and fascinated. An ashtray held the short stub of a thin cigar. After a brief struggle with her conscience, she walked toward the kitchen. She wasn't prying, she told herself, only making certain he wasn't home. After all, his car was here and the door had been unlocked.

There was a cup in the sink and a half pot of cold coffee on the stove. He had spilled some on the counter and neglected to wipe it up. Megan curtailed the instinctive move to reach for a dish towel. As she turned to leave, a low mechanical hum from outside caught her attention. She walked to the window and saw him.

He was coming from the south side of the lawn, striding behind a power mower. He was naked to the waist, with jeans low and snug at his hips. He was tanned, a deep honey gold that glistened now with the effort of manual labor. She admired the play of muscles rippling down his arms and across his back.

Stepping back from the window with a jerk, she stormed through the side kitchen door and raced across the lawn.

The flurry of movement and a flash of crimson caught his eye. Katch glanced over as Megan moved toward him in a red tailored shirt and white jeans. Squinting against the sun, he wiped the back of his hand across his brow. He reached down and shut off the mower as she came to him.

"Hello, Meg," he said lightly, but his eyes weren't as casual.

"You have nerve, Katcherton," she began. "But even I didn't think you'd take advantage of a trusting old man."

He lifted a brow and leaned against the mower's handle. "Once more," he requested, "with clarity."

"You're the type who has to poke your fingers into other people's business," she continued. "You just had to be at the park, you just had to make a magnanimous offer with your tidy little pile of money."

"Ah, a glimmer of light." He stretched his back. "I didn't think you'd be thrilled the money came from me. It seems I was right."

"You knew I'd never allow it," she declared.

"I don't believe I considered that." He leaned on the mower again, but there was nothing restful in the gesture. "You don't run Pop's life from what I've seen, Meg, and you certainly don't run mine."

She did her best to keep her tone even. "I have a great deal of interest in the park and everything that pertains to it."

"Fine, then you should be pleased that you have the money for the repairs quickly, and at a low rate of interest." His tone was cool and businesslike.

"Why?" she demanded. "Why did you lend us the money?"

"I don't," Katch said after a long, silent moment, "owe you any explanation."

"Then I'll give you one," Megan tossed back. There was passion in her voice. "You saw an opportunity and grabbed it. I suppose that's what people do in your sort of world. Take, without the least thought of the people involved."

"Perhaps I'm confused." His eyes were slate, opaque and unreadable. His voice matched them. "I was under the impression that I gave something."

"*Lent* something," Megan corrected. "With the park as collateral."

"If that's your problem, take it up with your grandfather." Katch bent down, reaching for the cord to restart the mower.

"You had no right to take advantage of him. He trusts everyone."

Katch released the cord again with a snap. "A shame it's not an inherited quality."

"I've no reason to trust you."

"And every reason, it appears, to mistrust me since

the first moment." His eyes had narrowed as if in speculation. "Is it just me or a general antipathy to men?"

She refused to dignify the question with an answer. "You want the park," she began.

"Yes, and I made that clear from the beginning." Katch shoved the mower aside so that there was no obstacle between them. "I still intend to have it, but I don't need to be devious to get it. I still intend to have you." She stepped back but he was too quick. His fingers curled tightly around her upper arm. "Maybe I made a mistake by letting you go the other night."

"You didn't want me. It's just a game."

"Didn't want you?" She made another quick attempt to pull away and failed. "No, that's right, I didn't want you." He pulled her against him and her mouth was crushed and conquered. Her mind whirled with the shock of it. "I don't want you now." Before she could speak, his mouth savaged hers again. There was a taste of brutality he had never shown her. "Like I haven't wanted you for days." He pulled her to the ground.

"No," she said, frightened, "don't." But his lips were silencing hers again.

There was none of the teasing persuasion he had shown her before, no light arrogance. These were primordial demands, eliciting primordial responses from her. He would take what he wanted, his way. He plundered, dragging her with him as he raced for more. Then his lips left hers, journeying to her throat before traveling downward. Megan felt she was suffocating, suffused with heat. Her breath caught in her lungs, emerging in quick gasps or moans. His fingers ran a bruising trail over her quivering flesh. He ran his thumb over the point of her breast, back and forth, until she was beyond fear, beyond thought. His mouth came back to hers, fever hot, desperate. She murmured mindlessly, clinging to him as her body shuddered with waves of need.

Katch lifted his head, and his breath was warm and erratic on her face. Megan's lids fluttered open, revealing eyes dazed with passion, heavy with desire. Silently, she trembled. If words had been hers, she would have told him that she loved him. There was no pride in her, no shame, only soaring need and a love that was painful in its strength.

"This isn't the place for you." His voice was rough as he rolled over on his back. They lay there a moment, side by side, without touching. "And this isn't the way."

Her mind was fogged, and her blood surging. "Katch," Megan managed his name and struggled to sit up. His eyes lingered on her form, then slid up slowly to brood on her face. It was flushed and aware. She wanted to touch him but was afraid.

For a moment their eyes met. "Did I hurt you?"

She shook her head in denial. Her body ached with longing.

"Go home then." He rose, giving her a last, brief glance. "Before I do." He turned and left her.

Megan heard the slam of the kitchen door.

Chapter 8

It was difficult for Megan to cope with the two-week influx of tourists and sun seekers. They came, as they did every Easter, in droves. It was a preview of what the summer would hold. They came to bake on the beach and impress those left at home with a spring tan. They came to be battered and bounced around by the waves. They came to have fun. And what better place to find it than on white sand beaches or in an ocean with a gentle undertow and cresting waves? They came to laugh and sought their entertainment on spiraling water slides, in noisy arcades or crowded amusement parks.

For the first time in her life, Megan found herself resenting the intrusion. She wanted the quiet, the solitude that went with a resort town in its off-season. She wanted to be alone, to work, to heal. It seemed her art was the only thing she could turn to for true comfort.

She was unwilling to speak of her feelings to her grandfather. There was still too much to be sorted out in her own mind. Knowing her, and her need for privacy, Pop didn't question.

The hours she spent at the park were passed mechanically. The faces she saw were all strangers. Megan resented it. She resented their enjoyment when her own life was in such turmoil. She found solace in her studio. If the light in her studio burned long past midnight, she never noticed the time. Her energy was boundless, a nervous, trembling energy that kept her going.

It was afternoon at the amusement park. At the kiddie cars Megan was taking tickets and doing her best to keep the more aggressive youngsters from trampling others. Each time the fire engines, race cars, police cruisers and ambulances were loaded, she pushed the lever which sent the caravan around in its clanging, roaring circle. Children grinned fiercely and gripped steering wheels.

One toddler rode as fire chief with eyes wide with stunned pleasure. Even though she'd been on duty nearly four hours, Megan smiled.

"Excuse me." Megan glanced over at the voice, prepared to answer a parental question. The woman was an exquisite blonde, with a mane of hair tied back from a delicately molded face. "You're Megan, aren't you? Megan Miller?"

"Yes. May I help you?"

"I'm Jessica Delaney."

Megan wondered that she hadn't seen it instantly. "Katch's sister."

"Yes." Jessica smiled. "How clever of you—but Katch

told me you were. There is a family resemblance, of course, but so few people notice it unless we're standing together."

Megan's artist eyes could see the similar bone structure beneath the surface differences. Jessica's eyes were blue, as Katch had said, and the brows above them more delicate than his, but there were the same thick lashes and long lids.

"I'm glad to meet you." Megan reached for something to say. "Are you visiting Katch?" She didn't look like a woman who would patronize amusement parks, more likely country clubs or theaters.

"For a day or so." Jessica gestured to the adjoining ride where children flew miniature piper cubs in the inevitable circle. "My family's with me. Rob, my husband." Megan smiled at a tall man with a straight shock of dark hair and an attractive, angular face. "And my girls, Erin and Laura." She nodded to the two caramel-haired girls of approximately four and six riding double in a plane.

"They're beautiful."

"We like them," Jessica said comfortably. "Katch didn't know where I might find you in the park, but he described you very accurately."

"Is he here?" Megan asked, trying without much success to sound offhanded even as her eyes scanned the crowd.

"No, he had some business to attend to."

The timer rang, signaling the ride's end. "Excuse me a moment," Megan murmured. Grateful for the interruption, she supervised the unloading and loading of children. It gave her the time she needed to steady herself. Her two final customers were Katch's nieces.

Erin, the elder, smiled at her with eyes the identical shade of her uncle's.

"I'm driving," she said positively as her sister settled beside her. "She only rides."

"I do not." Laura gripped the twin steering wheel passionately.

"It runs in the family," Jessica stated from behind her. "Stubbornness." Megan hooked the last safety belt and returned to the controls. "You've probably noticed it."

Megan smiled at her. "Yes, once or twice." The lights and noise spun and circled behind her.

"I know you're busy," Jessica stated, glancing at the packed vehicles.

Megan gave a small shrug as she followed her gaze. "It's mostly a matter of making certain everyone stays strapped in and no one's unhappy."

"My little angels," Jessica said, "will insist on dashing off to the next adventure the moment the ride's over." She paused. "Could we talk after you're finished here?"

Megan frowned. "Well, yes, I suppose… I'm due relief in an hour."

"Wonderful." Jessica's smile was as charming as her brother's. "I'd like to go to your studio, if that suits you. I could meet you in an hour and a half."

"At my studio?"

"Wonderful!" Jessica said again and patted Megan's hand. "Katch gave me directions."

The timer rang again, recalling Megan to duty. As she started yet another round of junior rides she wondered why Jessica had insisted on a date in her studio.

* * *

With a furrowed brow, Megan studied herself in the bedroom mirror. Would a man who admired Jessica's soft, delicate beauty be attracted to someone who seemed to be all planes and angles? Megan shrugged her shoulders as if it didn't matter. She twirled the stem of the brush idly between her fingers. She supposed that he, like the majority of people who came here, was looking for some passing entertainment.

"You are," she said softly to the woman in the glass, "such a fool." She closed her eyes, not wanting to see the reflected accusation. Because you can't let go, her mind continued ruthlessly. Because it doesn't really matter to you why he wanted you with him, just that he wanted you. And you wish, you wish with all your heart that he still did.

She shook her head, disturbing the work she had done with the brush. It was time to stop thinking of it. Jessica Delaney would be arriving any moment.

Why? Megan set down her brush and frowned into middle distance. Why was she coming? What could she possibly want? Megan still had no sensible answer. I haven't heard from Katch in two weeks, she reflected. Why should his sister suddenly want to see me?

The sound of a car pulling into the drive below interrupted her thoughts. Megan walked to the window in time to see Jessica get out of Katch's Porsche.

Megan reached the back stoop before Jessica, as she had been taking a long, leisurely look at the yard. "Hello." Megan felt awkward and rustic. She hesitated briefly before stepping away from the door.

"What a lovely place." Jessica's smile was so like

Katch's that Megan's heart lurched. "How I wish my azaleas looked like yours."

"Pop—my grandfather babies them."

"Yes." The blue eyes were warm and personal. "I've heard wonderful things about your grandfather. I'd love to meet him."

"He's still at the park." Her sense of awkwardness was fading. Charm definitely ran in the Katcherton family. "Would you like some coffee? Tea?"

"Maybe later. Let's go up to the studio, shall we?"

"If you don't mind my asking, Mrs. Delaney—"

"Jessica," she interrupted cheerfully and began to climb the open back stairs.

"Jessica," Megan agreed, "how did you know I had a studio, and that it was over the garage?"

"Oh, Katch told me," Jessica said breezily. "He tells me a great many things." She stood to the side of the door and waited for Megan to open it. "I'm very anxious to see your work. I dabble in oil from time to time."

"Do you?" Jessica's interest now made more sense. Artistic kinship.

"Badly, I'm afraid, which is a constant source of frustration to me." Again the Katcherton smile bloomed on her face.

Megan's reaction was unexpectedly sharp and swift. She fumbled for the doorknob. "I've never had much luck on canvas," she said quickly. She needed words, lots of words to cover what she feared was much too noticeable. "Nothing seems to come out the way I intend," she continued as they entered the studio. "It's maddening not to be able to express yourself properly. I do some airbrushing during the summer rush, but..."

Jessica wasn't listening. She moved around the room

much the same way her brother had—intently, grace-
fully, silently. She fingered a piece here, lifted a piece
there. Once, she studied a small ivory unicorn for so
long, Megan fidgeted with nerves.

What was she doing? she wondered. *And why?*

Sunlight stippled the floor. Dust motes danced in the
early evening light. Too late, Megan recalled the bust
of Katch. One slanted beam of sun fell on it, highlight-
ing the planes the chisel had already defined. Though
it was still rough hewn and far from finished, it was
unmistakably Katch. Feeling foolish, Megan walked
over to stand in front of it, hoping to conceal it from
Jessica's view.

"Katch was right," Jessica murmured. She still held
the unicorn, stroking it with her fingertips. "He invariably is. Normally that annoys me to distraction, but not
this time." The resemblance to Katch was startling now.
Megan's fingers itched to make a quick sketch even as
she tried to follow the twisting roads in Jessica's conversation.

"Right about what?"

"Your extraordinary talent."

"What?" Meg's eyes widened.

"Katch told me your work was remarkable," she went
on, giving the unicorn a final study before setting it
down. "I agreed when I received the two pieces he sent
up to me, but they were only two, after all." She picked
up a chisel and tapped it absently against her palm while
her eyes continued to wander. "This is astonishing."

"He sent you the sculptures he bought from me?"

"Yes, a few weeks ago. I was very impressed." Jessica set down the chisel with a clatter and moved to a
nearly completed study in limestone of a woman rising

from the sea. It was the piece Megan had been working on before she had set it aside to begin Katch's bust. "This is fabulous!" Jessica declared. "I'm going to have to have it as well as the unicorn. The response to the two pieces Katch sent me has been very favorable."

"I don't understand what you're talking about." Try as she might, Megan couldn't keep up with Jessica's conversation. "Whose response?"

"My clients'," said Jessica. "At my gallery in New York." She gave Megan a brilliant smile. "Didn't I tell you I run my own gallery?"

"No," Megan answered. "No, you didn't."

"I suppose I thought Katch did. I'd better start at the beginning then."

"I'd really appreciate it if you would," Megan told her, and waited until she had settled herself in the small wooden chair beside her.

"Katch sent me two of your pieces a few weeks ago," Jessica began briskly. "He wanted a professional opinion. I may only be able to dabble in oil, but I know art." She spoke with a confidence that Megan recognized. "Since I knew I'd never make it as a working artist, I put all the years of study to good use. I opened a gallery in Manhattan. *Jessica's.* Over the past six years, I've developed a rather nice clientele." She smiled. "So naturally, when my wandering brother saw your work, he sent it off to me. He always has his instincts verified by an expert, then plunges along his own way notwithstanding." She sighed indulgently. "I happen to know he was advised against building that hospital in Central Africa last year but he did it anyway. He does what he wants to."

"Hospital." Megan barely made the jump to Jessica's new train of thought.

"Yes, a children's hospital. He has a soft spot for kids." Jessica tried to speak teasingly, but the love came through. "He did some astonishing things for orphaned refugees after Vietnam. And there was the really fabulous little park he built in New South Wales."

Megan sat dumbly. Could they possibly be speaking about the same David Katcherton? Was this the man who had brashly approached her in the local market?

She remembered with uncomfortable clarity that she had accused him of trying to cheat her grandfather. She had told herself that he was an opportunist, a man spoiled by wealth and good looks. She'd tried to tell herself he was irresponsible, undependable, a man in search of his own pleasure.

"I didn't know," she murmured. "I didn't know anything about it."

"Oh, Katch keeps a low profile when he chooses," Jessica told her. "And he chooses to have no publicity when he's doing that sort of thing. He has incredible energy and outrageous self-confidence, but he's also very warm." Her gaze slipped beyond Megan's shoulder. "But then, you appear to know him well."

For a moment, Megan regarded Jessica blankly. Then she twisted her head and saw Katch's bust. In her confusion, she had forgotten her desire to conceal it. Slowly, she turned her head back, trying to keep her voice and face passive.

"No. No, really I don't think I know him at all. He has a fascinating face. I couldn't resist sculpting it."

She noted a glint of understanding in Jessica's eyes. "He's a fascinating man," Jessica murmured.

Megan's gaze faltered.

"I'm sorry," Jessica said immediately. "I've intruded, a bad habit of mine. We won't talk about Katch. Let's talk about your showing."

Megan lifted her eyes again. "My what?"

"Your showing," Jessica repeated, dashing swiftly up a new path. "When do you think you'll have enough pieces ready? You certainly have a tremendous start here, and Katch mentioned something about a gallery in town having some of your pieces. I think we can shoot for the fall."

"Please, Jessica, I don't know what you're talking about." A note of panic slipped into Megan's voice. It was faint, almost buried, but Jessica detected it. She reached over and took both of Megan's hands. The grip was surprisingly firm.

"Megan, you have something special, something powerful. It's time to share it." She rose then, urging Megan up with her. "Let's have that coffee now, shall we? And we'll talk about it."

An hour later, Megan sat alone in the kitchen. Darkness was encroaching, but she didn't rise from the table to switch on the light. Two cups sat, her own half-filled with now cold coffee, Jessica's empty but for dregs. She tried to take her mind methodically over what had happened in the last sixty minutes.

A showing at Jessica's, an art gallery in Manhattan. New York. A public show. Of her work.

It didn't happen, she thought. I imagined it. Then she looked down at the empty cup across from her. The air still smelled faintly of Jessica's light, sophisticated scent.

Half-dazed, Megan took both cups to the sink and

automatically began rinsing them. How did she talk me into it? she wondered. I was agreeing to dates and details before I had agreed to do the showing. Does anyone ever say no to a Katcherton? She sighed and looked down at her wet hands. I have to call him. The knowledge increased the sense of panic. *I have to.*

Carefully, she placed the washed cups and saucers in the drainboard. I have to thank him. Nerves fluttered in her throat, but she made a pretense, for herself, of casually drying her damp hands on the hips of her jeans. She walked to the wall phone beside the stove.

"It's simple," she whispered, then bit her lip. She cleared her throat. "All I have to do is thank him, that's all. It'll only take a minute." Megan reached for the phone, then drew her hand away. Her mind raced on with her heartbeat.

She lifted the receiver. She knew the number. Hadn't she started to dial it a dozen times during the past two weeks? She took a long breath before pushing the first digit. It would take five minutes, and then, in all probability, she'd have no reason to contact him again. It would be better if they erased the remnants of their last meeting. It would be easier if their relationship ended on a calmer, more civilized note. Megan pressed the last button and waited for the click of connection, the whisper of transmitters and the ring.

It took four rings—four long, endless rings before he picked up the phone.

"Katch." His name was barely audible. She closed her eyes.

"Meg?"

"Yes, I…" She fought herself to speak. "I hope I'm

not calling you at a bad time." How trite, she thought desperately. How ordinary.

"Are you all right?" There was concern in the question.

"Yes, yes, of course." Her mind fretted for the simple, casual words she had planned to speak. "Katch, I wanted to talk to you. Your sister was here—"

"I know, she got back a few minutes ago." There was a trace of impatience in his tone. "Is anything wrong?"

"No, nothing's wrong." Her voice refused to level. Megan searched for a quick way to end the conversation.

"Are you alone?"

"Yes, I…"

"I'll be there in ten minutes."

"No." Megan ran a frustrated hand through her hair. "No, please—"

"Ten minutes," he repeated and broke the connection.

Chapter 9

Megan stared at the dead receiver for several silent moments. How had she, in a few uncompleted sentences, managed to make such a mess of things? She didn't want him to come. She never wanted to see him again. *That is a lie.*

Carefully, Megan replaced the receiver. I do want to see him, she admitted, have wanted to see him for days. It's just that I'm afraid to see him. Turning, she gazed blindly around the kitchen. The room was almost in complete darkness now. The table and chairs were dark shadows. She walked to the switch, avoiding obstacles with the knowledge of years. The room flooded with brightness. That's better, she thought, more secure in the artificial light. Coffee, she decided, needing something, anything, to occupy her hands. I'll make fresh coffee.

Megan went to the percolator and began a step-by-step preparation, but her nerves continued to jump. In a few moments, she hoped, she'd be calm again. When he arrived, she would say what she needed to say, and then they would part.

The phone rang, and she jolted, juggling the cup she held and nearly dropping it. Chiding herself, Megan set it down and answered the call.

"Hello, Megan." Pop's voice crackled jovially across the wire.

"Pop…are you still at the park?" What time is it? she wondered distractedly and glanced down at her watch.

"That's why I called. George stopped by. We're going to have dinner in town. I didn't want you to worry."

"I won't." She smiled as the band of tension around her head loosened. "I suppose you and George have a lot of fish stories to exchange."

"His have gotten bigger since he retired," Pop claimed. "Hey, why don't you run into town, sweetheart? We'll treat you."

"You two just want an audience," she accused and her smile deepened with Pop's chuckle. "But I'll pass tonight, thanks. As I recall, there's some leftover spaghetti in the fridge."

"I'll bring you back dessert." It was an old custom. For as long as Megan could remember, if Pop had dinner without her, he'd bring her back some treat. "What do you want?"

"Rainbow sherbet," she decided instantly. "Have a good time."

"I will, darling. Don't work too late."

As she hung up the phone, Megan asked herself why she hadn't told her grandfather of Katch's impending visit. Why hadn't she mentioned Jessica or the incredible plans that had been made? It has to wait until we can talk, she told herself. Really talk. It's the only way I'll be certain how he really feels—and how everything will affect him.

It's probably a bad idea. Megan began to fret, pushing a hand through her hair in agitation. It's a crazy idea. How can I go to New York and—

Her thoughts were interrupted by the glaring sweep of headlights against the kitchen window. She struggled to compose herself, going deliberately to the cupboard to close it before heading to the screen door.

Katch stepped onto the stoop as she reached for the handle. For a moment, in silence, they studied each other through the mesh. She heard the soft flutter of moths' wings on the outside light.

Finally he turned the knob and opened the door. After he had shut it quietly behind him, he reached up to touch her cheek. His hand lingered there while his eyes traveled her face.

"You sounded upset."

Megan moistened her lips. "No, no, I'm fine." She stepped back so that his palm no longer touched her skin. Slowly, his eyes on hers, Katch lowered his hand. "I'm sorry I bothered you—"

"Megan, stop it." His voice was quiet and controlled. Her eyes came back to his, a little puzzled, a little desperate. "Stop backing away from me. Stop apologizing."

Her hands fluttered once before she could control the movement. "I'm making coffee," she began. "It should be ready in a minute." She would have turned to arrange the cups and saucers, but he took her arm.

"I didn't come for coffee." His hand slid down until

it encircled her wrist. Her pulse vibrated against his fingers.

"Katch, please, don't make this difficult."

Something flared in his eyes while she watched. Then it was gone, and her hand was released. "I'm sorry. I've had some difficulty the past couple of weeks dealing with what happened the last time I saw you." He noted the color that shot into her cheeks, but she kept her eyes steady. He slipped his hands into his pockets. "Megan, I'd like to make it up to you."

Megan shook her head, disturbed by the gentleness in his voice, and turned to the coffee pot.

"Don't you want to forgive me?"

The question had her turning back, her eyes darkened with distressed confusion. "No...that is, yes, of course."

"Of course you don't want to forgive me?" There was a faint glimmer of a smile in his eyes and the charm was around his mouth. She could feel herself sinking.

"Yes, of course I forgive you," she corrected and this time did turn to the coffee. "It's forgotten." He laid his hands on her shoulders, and she jumped.

"Is it?" Katch turned her until they were again face-to-face. The glimpse of humor in his eyes was gone. "You can't seem to abide my touching you. I don't much like thinking I frighten you."

She made a conscious effort to relax under his hands. "You don't frighten me, Katch," Megan murmured. "You confuse me. Constantly."

She watched his brow lift in consideration. "I don't have any intention of confusing you. I am sorry, Megan."

"Yes." She smiled, recognizing the simple sincerity. "I know you are."

He drew her closer. "Can we kiss and make up then?"

Megan started to protest, but his mouth was already on hers, light and gentle. Her heart began to hammer in her throat. He made no attempt to deepen the kiss. His hands were easy on her shoulders. Against all the warnings of her mind, she relaxed against him, inviting him to take whatever he chose. But he took no more.

Katch drew her away, waiting until her heavy lids fluttered open before he touched her hair. Without speaking, he turned and paced to the window. Megan struggled to fill the new gap.

"I wanted to talk to you about your sister." She busied her hands with the now noisy percolator. "Or, more accurately, about what Jessica came to see me about."

Katch turned his head, watching her pour the coffee into the waiting cups. He walked to the refrigerator and took out the milk.

"All right." Standing beside her now, he poured milk into one cup and, at her nod, into the second.

"Why didn't you tell me you were sending my work to your sister?"

"I thought it best to wait until I had her opinion." Katch sat beside Megan and cradled the cup in both hands. "I trust her.... And I thought you'd trust her opinion more than mine. Are you going to do the showing? Jessica and I didn't have time to talk before you called."

She shifted in her chair, studied her coffee, then looked directly at him. "She's very persuasive. I was agreeing before I realized it."

"Good," Katch said simply and drank.

"I want to thank you," Meg continued in a stronger voice, "for arranging things."

"I didn't arrange anything," he responded. "Jessica makes her own decisions, personal and professional. I simply sent her your sculptures for an opinion."

"Then I'll thank you for that, for making a move I might never have made for the hundreds of reasons which occurred to me five minutes after she'd left."

Katch shrugged. "All right, if you're determined to be grateful."

"I am," she said. "And I'm scared," she continued, "really terrified at the thought of putting my work on public display." Megan let out a shaky breath at the admission. "I may despise you when all this is over and art critics stomp all over my ego, so you'd better take the gratitude now."

Katch crossed to her, and her heart lifted dizzily, so sure was she that he would take her into his arms. He merely stroked her cheek with the back of his hand. "When you're a smashing success, you can give it to me again." He smiled at her, and the world snapped into sharp focus. Until that moment, she hadn't realized how dull everything had been without him.

"I'm so glad you came," she whispered and, unable to resist, slipped her arms around him, pressing her face into his shoulder. After a moment, he rested his hands lightly at her waist. "I'm sorry for the things I said… about the loan. I didn't mean any of it really, but I say horrible things when I lose my temper."

"Is this your turn to be penitent?"

He made her laugh. "Yes." She smiled and tilted back her head. Her arms stayed around him. He kissed her and drew away. Reluctantly, she let him slip out of her arms. Then he stood silently, staring down at her.

"What are you doing?" she asked with a quick, self-conscious smile.

"Memorizing your face. Have you eaten?"

She shook her head, wondering why it should come as a surprise that he continued to baffle her. "No, I was going to heat up some leftovers."

"Unacceptable. Want a pizza?"

"*Mmm,* I'd love it, but you have company."

"Jessica and Rob took the kids to play miniature golf. I won't be missed." Katch held out his hands. "Come on."

His eyes were smiling, and her heart was lost. "Oh wait," she began even as she put her hand into his. Quickly, Megan scrawled a message on the chalkboard by the screen door.

OUT WITH KATCH

It was enough.

Chapter 10

Katch drove along Ocean Boulevard so they could creep along in the traffic filled with tourists and beachers. Car radios were turned up high and windows rolled down low. Laughter and music poured out everywhere. The lights from a twin Ferris wheel glittered red and blue in the distance. People sat out on their hotel balconies, with colorful beach towels flapping over the railings, as they watched the sluggish flow of cars and pedestrians. To the left, there were glimpses of the sea in between buildings.

Sleepily content after pizza and Chianti, Megan snuggled deeper into the soft leather seat. "Things'll quiet down after this weekend," she commented. "Until Memorial Day."

"Do you ever feel as though you're being invaded?" Katch asked her with a gesture at the clogged traffic.

"I like the crowds," she said immediately, then laughed. "And I like the winter when the beaches are deserted. I suppose there's something about the honky-tonk that appeals to me, especially since I know I'm going to have a few isolated months in the winter."

"That's your time," Katch murmured, glancing back at her. "The time you give yourself for sculpting."

She shrugged, a bit uncomfortable with the intense look. "I do some in the summer, too—when I can. Time's something I forgot when Jessica was talking about a showing and making all those plans..." Megan trailed off, frowning. "I don't know how I can possibly get things ready."

"Not backing out, are you?"

"No, but—" The look in his eyes had her swallowing excuses. "No," she said more firmly. "I'm not backing out."

"What're you working on now?"

"I, ah..." Megan looked fixedly out the window, thinking of the half-formed bust of Katch's head. "It's just..." She shrugged and began to fiddle with the dial of the radio. "It's just a wood carving."

"Of what?"

Megan made a few inarticulate mumbles until Katch turned to grin at her. "A pirate," she decided as the light from a street lamp slanted over his face, throwing it into planes and shadows. "It's the head of a pirate."

His brow lifted at the sudden, narrow-eyed concentration with which she was studying him. "I'd like to see it."

"It's not finished," she said quickly. "I've barely got the clay model done. In any case, I might have to put it off if I'm going to get the rest of my pieces organized for your sister."

"Meg, why don't you stop worrying and just enjoy it?"

Confused, she shook her head and stared at him. "Enjoy it?"

"The show," he said, ruffling her hair.

"Oh, yes." She fought to get her thoughts back into some kind of order. "I will…after it's over," she added with a smile. "Do you think you'll be in New York, then?"

As the rhythm of the traffic picked up, he shifted into third. "I'm considering it."

"I'd like you to be there if you could arrange it." When he laughed, shaking his head, she continued, "It's just that I'm going to need all the friendly faces I can get."

"You're not going to need anything but your sculptures," Katch corrected, but the amusement was still in his eyes. "Don't you think I'd want to be around the night of your opening so that I can brag I discovered you?"

"Let's just hope we both don't live to regret it," Megan muttered, but he only laughed again. "You just can't consider the possibility that you might have made a mistake," she accused testily.

"You can't consider the possibility that you might be successful," he countered.

Megan opened her mouth, then shut it again. "Well," she said after a moment, "we're both right." Waiting until they were stopped in traffic again, Megan touched his shoulder. "Katch?"

"Hmm?"

"Why did you build a hospital in Central Africa?"

He turned to her then, a faint frown between his brows. "It was needed," he said simply.

"Just that?" she persisted, though she could see he wasn't pleased with her question. "I mean, Jessica said you were advised against it, and—"

"As it happens, I have a comfortable amount of money." He cut her off with an annoyed movement of his shoulder. "I do what I choose with it." Seeing her expression, Katch shook his head. "There are things I want to do, that's all. Don't canonize me, Meg."

She relaxed again and found herself brushing at the curls over his ear. "I wouldn't dream of it." He'd rather be thought of as eccentric than benevolent, she mused. And how much simpler it was to love him, knowing that one small secret. "You're much easier to like than I thought you'd be when you made a nuisance of yourself in the market."

"I tried to tell you," he pointed out. "You were too busy pretending you weren't interested."

"I wasn't interested," Megan insisted, "in the least." He turned to grin at her and she found herself laughing. "Well, not very much anyway." When he swung the car onto a side street, she looked back at him in question. "What are you doing?"

"Let's go out on the boardwalk." Expertly, he slid the Porsche into a parking space. "Maybe I'll buy you a souvenir." He was already out of the car—primed, impatient.

"Oh, I love rash promises," Megan crowed as she joined him.

"I said maybe."

"I didn't hear that part. And," she added as she laced her fingers with his, "I want something extravagant."

"Such as?" They jaywalked, maneuvering around stopped cars.

"I'll know when I see it."

The boardwalk was crowded, full of people and light and noise. The breeze off the ocean carried the scent of salt to compete with the aroma of grilling meat from concessions. Instead of going into one of the little shops, Katch pulled Megan into an arcade.

"Big talk about presents and no delivery," Megan said in disgust as Katch exchanged bills for tokens.

"It's early yet. Here." He poured a few tokens into her hand. "Why don't you try your luck at saving the galaxy from invaders?"

With a smirk, Megan chose a machine, then slipped two tokens into the slot. "I'll go first." Pressing the start button, she took the control stick in hand and began systematically to vaporize the enemy. Brows knit, she swung her ship right and left while the machine exploded with color and noise with each hit. Amused, Katch dipped his hands into his pockets and watched her face. It was a more interesting show than the sophisticated graphics.

She chewed her bottom lip while maneuvering into position, narrowing her eyes when a laser blast headed her way. Her breath hissed through her teeth at a narrow escape. But all the while, her face held that composed, almost serious expression that was so much a part of her. Fighting gamely to avoid being blown up in cross fire, Megan's ship at last succumbed.

"Well," Katch murmured, glancing at her score as

she wiped her hands on the back of her jeans. "You're pretty good."

"You have to be," Megan returned soberly, "when you're the planet's last hope."

With a chuckle, he nudged her out of the way and took the control.

Megan acknowledged his skill as Katch began to blast away the invaders with as much regularity as she had, and a bit more dash. He likes to take chances, she mused as he narrowly missed being blown apart by laser fire in order to zap three ships in quick succession. As his score mounted, she stepped a bit closer to watch his technique.

At the brush of her arm against his, Megan noticed a quick, almost imperceptible break in his rhythm. Now, that was interesting, she reflected. Feeling an irrepressible surge of mischief, she edged slightly closer. There was another brief fluctuation in his timing. Softly, she touched her lips to his shoulder, then smiled up into his face. She heard rather than saw the explosion that marked his ship's untimely end.

Katch wasn't looking at the screen either, but at her. She saw something flash into his eyes—something hot, barely suppressed, before his hand released the control to dive into her hair.

"Cheat," he murmured.

For a moment, Megan forgot the cacophony of sound, forgot the crowds of people that milled around them. She was lost somewhere in those smoky gray eyes and her own giddy sense of power.

"Cheat?" she repeated, and her lips stayed slightly parted. "I don't know what you mean."

The hand on her hair tightened. He was struggling,

she realized, surprised and excited. "I think you do," Katch said quietly. "And I think I'm going to have to be very careful now that you know just what you can do to me."

"Katch." Her gaze lowered to his mouth as the longings built. "Maybe I don't want you to be careful anymore."

Slowly, his hand slid out of her hair, over her cheek, then dropped. "All the more reason I have to be," he muttered. "Come on." He took her arm and propelled her away from the machine. "Let's play something else."

Megan flowed with his mood, content just to be with him. They pumped tokens into machines and competed fiercely—as much with each other as with the computers. Megan felt the same lighthearted ease with him that she'd experienced that night at the carnival. Spending time with him was much like a trip on one of the wild, breathless rides at the park. Quick curves, fast hills, unexpected starts and stops. No one liked the windy power of a roller coaster better than Megan.

Hands on hips, she stood back as he consistently won coupons at Skee Ball. She watched another click off on the already lengthy strip as he tossed the ball neatly into the center hole.

"Don't you ever lose?" she demanded.

Katch tossed the next ball for another forty points. "I try not to make a habit of it. Wanna toss the last two?"

"No." She brushed imaginary lint from her shirt. "You're having such a good time showing off."

With a laugh, Katch dumped the last two balls for ninety points, then leaned over to tear off his stream of coupons. "Just for that, I might not turn these in for your souvenir."

"These?" Megan gave the ream of thin cardboard an arched-brow look. "You were supposed to *buy* me a souvenir."

"I did." He grinned, rolling them up. "Indirectly." Slipping an arm companionably around her shoulder, he walked to the center counter where prizes were displayed. "Let's see... I've got two dozen. How about one of those six-function penknives?"

"Just who's this souvenir for?" Megan asked dryly as she scanned the shelves. "I like that little silk rose." She tapped the glass counter to indicate a small lapel pin. "I have all the tools I need," she added with an impish grin.

"Okay." Katch nodded to the woman behind the counter, then tore off all but four of the tickets. "That leaves us these. Ah..." With a quick scan of the shelves, he pointed. "That."

Thoughtfully, Megan studied the tiny shell figure the woman lifted down. It seemed to be a cross between a duck and a penguin. "What're you going to do with that?"

"Give it to you." Katch handed over the rest of the tickets. "I'm a very generous man."

"I'm overwhelmed," she murmured. Megan turned it over in the palm of her hand as Katch pinned the rose to the collar of her shirt. "But what is it?"

"It's a mallard." Draping his arm over her shoulder again, he led her out of the arcade. "I'm surprised at your attitude. I figured, as an artist, you'd recognize its aesthetic value."

"Hmm." Megan took another study, then slipped it into her pocket. "Well, I do recognize a certain winsome charm. And," she added, rising on her toes to

kiss his cheek, "it was sweet of you to spend all your winnings on me."

Smiling, Katch ran a finger down her nose. "Is a kiss on the cheek the best you can do?"

"For a shell penguin it is."

"It's a mallard," he reminded her.

"Whatever." Laughing, Megan slipped an arm around his waist as they crossed the boardwalk and walked down the slope to the beach.

The moon was only a thin slice of white, but the stars were brilliant and mirrored in the water. There was a quiet swish of waves flowing and ebbing over the sand. Lovers walked here and there, arm in arm, talking quietly or not speaking at all. Children dashed along with flashlights bobbing, searching the sand and the surf for treasures.

Bending, Megan slipped out of her shoes and rolled up the hem of her jeans. In silent agreement, Katch followed suit. The water lapped cool over their ankles as they began to walk north, until the laughter and music from the boardwalk was only a background echo.

"Your sister's lovely," Megan said at length. "Just as you said."

"Jessica was always a beauty," he agreed absently. "A little hardheaded, but always a beauty."

"I saw your nieces at the park." Megan lifted her head so that the ocean breeze caught at her hair. "They had chocolate all over their faces."

"Typical." He laughed, running a hand up and down her arm as they walked. Megan felt the blood begin to hum beneath her flesh. "Before they left tonight, they were out digging for worms. I've been drafted to take them fishing tomorrow."

"You like children."

He twisted his head to glance down at her, but Megan was looking out to sea. "Yes. They're a constant adventure, aren't they?"

"I see so many of them in the park every summer, yet they never cease to amaze me." She turned back then with her slow, serious smile hovering on her lips. "And I see a fair number of harassed or long-suffering parents."

"When did you lose yours?"

He saw the flicker of surprise in her eyes before she looked down the stretch of beach again. "I was five."

"It's difficult for you to remember them."

"Yes. I have some vague memories—impressions really, I suppose. Pop has pictures, of course. When I see them, it always surprises me how young they were."

"It must have been hard on you," Katch murmured. "Growing up without them."

The gentleness in his voice had her turning back to him. They'd walked far down the beach so that the only light now came from the stars. His eyes caught the glitter of reflection as they held hers. "It would have been," Megan told him, "without Pop. He did much more than fill in." She stopped to take a step farther into the surf. The water frothed and bubbled over her skin. "One of my best memories is of him struggling to iron this pink organdy party dress. I was eight or nine, I think." With a shake of her head, she laughed and kicked the water. "I can still see him."

Katch's arms came around her waist, drawing her back against him. "So can I."

"He was standing there, struggling with frills and flounces—and swearing like a sailor because he didn't know I was there. I still love him for that," she murmured. "For just that."

Katch brushed his lips over the top of her hair. "And I imagine you told him not long afterward that you didn't care much for party dresses."

Surprised, Megan turned around. "How did you know that?"

"I know you." Slowly, he traced the shape of her face with his fingertip.

Frowning, she looked beyond his shoulder. "Am I so simple?"

"No." With his fingertip still on her jaw, he turned her face back to his. "You might say I've made a study of you."

She felt her blood begin to churn. "Why?"

Katch shook his head and combed his fingers through her hair. "No questions tonight," he said quietly. "I don't have the answers yet."

"No questions," she agreed, then rose on her toes to meet his mouth with hers.

It was a soft, exploring kiss—a kiss of renewal. Megan could taste the gentleness. For the moment, he seemed to prize her, to find her precious and rare. He held her lightly, as though she would break at the slightest pressure. Her lips parted, and it was she who entered his mouth first, teasing his tongue with hers. His sound of pleasure warmed her. The water swayed, soft and cool, on her calves.

She ran her hands up his back, letting her strong, artist's fingers trail under his hair to caress the nape of his neck. There was tension there, and she murmured against his lips as if to soothe it. Megan felt both his resistance and the tightening of his fingers against her skin. Her body pressed more demandingly into his.

Passion began to smolder quietly. Megan knew she was drawing it from him without his complete consent. The wonder of her own power struck her like a flash. He was holding back, letting her set the pace, but she could feel the near-violence of need in him. It tempted her. She wanted to undermine his control as he had undermined hers. She wanted to make him need as blindly as she needed. It wasn't possible to make him love her, but she could make him want. If it was all she could have from him, then she would be satisfied with his desire.

Megan felt his control slipping. His arms tightened around her, drawing her close so they were silhouetted as one. The kiss grew harder, more urgent. He lifted a hand to her hair, gripping it, pulling her head back as if now he would take command. There was fire now, burning brightly. Heat rose in her, smoking through her blood. She caught his bottom lip between her teeth and heard his quiet moan. Abruptly, he drew her away.

"Meg."

She waited, having no idea what she wanted him to say. Her head was tossed back, her face open to his, her hair free to the breeze. She felt incredibly strong. His eyes were nearly black, searching her face deeply. She could feel his breath feather, warm and uneven, on her lips.

"Meg." He repeated her name, bringing his hands back to her shoulders slowly. "I have to go now."

Daring more than she would have believed possible, Megan pressed her lips to his again. Hers were soft and hungry and drew instant response from him. "Is that what you want?" she murmured. "Do you want to leave me now?"

His fingers tightened on her arms convulsively, then he pulled her away again. "You know the answer to that," he said roughly. "What are you trying to do, make me crazy?"

"Maybe." Desire still churned in her. It smoldered in her eyes as they met his. "Maybe I am."

He caught her against him, close and tight. She could feel the furious race of his heart against hers. His control, she knew, balanced on a razor's edge. Their lips were only a whisper apart.

"There'll be a time," he said softly, "I swear it, when it'll just be you and me. Next time, the very next time, Meg. Remember it."

It took no effort to keep her eyes level with his. The power was still flowing through her. "Is that a warning?"

"Yes," he told her. "That's just what it is."

Chapter 11

It took two more days for Megan to finish the bust of Katch. She tried, when it was time, to divorce herself from emotion and judge it objectively.

She'd been right to choose wood. It was warmer than stone. With her tongue caught between her teeth, she searched for flaws in her workmanship. Megan knew without conceit it was one of her better pieces. Perhaps the best.

The face wasn't stylishly handsome, but strong and compelling. Humor was expressed in the tilt of the brows and mouth. She ran her fingertips over his lips. An incredibly expressive mouth, she mused, remembering the taste and texture. I know just how it looks when he's amused or angry or aroused. And his eyes. Hers drifted up to linger. I know how they look, how they change shades and expression with a mood. Light for pleasure, turning smoky in anger, darker in passion.

I know his face as well as my own…but I still don't know his mind. That's still a stranger. With a sigh she folded her arms on the table and lowered her chin to them.

Would he ever permit me to know him? she wondered. Tenderly, she touched a lock of the disordered hair. Jessica knows him, probably better than anyone else. If he loved someone…

What would happen if I drew up the courage to tell him that I love him? What would happen if I simply walked up to him and said *I love you?* Demanding nothing, expecting nothing. Doesn't he perhaps have the right to know? Isn't love too special, too rare to be closed up? Then Megan imagined his eyes with pity in them.

"I couldn't bear it," she murmured, lowering her forehead to Katch's wooden one. "I just couldn't bear it." A knock interrupted her soul-searching. Quickly, Megan composed her features and swiveled in her chair. "Come in."

Her grandfather entered, his fishing cap perched jauntily on his mane of white hair. "How do you feel about fresh fish for supper?" His grin told her that his early morning expedition had been a success. Megan cocked her head.

"I could probably choke down a few bites." She smiled, pleased to see his eyes sparkling and color in his cheeks. She sprang up and wound her arms around his neck as she had done as a child. "Oh, I love you, Pop!"

"Well, well." He patted her hair, both surprised and pleased. "I love you too, Megan. I guess I should bring you home trout more often."

She lifted her face from the warm curve of his neck

and smiled at him. "It doesn't take much to make me happy."

His eyes sobered as he tucked her hair behind her ear. "No.... It never has." His wide, blunt hand touched her cheek. "You've given me so much pleasure over the years, Megan, so much joy. I'm going to miss you when you're in New York."

"Oh, Pop." She buried her face again and clung. "It'll only be for a month or two, then I'll be home." She could smell the cherry-flavored scent of the tobacco he carried in his breast pocket. "You could even come with me—the season'll be over."

"Meg." He stopped her rambling and drew her up so that their eyes met. "This is a start for you. Don't put restrictions on it."

Shaking her head, Megan rose to pace nervously. "I'm not. I don't know what you mean…"

"You're going to make something of yourself, something important. You have talent." Pop glanced around the room at her work until his eyes rested on the bust of Katch. "You've got a life to start. I want you to go after it at full speed."

"You make it sound as if I'm not coming home." Megan turned and, seeing where his eyes rested, clasped her hands together. "I've just finished that." She moistened her lips and struggled to keep her voice casual. "It's rather good, don't you think?"

"Yes, I think it's very good." He looked at her then. "Sit down, Megan, I need to talk to you."

She recognized the tone and tensed. Without a word, she obeyed, going to the chair across from him. Pop waited until she was settled, then studied her face carefully.

"Awhile back," he began, "I told you things change. Most of your life, it's been just the two of us. We needed each other, depended on each other. We had the park to keep a roof over our heads and to give us something to work for." His tone softened. "There hasn't been one minute in the eighteen years I've had you with me that you've been a burden. You've kept me young. I've watched you through all the stages of growing up, and each time, you've made me more proud of you. It's time for the next change."

Because her throat was dry as dust, Megan swallowed. "I don't understand what you're trying to tell me."

"It's time you moved out into the world, Megan, time I let you." Pop reached in the pocket of his shirt and took out carefully folded papers. After spreading them out, he handed them to Megan.

She hesitated before accepting them, her eyes clinging to his. The instant she saw the papers, she knew what they were. But when she read, she read each sentence, each word, until the finish. "So," she said, dry-eyed, dry-voiced. "You've sold it to him."

"When I sign the papers," Pop told her, "and you witness it." He saw the look of devastation in her eyes. "Megan, hear me out. I've given this a lot of thought." Pop took the papers and set them on the table, then gripped her hands. "Katch isn't the first to approach me about selling, and this isn't the first time I've considered it. Everything didn't fit the way I wanted before—this time it does."

"What fits?" she demanded, feeling her eyes fill.

"It's the right man, Meg, the right time." He soothed her hands, hating to watch her distress. "I knew it when all those repairs fell on me. I'm ready to let it go, to let someone younger take over so I can go fishing. That's what I want now, Megan, a boat and a rod. And he's the man I want taking over." He paused, fumbling in his pocket for a handkerchief to wipe his eyes. "I told you I trusted him and that still holds. Managing the park for Katch won't keep me from my fishing, and I'll have the stimulation without the headaches. And you," he continued, brushing tears from her cheeks, "you need to cut the strings. You can't do what you're meant to do if you're struggling to balance books and make payroll."

"If it's what you want," Megan began, but Pop cut her off.

"No, it has to be what you want. That's why the last lines are still blank." He looked at her with his deep-set eyes sober and quiet. "I won't sign it, Megan, unless you agree. It has to be what's best for both of us."

Megan stood again, and he released her hands to let her walk to the window. At the moment, she was unable to understand her own feelings. She knew agreeing to do a show in New York was a giant step away from the life she had led. And the park was a major part of that life. She knew in order to pursue her own career, she couldn't continue to tie herself to the business end of Joyland.

The park had been security—her responsibility, her second home—as the man behind her had been both mother and father to her. She remembered the look of weariness on his face when he had come to tell her that the park needed money. Megan knew the hours and endless demands that summer would bring.

He was entitled to live his winter years as he chose, she decided. With less worry, less responsibility. He was entitled to fish, and to sleep late and putter around his azaleas. What right did she have to deny him that because she was afraid to cut the last tie with her childhood? He was right, it was time for the change.

Slowly, she walked to her workbox and searched out a pen. Going to Pop, Megan held it out to him. "Sign it. We'll have champagne with the trout."

Pop took the pen, but kept his eyes on her. "Are you sure, Meg?"

She nodded, as sure for him as she was uncertain for herself. "Positive." She smiled and watched the answering light in his eyes before he bent over the paper.

He signed his name with a flourish, then passed her the pen so that she could witness his signature. Megan wrote her name in clear, distinct letters, not allowing her hand to tremble.

"I suppose I should call Katch," Pop mused, sighing as though a weight had been lifted. "Or take the papers to him."

"I'll take them." Carefully, Megan folded them again. "I'd like to talk to him."

"That's a good idea. Take the pickup," he suggested as she headed for the door. "It looks like rain."

Megan was calm by the time she reached Katch's house. The papers were tucked securely in the back pocket of her cutoffs. She pulled the truck behind his car and climbed out.

The air was deadly still and heavy, nearly shimmering with restrained rain. The clouds overhead were black and bulging with it. She walked to the front door and knocked as she had many days before. As before, there was no answer. She walked back down the steps and skirted the house.

There was no sign of him in the yard, no sound but the voice of the sea muffled by the tall hedges. He'd planted a willow, a young, slender one near the slope which led to the beach. The earth was still dark around it, freshly turned. Unable to resist, Megan walked to it, wanting to touch the tender young leaves. It was no taller than she, but she knew one day it would be magnificent…sweeping, graceful, a haven of shade in the summer. Instinct made her continue down the slope to the beach.

Hands in his pockets, he stood, watching the swiftly incoming tide. As if sensing her, he turned.

"I was standing here thinking of you," he said. "Did I wish you here?"

She took the papers and held them out to him. "It's yours," she told him calmly. "Just as you wanted."

He didn't even glance down at the papers, but she saw the shift of expression in his eyes. "I'd like to talk to you, Meg. Let's go inside."

"No." She stepped back to emphasize her refusal. "There really isn't anything more to say."

"That might be true for you, but I have a great deal to say. And you're going to listen." Impatience intruded into his tone. Megan heard it as she felt the sudden gust of wind which broke the calm.

"I don't want to listen to you, Katch. This is what Pop wants, too." She thrust the papers into his hands as the first spear of lightning split the sky. "Take them, will you?"

"Megan, wait." He grabbed her arm as she turned to go. The thunder all but drowned out his words.

"I will not wait!" she tossed back, jerking her arm free. "And stop grabbing me. You have what you wanted—you don't need me anymore."

Katch swore, thrust the papers in his pocket and caught her again before she'd taken three steps. He whirled her back around. "You're not that big an idiot."

"Don't tell me how big an idiot I am." She tried to shake herself loose.

"We have to talk. I have things to say to you. It's important." A gust of wind whipped violently across Megan's face.

"Don't you understand a simple no?" she shouted at him, her voice competing with pounding surf and rising wind. She struggled against his hold. "I don't want to talk. I don't want to hear what you have to say. I don't *care* about what you have to say."

The rain burst from the clouds and poured over them. Instantly, they were drenched.

"Tough," he retorted, every bit as angry as she. "Because you're going to hear it. Now, let's go inside."

He started to pull her across the sand, but she swung violently away and freed herself. Rain gushed down in torrents, sheeting around them. "No!" she shouted. "I won't go inside with you."

"Oh yes you will," he corrected.

"What are you going to do?" she demanded. "Drag me by the hair?"

"Don't tempt me." Katch took her hand again only to have her pull away. "All right," he said. "Enough." In a swift move that caught her off guard, he swept her up into his arms.

"Put me down." Megan wriggled and kicked, blind with fury. He ignored her, dealing with her struggles by shifting her closer and climbing the slope without any apparent effort. Lightning and thunder warred around them. "Oh, I hate you!" she claimed as he walked briskly across the lawn.

"Good. That's a start." Katch pushed open the door with his hip, then continued through the kitchen and into the living room. A trail of rain streamed behind them. Without ceremony, he dumped her on the sofa. "Sit still," he ordered before she could regain her breath, "and just be quiet a minute." He walked to the hearth. Taking a long match, he set fire to the paper waiting beneath kindling and logs. Dry wood crackled and caught almost instantly.

Regaining her breath, Megan rose and bounded for the door. Katch stopped her before her fingers touched the knob. He held her by the shoulders with her back to the door. "I warn you, Meg, my tolerance is at a very low ebb. Don't push me."

"You don't frighten me," she told him, impatiently flipping her dripping hair from her eyes.

"I'm not trying to frighten you. I'm trying to reason with you. But you're too stubborn to shut up and listen."

Her eyes widened with fresh fury. "Don't you talk to me that way! I don't have to take that."

"Yes, you do." Deftly, he reached in her right front pocket and pulled out the truck keys. "As long as I have these."

"I can walk," she tossed back as he pocketed them himself.

"In this rain?"

Megan hugged her arms as she began to shiver. "Let me have my keys."

Instead of answering, he pulled her across the room in front of the fire. "You're freezing. You'll have to get out of those wet clothes."

"I will not. You're crazy if you think I'm going to take off my clothes in your house."

"Suit yourself." He stripped off his own sopping T-shirt and tossed it angrily aside. "You're the most hardheaded, single-minded, stubborn woman I know."

"Thanks." Barely, Megan controlled the urge to sneeze. "Is that all you wanted to say?"

"No." He walked to the fire again. "That's just the beginning—there's a lot more. Sit down."

"Then maybe I'll have my say first." Chills were running over her skin, and she struggled not to tremble. "I was wrong about you in a lot of ways. You're not lazy or careless or glory-seeking. And you were certainly honest with me." She wiped water from her eyes, a mixture of rain and tears. "You told me up front that you intended to have the park, and it seems perhaps for the best. What happened between then and now is my fault for being foolish enough to let you get to me." Megan swallowed, wanting to salvage a little pride. "But then you're a difficult man to ignore. Now you have what you wanted, and it's over and done."

"I only have part of what I wanted." Katch came to her and gathered her streaming hair in his hand. "Only part, Meg."

She looked at him, too tired to argue. "Can't you just let me be?" she asked.

"Let you be? Do you know how many times I've walked that beach at three in the morning because wanting you kept me awake and aching? Do you know how hard it was for me to let you go every time I had you in my arms?" The fingers in her hair tightened, pulled her closer.

Her eyes were huge now while chills shivered over

her skin. *What was he saying?* She couldn't risk asking, couldn't risk wondering. Abruptly, he cursed her and dragged her into his arms.

Thin wet clothes were no barrier to his hands. He molded her breasts even while his mouth ravished hers. She made no protest when he lowered her to the floor, as his fingers worked desperately at the buttons of her blouse. Her chilled wet skin turned to fire under his fingertips. His mouth was hungry, hot as it roamed to her throat and downward.

There was only the crackle of wood and the splash of rain on the windows to mix with their breathing. A log shifted in the grate.

Megan heard him take a long, deep breath. "I'm sorry. I wanted to talk—there are things I need to tell you. But I need you. I've kept it pent up a long time."

Need. Her mind centered on the word. Need was infinitely different from want. Need was more personal— still apart from love—but she let her heart grip the word.

"It's all right." Megan started to sit up, but he leaned over her. Sparks flicked inside her at the touch of naked flesh to naked flesh. "Katch..."

"Please, Meg. Listen to me."

She searched his face, noting the uncharacteristically grave eyes and mouth. Whatever he had to say was important to him. "All right," she said, quieter now, ready. "I'll listen."

"When I first saw you, the first minute, I wanted you. You know that." His voice was low, but without its usual calm. Something boiled just under the surface. "The first night we were together, you intrigued me as much as you attracted me. I thought it would be a simple matter to have you…a casual, pleasant affair for a few weeks."

"I know," she spoke softly, trying not to be wounded by the truth.

"No—shh." He lay a finger over her lips a moment. "You don't know. It stopped being simple almost immediately. When I had you here for dinner, and you asked to stay…" He paused, brushing wet strands of hair from her cheeks. "I couldn't let you, and I wasn't completely sure why. I wanted you—wanted you more than any woman I'd ever touched, any woman I'd ever dreamed about—but I couldn't take you."

"Katch…" Megan shook her head, not certain she was strong enough to hear the words.

"Please." She had closed her eyes, and Katch waited until she opened them again before he continued. "I tried to stay away from you, Meg. I tried to convince myself I was imagining what was happening to me. Then you were charging across the lawn, looking outraged and so beautiful I couldn't think of anything. Just looking at you took my breath away." While she lay motionless, he lifted her hand and pressed it to his lips. The gesture moved her unbearably.

"Don't," she murmured. "Please."

Katch stared into her eyes for a long moment, then released her hand. "I wanted you," he went on in a voice more calm than his eyes. "Needed you, was furious with you because of it." He rested his forehead on hers and shut his eyes. "I never wanted to hurt you, Meg— to frighten you."

Megan lay still, aware of the turmoil in him. Firelight played over the skin on his arms and back.

"It seemed impossible that I could be so involved I couldn't pull away," he continued. "But you were so

tangled up in my thoughts, so wound up in my dreams.
There wasn't any escape. The other night, after I'd taken
you home, I finally admitted to myself I didn't want an
escape. Not this time. Not from you." He lifted his head
and looked down at her again. "I have something for
you, but first I want you to know I'd decided against
buying the park until your grandfather came to me last
night. I didn't want that between us, but it was what he
wanted. What he thought was best for you and for himself. But if it hurts you, I'll tear the papers up."

"No." Megan gave a weary sigh. "I know it's best. It's
just like losing someone you love. Even when you know
it's the best thing, it still hurts." The outburst seemed to
have driven out the fears and the pain. "Please, I don't
want you to apologize. I was wrong, coming here this
way, shouting at you. Pop has every right to sell the
park, and you have every right to buy it." She sighed,
wanting explanations over. "I suppose I felt betrayed
somehow and didn't want to think it all through."

"And now?"

"And now I'm ashamed of myself for acting like a
fool." She managed a weak smile. "I'd like to get up and
go home. Pop'll be worried."

"Not just yet." When Katch leaned back on his heels
to take something from his pocket, Megan sat up, pushing her wet, tangled hair behind her. He held a box,
small and thin. Briefly, he hesitated before offering it
to her. Puzzled, both by the gift and by the tension she
felt emanating from him, Megan opened it. Her breath
caught.

It was a dark, smoky green emerald, square cut and
exquisite in its simplicity. Stunned, Megan stared at it,
then at Katch. She shook her head wordlessly.

"Katch." Megan shook her head again. "I don't understand… I can't accept this."

"Don't say no, Meg." Katch closed his hand over hers. "I don't handle rejection well." The words were light, but she recognized, and was puzzled by, the strain in the tone. A thought trembled in her brain, and her heart leaped with it.

She tried to be calm and keep her eyes steady on his. "I don't know what you're asking me."

His fingers tightened on hers. "Marry me. I love you."

Emotions ran riot through her. He must be joking, she thought quickly, though no hint of amusement showed in his eyes. His face was so serious, she reflected, and the words so simple. Where were the carelessly witty phrases, the glib charm? Shaken, Megan rose with the box held tightly in her hand. She needed to think.

Marriage. Never had she expected him to ask her to share a lifetime. What would life be like with him? *Like the roller coaster.* She knew it instantly. It would be a fast, furious ride, full of unexpected curves and indescribable thrills. And quiet moments too, she reflected. Precious, solitary moments which would make each new twist and turn more exciting.

Perhaps he had asked her this way, so simply, without any of the frills he could so easily provide because he was as vulnerable as she. What a thought that was! She lifted her fingers to her temple. David Katcherton vulnerable. And yet… Megan remembered what she had seen in his eyes.

I love you. The three simple words, words spoken every day by people everywhere, had changed her life forever. Megan turned, then walking back, knelt beside him. Her eyes were as grave, as searching as his.

She held the box out, then spoke quickly as she saw the flicker of desperation.

"It belongs on the third finger of my left hand."

Then she was caught against him, her mouth silenced bruisingly. "Oh, Meg," he murmured her name as he rained kisses on her face. "I thought you were turning me down."

"How could I?" She wound her arms around his neck and tried to stop his roaming mouth with her own. "I love you, Katch." The words were against his lips. "Desperately, completely. I'd prepared myself for a slow death when you were ready to walk away."

"No one's going to walk away now." They lay on the floor again, and he buried his face in her rain-scented hair. "We'll go to New Orleans. A quick honeymoon before you have to come back and work on the show. In the spring, we'll go to Paris." He lifted his face and looked down on her. "I've thought about you and me in Paris, making love. I want to see your face in the morning when the light's soft."

She touched his cheek. "Soon," she whispered. "Marry me soon. I want to be with you."

He picked up the box that had fallen beside them. Drawing out the ring, he slipped it on her finger. Then, gripping her hand with his, he looked down at her.

"Consider it binding, Meg," he told her huskily. "You can't get away now."

"I'm not going anywhere." She lifted her mouth to meet his kiss.

Epilogue

Nervously, Megan twisted the emerald on her finger and tried to drink the champagne Jessica had pushed into her hand. She felt as though the smile had frozen onto her face. People, she thought. She'd never expected so many people. What was she doing, standing in a Manhattan gallery pretending she was an artist? What she wanted to do was creep into the back room and be very, very sick.

"Here now, Meg." Pop strolled over beside her, looking oddly distinguished in his best—and only—black suit. "You should try one of these—tasty little things." He held out a canapé.

"No." Megan felt her stomach roll and shook her head. "No, thanks. I'm so glad you flew up for the weekend."

"Think I'd miss my granddaughter's big night?" He ate the canapé and grinned. "How about this turnout?"

"I feel like an impostor," Megan murmured, smiling gamely as a man in a flowing cape moved past her to study one of her marble pieces.

"Never seen you look prettier." Pop plucked at the sleeve of her dress, a swirl of watercolored silk. "'Cept maybe at your wedding."

"I wasn't nearly as scared then." She made a quick scan of the crowd and found only strangers. "Where's Katch?"

"Last time I saw him he was cornered by a couple of ritzy-looking people. Didn't I hear Jessica say you were supposed to mingle?"

"Yes." Megan made a small, frustrated sound. "I don't think I can move."

"Now, Meg, I've never known you to be chicken-hearted."

With her mouth half-opened in protest, she watched him walk away. *Chicken-hearted,* she repeated silently. Straightening her shoulders, she drank some champagne. All right then, she decided, she wouldn't stand there cowering in the corner. If she was going to be shot down, she'd face it head on. Moving slowly, and with determined confidence, Megan walked toward the buffet.

"You're the artist, aren't you?"

Megan turned to face a striking old woman in diamonds and black silk. "Yes," she said with a fractional lift of her chin. "I am."

"Hmmm." The woman took Megan in with a long, sweeping glance. "I noticed the study of the girl with the sand castle isn't for sale."

"No, it's my husband's." After two months, the words still brought the familiar warmth to her blood. *Katch, my husband.* Megan's eyes darted around the room to find him.

"A pity," the woman in black commented.

"I beg your pardon?"

"I said it's a pity—I wanted it."

"You—" Stunned, Megan stared at her. "You wanted it?"

"I've purchased 'The Lovers,'" she went on as Megan only gaped. "An excellent piece, but I want to commission you to do another sand castle. I'll contact you through Jessica."

"Yes, of course." *Commission?* Megan thought numbly as she automatically offered her hand. "Thank you," she added as the woman swept away.

"Miriam Tailor Marcus," a voice whispered beside her ear. "A tough nut to crack."

Megan half turned and grabbed Katch's arm. "Katch, that woman, she—"

"Miriam Tailor Marcus," he repeated and bent down to kiss her astonished mouth. "And I heard. I've just been modestly accepting compliments on my contribution to the art world." He touched the rim of his glass to hers. "Congratulations, love."

"They like my work?" she whispered.

"If you hadn't been so busy trying to be invisible, you'd know you're a smashing success. Walk around with me," he told her as he took her hand. "And look at all the little blue dots under your sculptures that mean SOLD."

"They're buying?" Megan gave a wondering laugh as she spotted sale after sale. "They're really buying them?"

"Jessica's frantically trying to keep up. Three people've

tried to buy the alabaster piece she bought from you herself—at twice what you charged her. And if you don't talk to a couple of the art critics soon, she's going to go crazy."

"I can't believe it."

"Believe it." He brought Megan's hand to his lips. "I'm very proud of you, Meg."

Tears welled up, threatening to brim over. "I have to get out of here for a minute," she whispered. "Please."

Without a word, Katch maneuvered his way through the crowd, taking Megan into the storage room and shutting the door behind them.

"This is silly," she said immediately as the tears rolled freely down her cheeks. "I'm an idiot. I have everything I've ever dreamed of and I'm crying in the back room. I'd have handled failure better than this."

"Megan." With a soft laugh, he gathered her close. "I love you."

"It doesn't seem real," she said with a quaver in her voice. "Not just the showing…it's everything. I see your ring on my finger and I keep wondering when I'm going to wake up. I can't believe that—"

His mouth silenced her. With a low, melting sigh, she dissolved against him. Even after all the days of her marriage, and all the intimate nights, he could still turn her to putty with only his mouth. The tears vanished as her blood began to swim. Pulling him closer, she let her hands run up the sides of his face and into his hair.

"It's real," he murmured against her mouth. "Believe it." Tilting his head, he changed the angle of the kiss and took her deeper. "It's real every night when you're in my arms, and every morning when you wake there." Katch drew her away slowly, then kissed both her damp cheeks until her lashes fluttered up. "Tonight," he said with a smile, "I'm going to make love to the newest star in the New York art world. And when she's still riding high over the reviews in the morning papers, I'm going to make love to her all over again."

"How soon can we slip away?"

Laughing, he caught her close for a hard kiss. "Don't tempt me. Jessica'd skin us both if we didn't stay until the gallery closes tonight. Now, fix your face and go bask in the admiration for a while. It's good for the soul."

"Katch." Megan stopped him before he could open the door. "There's one piece I didn't put out tonight."

Curious, he lifted a brow. "Oh?"

"Yes, well…" A faint color rose to her cheeks. "I was afraid things might not go well, and I thought I could handle the criticism. But this piece—I knew I couldn't bear to have anyone say it was a poor attempt or amateurish."

Puzzled, he slipped his hands into his pockets. "Have I seen it?"

"No." She shook her head, tossing her bangs out of her eyes. "I'd wanted to give it to you as a wedding present, but everything happened so fast and it wasn't finished. After all," she added with a grin, "we were only engaged for three days."

"Two days longer than if you'd agreed to fly to Vegas," he pointed out. "All in all, I was very patient."

"Be that as it may, I didn't have time until later to finish it. Then I was so nervous about the showing that I couldn't give it to you." She took a deep breath. "I'd like you to have it now, tonight, while I'm feeling—really feeling like an artist."

"Is it here?"

Turning around, Megan reached up on the shelf where the bust was carefully covered in cloth. Wordlessly, she handed it to him. Katch removed the cloth, then stared down into his own face.

Megan had polished the wood very lightly, wanting it to carry that not-quite-civilized aura she perceived in the model. It had his cockiness, his confidence and the warmth the artist had sensed in him before the woman had. He stared at it for so long, she felt the nerves begin to play in her stomach again. Then he looked up, eyes dark, intense.

"Meg."

"I don't want to put it out on display," she said hurriedly. "It's too personal to me. There were times," she began as she took the bust from him and ran a thumb down a cheekbone, "when I was working on the clay model, that I wanted to smash it." With a half-laugh, she set it down on a small table. "I couldn't. When I started it, I told myself the only reason I kept thinking about you was because you had the sort of face I'd like to sculpt." She lifted her eyes then to find his fixed on hers. "I fell in love with you sitting in my studio, while my hands were forming your face." Stepping forward, Megan lifted her hands and traced her fingers over the planes and bones under his flesh. "I thought I couldn't love you more than I did then. I was wrong."

"Meg." Katch brought his hands to hers, pressing her palms to his lips. "You leave me speechless."

"Just love me."

"Always."

"That just might be long enough." Megan sighed as she rested her head against his shoulder. "And I think I'll be able to handle success knowing it."

Katch slipped an arm around her waist as he opened the door. "Let's go have some more champagne. It's a night for celebrations."

* * * * *